Small Bird,

Tell Me

Helen Papanikolas

Small Bird,

Tell Me

STORIES OF

GREEK IMMIGRANTS

Swallow Press/Ohio University Press
Athens

First paperback edition published 1994

Swallow Press/Ohio University Press books are printed on acid-free paper ∞

01 00 99 98 97   5 4 3 2 (pbk.)

Library of Congress Cataloging-in-Publication Data

Papanikolas, Helen Zeese.
  Small bird, tell me / Helen Papanikolas.
    p.   cm.
    Contents: The letter writer — A mother's curse — Old Jim — The Greek pioneer of 1902 — A fine marriage — The coffeehouse election of 1922 — Crying Kostas — Mother and son — Father Gregory and the stranger — My son the monk — The first meeting of the group — The great day.
  ISBN 0-8040-0974-0 (cl.) 0-8040-0982-1 (pbk.)
  1. Greek Americans — Fiction I. Title
PS3566.A612S6   1993
813'.54—dc20
                                                               93-8426
                                                               CIP

For my children, Thalia Smart and Zeese Papanikolas

Contents

Small bird, there where you fly to *Ameriki,*
Tell me, where does my son lie down to sleep,
When he is sick, who tends him?

—*Greek folksong of immigration*

The Letter Writer

Yiannis fourteen years of age, but more the size of a ten-year-old, arrived at Ellis Island in 1908 clutching the baptismal cross around his neck and thanking the Virgin that he had escaped a horrible fate. When the ship had stopped in Spain, he thought he was in America and went down the gangplank carrying his possessions wrapped in a woven rug. His father's village friend was not there to meet him, and he began wandering about the docks and then the streets looking for him, panic drumming in his ears. Heavy footsteps followed him. He turned around with a gasp of hope that he would face his savior. A big, dark man with a great hooked nose grabbed him, dragged him down alleys while children, women, a few men looked on, and threw him down a chute leading to a dark cellar.

Ten boys were crouched there, one a black with bulging frightened eyes, two others younger but bigger than Yiannis who were crying. Immediately Yiannis began clawing at the rough rock walls, and after bruising his hands and tearing off his fingernails, he was able to reach the chute. Straddling it with his feet, he lifted the lid with his head and escaped. He ran from one alley to another calling in Greek, "Save me! Save me!" A carriage stopped, and a man wearing pince-nez eyeglasses beckoned and spoke in Greek. Breathlessly he told his story to the man. It was a miracle. The man was from the Greek embassy.

Again Yiannis was put on board ship but without his possessions, left behind in the cellar. He arrived in Ellis island with fleas and lice. After being deloused, his clothes fumigated, he waited over a week until his father's friend could be found to meet him. He waited in stark fear that the man would not come and he would have to return to the village and his mother. Her screams pierced his ears: "Quickly send your sisters dowries! Don't go to street women! You'll get skoulamentria! Come back soon, and we'll have a proper bride for you!"

Just as Yiannis had decided he was doomed, that no one would come to rescue him, his father's friend appeared. He had just signed up with a labor agent for a western railroad gang and had asked the padrone if he could put his friend's son on as a water boy. But seeing how puny Yiannis was, his father's friend sent him to a cousin in Chicago's Halsted Street to wash dishes. Tears dropped off Yiannis's nose and into the dishwater. He wanted to cry wholeheartedly at night, but the minute his head lay on the fetid mattress, he fell asleep from exhaustion.

After his ten-hour shift one Sunday, he timidly ventured into the Peloponnesian coffeehouse, the Athena. A large, gray-haired man spoke to him. He told Yiannis he had come to America in the 1880s, one of the first Greek immigrants to arrive, and was a correspondent for the Greek-language newspaper the *Greek Star.* "Study your English lessons and learn a trade," Davalis told Yiannis, "or else you'll be stuck in restaurants and live in stinking hovels all your life." Yiannis had more schooling than most immigrants, six full years, and learned quickly from the method book he bought at a Greek importing store. Sometimes he showed his Greek-English dictionary to Davalis, who ostensibly—he accented the wrong syllables—corrected his pronunciation. Yiannis worked, studied his method book, attended liturgy on his nameday, and thanked his patron saint, John the Baptist, for helping him escape the dark cellar.

Often, when he left the restaurant and the nights were cool, when stars swept over the black sky, he thought of his village. He had been fascinated by stars as a small boy. It had seemed to him that when he was taller he would be able to reach them, so close they looked to his mountain village. The black, starry American skies gave him no joy. Instead they pulled him deeper into a numbing darkness where he would not eat, would not talk. His hands in the greasy dishwater reminded him that in his village, cool, clear streams were flowing down the mountain. The steamy kitchen brought remembrances of his mother, kerchief about her head, putting paddles of dough into the outdoor earth oven, his sisters hoeing the vineyard, and the scent of thyme in the air.

"Be careful," Davalis lectured him. "You know that boy from Messenia? Homesickness sapped out his life and he died of it."

Two years later Yiannis was promoted to waiting on tables. By then he had made a habit of going to the coffeehouse after work and on Sundays. In the company of men quarreling, laughing, and telling stories, his homesickness, though not cured, was blunted. He carried his mother's latest demanding letter in his pocket: "Your sister will soon go beyond marriageable age!" He was able to pacify her with slightly larger money orders.

Davalis advised Yiannis to learn photography. In America, he said, people had enough money to pay for photographs, not like it was in *patridha*. The main reason Yiannis took Davalis's advice was his size; labor agents passed him over. Still too small, they told him, to work in mines and on railroads in the West. Yiannis was disappointed: wages there were as high as a dollar and seventy-five cents a day in certain places. It would take him longer to make enough money for his three sisters' dowries.

In the daytime Yiannis waited on tables and at night attended photography school. He relished the classes: they would lead to a quicker return to the fatherland, and this thought mellowed his homesickness for his family to nostalgia for church, language, king, and Greece. At Davalis's suggestion he changed his name to John. Several others in the coffeehouse had also done this, but a bad-tempered immigrant from Mani ranted only at him, called him a *bastardello,* ashamed of being a Greek. John was the smallest man in the coffeehouse and had not a single fellow villager to stand up for him. Davalis did not allow the men to make John a scapegoat and the butt of jokes, but he was often gone weeks at a time.

There were already other photographers on Halsted Street in Chicago's Greek Town, and after receiving his diploma a year and a half later, John bought a railroad coach ticket to the West. He had read in the *Greek Star* that there were thousands of Greek laborers there. After taking care of every detail, he went to church to light a candle for Davalis, who had died somewhere in Nevada, then wrote a stinging letter to the *Maniotis*, his coffeehouse tormentor. John called him an assless Turk, a *mangas*, a rogue, and sent him to the devil.

He arrived in Salt Lake City in 1911. He had sat up three nights and two days but looked well-groomed and unwrinkled when he stepped down from the train. "Greek Town?" he asked the conductor, who made a wide circle with his arm. "Greek Town all around," the conductor said smiling indulgently at him as if he were a child. He went directly up the street and to the first coffeehouse he came to, the Corinthos.

In the cubbyhole studio with a backdrop of a murky Italian garden, a camera on tripod, and glass plates, he quickly established himself in Greek Town. He lived in a Greek hotel opposite the Denver & Rio Grande Western depot and ate frugal meals at the Stadium Cafe where Stellios the Cretan cooked food even more flavorful than his mother had. He used plenty of meat in his cooking. It was cheap in America. He ate alone: he could not join in the camaraderie of the men—they laughed so much; they were so carefree. He often thought of Davalis and yearned to have him seated across from him. He sighed less often for his mother and sisters.

Often John made forays into the copper mining town west and the coal mining camps south of the city. By then he had become a dapper little man who wore a bow tie and, cocked over one eye, a straw boater in summer and a fedora in winter. He was not only in great demand by the Greeks, but also by Slavic, Lebanese, and Italian immigrants. Watching him hurrying with his tripod and camera, the immigrants wondered when he had time to eat.

A year after his arrival, the Cretans had gone on strike at the copper mines to rid themselves of their Greek labor agent. John took pictures of the coffeehouse where the strikers met, of their handsome mustached leader, of the long winding street between two mountains where houses clung all the way to the top, and of businesses on both sides of the street, including the brothels.

At the same time the Balkan Wars began, and he was thankful he had left Greece before having to endure the three years' army service.

Otherwise he would have had to return to fight, and his sisters would languish away without dowries. On Palm Sunday he took pictures of a large group of former soldiers called back to service. He placed them in front of the small brick church with its one dome and arched door. On each side a man held up a large flag, Greek on the right, American on the left. The men wore their Sunday suits, and all held palms in their hands. John made almost two hundred dollars from that single photograph. The men wanted pictures to send to their families in Greece, and *patriotes* left behind ordered copies as a memento. His oldest sister's dowry was complete. He would never have such luck again.

The year 1912 was also the year a rush of picture brides started coming on every train. John took careful, and to his mind artistic, photographs of the men to impress the prospective brides' relatives in Greece. When the women's pictures arrived, he examined them critically and found Greek photographers wanting.

John had taken to sighing deeply when he took the wedding pictures. The faces of the brides, especially that of a petite young woman from a village not far from Elasson, where he was born, stayed with him for days. He often had dreams in which he was a taller man and unclothed women were near him. He could not remember the details of the dreams when he woke up, except that they were erotic. Once he thought he ought to confess to the priest who wandered the streets of Greek Town in spotted black robes and tall black priest hat, like royalty never paying for anything: drinking Turkish coffee in the coffeehouses, eating at the restaurants, returning to his rooming house next to the church with a bottle of Kalamata olives and feta cheese from the grocery store, and a ring of bread from the Athens Bakery. But John reasoned he did not have to go to the priest: he hadn't killed anyone, hadn't slandered anyone, and hadn't gone to the *poutanes* in the red-light district that was almost in the heart of Greek Town. Having erotic dreams was the kind of thing Catholics ran to confess to their priests.

About this time he began to write letters. He was meticulous in expressing himself, and ordered a grammar book from the New York Atlas Company to help him be even more concise. He thumbed through it incessantly. When he finished a letter, he fell asleep quickly and hardly ever dreamed.

Nine months or so after the weddings, babies were born and yearly thereafter. John took pictures of all of them, the boys naked, propped up against pillows, showing their little penises, the girls in modest baptismal dress. He asked to become godfather to a son of the woman who came from the village near Elasson; he even allowed her to choose the name. Miltiades, she said gratefully, the name of her father; a first-grade teacher would later change it to Milt. Milt's mother grew plump, fat, then stout, and always insisted that John eat dinner with her family on the great feast days of the church. John would have liked to become a godfather to other children of men he met in Stellios's restáurant or in the coffeehouses, but the cost would have reduced the dowry money he was accumulating.

Regularly, too, young men were killed in mine accidents. Photographs of the weddings, baptisms, and the dead in open caskets were needed for friends in America and families in Greece. Twice he had taken pictures of a wedding, baptism, and a funeral in the same day. He was so busy coffeehouse habitués kept wondering aloud when he found time to write letters. He wrote weekly to the church board and more often to the Greek-language newspapers published in the city, first the *Evzone* and later its successor *The Light*. Being better schooled than the workers, he explained Greek political upheavals succinctly, showing the groundwork laid by past historical events. He never failed to bring in the hated Turks, no matter how farfetched their connection. Although he was capable of writing in the purist, the *katharevousa*, he wrote in the demotic. Immigrants with a few years' schooling comprised the church boards and, as John explained to the well-educated editor, if readers were to understand his letters, he had to write in the everyday language.

He became melancholy. It would take longer than he had expected to provide his younger sisters with dowries and save enough for himself to set up a shop in *patridha*. He began writing about conditions among the Greeks in America. It kept his mind off seeing other immigrants marrying and having children. Men teased him when he passed by the coffeehouses, called out to him to become a priest. All because he wanted people to be better than they were. He wanted bosses at the mines, mills, and smelters to do away with the *mesitis*, the agents who bled the laborers. He wanted the Panhellenic Unions and the Greek lodges to give better benefits to the injured and the survivors of the dead. He wanted the laborers to stay away from prostitutes and gamblers. He wanted them to send more of their money back to their families for their sisters' dowries just as he had come to America to do and was doing.

His letters were duly read to the church board, and at intervals when, as the editor told him, there was space in the newspaper, his letters were published. At times the editor thanked him in editorials for a letter and paraphrased it. But this was not enough. John sat up until late at night and under a dangling light globe made copies of his letters and sent them to prominent or more educated men: the Athenian doctor with a degree from a German university, the attorney who had made friends with the county sheriff, and the Greek schoolteacher who enticed him into coffeehouses to argue with him before an attentive audience whenever he saw him walking with the tripod over his shoulder. He enjoyed talking with the current Greek priest, though John thought him more interested in the collection plate than in his duties. There were times, John knew, when he left out parts of the liturgy. He wrote the priest a carefully worded letter suggesting he cut his long hair and not wear his robes and tall black priest hat outside the church. "When you go back to Greece," John ended with kindly advice, "you can let your hair grow again and wear your *rassa* and *kalimafkion*." The priest stopped speaking to him.

While other bachelors continued bringing wives from their villages or, to his distaste, marrying American women, John steadfastly made the rounds of the mining towns, read both American and Greek newspapers voraciously, and wrote letters. The letters became more frequent, longer, with straight pins to keep the pages together. He widened his concerns. The letters began to include his insights on American politics and situations that needed reform. Each night he went to bed exhausted and fell asleep immediately.

There was so much to write about in the second decade of the 1900s and the early 1920s. John was almost drafted in the World War. He was saved by his short height and a hernia, kept in place by a truss which the Greek doctor who had trained in Germany prescribed for him. The war was lucrative for John. At first the Greeks balked at serving because they were not yet citizens, especially after reading John's letter in the Greek newspaper demanding that "The Allies better make known immediately what will happen to Greek lands after the war. Will the Great Powers again use this opportunity to cut up Greece under the ruse of protecting her?" The men began to enlist when the Americans raised fists at them or when they were drafted, and all wanted pictures of themselves in their ill-fitting uniforms to send to their villages. By the time of the Armistice, John had finished paying for his second sister's dowry.

Then came the repressive immigration laws; strikes; the Ku Klux Klan attacks on immigrants—burning crosses, marches, beatings; a mine explosion that killed 171 miners, 49 of them Greeks. Many of the miners were mangled, unrecognizable, and could not be photographed. John took pictures of the others in their open caskets and, if they were unmarried, with wedding crowns on their heads.

By then the babies he had photographed at baptism were now children attending church and the Greek school in its basement. Teachers and priests came and went; he took pictures of all of them standing alongside their students. He was busy taking photographs of grocery stores, restaurants, and shoeshine and hat-cleaning parlors the immigrants were opening with their savings from the mines, mills, and smelters.

Greek Town was breaking up by the mid-twenties, and an exodus had begun toward the eastside of town. John took photographs of the new houses and was able to send a dowry for his youngest sister, who had been two years old when he left Greece. The groom had come from a village outside Elasson, John's nearly illiterate father had written, but he told John nothing more, not even the groom's family name. Then, unexpectedly, John had to pay off a mortgage his father had taken on his land because at the last moment the bridegroom demanded a completely furnished house. His father had a stroke and died the day after the wedding. John immediately wrote asking for the name and address of the bridegroom so he could send him to the devil. His family never answered his letter, and the next one made no mention of the groom's duplicity. "They're vultures! They think we shovel gold in America," he told Stellios over a plate of lamb stew. As soon as he had paid off his father's mortgage and saved some money for himself, he would return to Greece and fix that bastard, that gypsy!

Greek Town was changing rapidly. John's boardinghouse was torn down to make room for a sausage factory, and he was forced to move closer to Main Street. He found a first-floor apartment, dreary, dim, one room with kitchenette. He turned the room into a studio, with a cot in one corner where he slept. To save money for stamps and stationery and for the savings he would take with him to Greece, he began to cook most of his meals on a two-plate burner. Invariably he ate sardines, feta cheese, and a hunk of bread pulled off the round loaf he carried home through the crook of his elbow. He sometimes looked up from his plate and thought of Stellios's kitchen, where customers picked up the lids and peered inside pots while they decided what to order. And he missed Stellios, the good hearty Cretan, always ready to sit down when he'd served everyone and talk about everything that had gone on that day. Still, John would not put his letter-writing duties aside to linger about at Stellios's restaurant and the coffee-houses nearby. Once a month after liturgy he allowed himself a Sunday meal at Stellios's Stadium Cafe.

During the mid-twenties another Greek photographer set up shop. He had not gone to school as John had, but had paid a Mormon photographer ten dollars to show him his trade. Sometimes John read of a wedding in *The Light* and realized he had not been asked to take the traditional pictures. He contemplated the news for a few minutes, then went back to his letters.

He did attend the *horoesperidhes,* the evening dances in the church basement, but for little more than an hour. He loved the clarinet's soaring and descending notes as it vibrated with the old songs of treachery under the Turks. Now the children of the immigrants were in junior high school, and some could dance to the old village songs of laments and desires better than their elders. His overweight godson Milt was especially good, a showoff, but good. After fulfilling his godfatherly duties by dancing with Milt, John returned to his apartment to work on his letters.

Suddenly *The Light* stopped publication. John was so saddened that his heart pained off and on for weeks. The immigration restriction laws had drastically cut off the newspaper's biggest number of readers, the newest arrivals who had not yet become accustomed to America. John turned to writing letters to the New York *Atlantis* and *National Herald,* the *California,* and Chicago's two papers, all of which the immigrants seemed to prefer anyway. Sometimes his letters were printed with portions left out, and this kept John busy with correspondence explaining why they should be published again in full. He began to dislike newspaper editors. If they knew him, he thought, they would pay more attention to him, but they didn't think the West was important. The only newspaper man he knew was the *California* reporter who came through the city every two or three weeks. He left with local news and John's latest letter pressed upon him.

Of all his letters, his masterpiece was written during the Depression of the thirties. Of course, it was illogical to return to Greece under such conditions; they were suffering badly there, according to the begging letters he received from his sisters—his mother had died, weakened from malaria. Besides, he had to help provide his oldest sister's daughter with a dowry.

John's photography had become an annoyance to him; it kept him from his letter-writing. Even the dinners at his godson's house interfered with his letters, but he could do nothing about it. Milt's father, suspiciously not affected by the Depression, would drive John to his house in a bright new Studebaker. When his godson was old enough to drive, around twelve or thirteen, a dark down above his upper lip, he began picking John up. A sullen respect was on Milt's round face, but John, thinking about the letter he was writing, did not notice.

The masterpiece was written in longhand. John became a recluse while working on it. He had little else to do. Because of the Depression fewer people were marrying, and sometimes children were baptized without a photograph to celebrate the event. After he was satisfied with the letter, he took it to a young Greek whose uncle had brought him from Greece for a university education. John paid the student to translate his letter and then had a printer make 550 copies. He needed that many, he told the young man, because he intended to send his Depression plan to the president, his cabinet members, every senator, congressman, governor, and supreme court judge. John got the addresses in the federal offices on the second floor of the post office where he had taken his oath of citizenship. The letter was two pages long, single-spaced, and in small type. The title was "Social Security Pension and Unemployment Plan" by John H. Hagros. His address appeared beneath this.

The letter began: "I have given serious consideration to the Townsend Plan as well of other forms of social security but . . . ." He then went on to describe his plan, which "if the best minds think it necessary to put it in effect, a constitutional amendment should be proposed." Every male and female over the age of sixty should retire to give the younger unemployed work and in return receive one hundred dollars a month, except for divorced persons. They should receive only fifty dollars a month to discourge divorce. It is reported, his letter went on, "that fifty percent of the inmates in the penitentiaries throughout the land come from divorced families."

John's plan included a three and one-half percent tax on the hundred dollars and a complicated paying-in of fifteen dollars a month to pension funds by all working people. In great detail he described how the plan would work, down to a pension book each person would carry at all times. He finished with the sentence: "We must act; we must persist if we are to keep intact the American ideals and American economic independence." He received a number of form letters thanking him for his concern, and all ended with "Your letter will be taken under consideration."

As the months passed and his plan was still being considered, John wrote another, stronger letter. He began: "The working man's enemies are the machine and the women who hold positions that he, as a man, is entitled to and can not obtain. The modern working woman has deprived men and boys from millions of jobs. All married women, regardless of age, should not be allowed to work for the Government or any private firm whatsoever. (Not to include widows and divorcees)."

After several paragraphs, he gave his second point: factory owners should set prices for their goods, and retail stores could only advertise their names and addresses. This would stop raising prices that put people at the mercy of retailers. His last point was a castigation of chain stores "that have completely ruined the small dealer. It should be enforced that drug stores be equipped only with drugs, clothing stores only with clothes, shoe stores only with shoes, etc."

He sent the letter to the same politicians as those who had received his social security plan and this time included Eleanor Roosevelt. Because the president allowed her to travel about instead of staying in the White House, it showed she had influence on him. That's how some American men were; they listened to their wives.

While Washington politicians were studying his plan and subsequent letter, he wrote a long letter to the current church board proposing a sickness and death benefit plan that would ensure every member of the congregation peace of mind during economic slumps. Nothing was done about it. "Just wait," he accosted them after liturgies, "you'll remember my advice some day, but 'does the deaf man hear the bell?' "

Still waiting for word from Washington, delayed, John was certain, by World War II, which had obliterated the Depression, John began a campaign in 1946 to keep the Greek language alive among the immigrants' children. He wrote the archbishop of the great danger the Greek Orthodox religion faced in America; children were not taking the Greek lanaguage to heart. His letter was four ledger pages long, single-spaced, and in Greek typescript. He had bought the typewriter from the former editor of *The Light*.

It was hard work for John to peck out the Greek type, but he had all day to do it. When he finished, he wrote out copies by hand because it was easier than using the typewriter, and asked the current priest for permission to copy the addresses of all Greek Orthodox churches in the United States from the archdiocese yearbook. He told the president of the Mothers Club that he would bring the letter to their next meeting and read it.

The immigrant mothers, now grandmothers, many in black for old-country dead, took their places on rows of folding chairs in the church basement. Holding their purses protectively on their laps, they listened to Kyrios Hagros, who had taken their family wedding, baptismal, and, for some, husbands' funeral pictures.

"I've invited you here today," he began, "because of the great danger we face with our new generation. Our religion that sustained our holy land during the centuries of Turkish tyranny is on the verge of vanishing. And you mothers have the responsibility . . . ." He went on exhorting the mothers to preserve the language and by all means to resist the translations of the liturgy into English which the American-born priests were carelessly allowing. This would be the first step, he said sternly, to oblivion for the Greek language in America.

A few women looked at him with alarm; most sighed, weary from years of telling their children, "In the house Greek!," weary from keeping grandchildren on the weekends to take them to church on Sunday while their parents slept, weary from lecturing their sons and daughters to send their children to Greek school. The mothers were also distracted by another matter. They were to vote that day on whether the Mothers Club would be disbanded in favor of joining the archdiocese organization, the Philoptochos. A strong group was against it, even after the young American-born priest patiently explained the benefits of affiliating with the Philoptochos. Long before John, now grayed, his mouth pursed permanently into a thin line, finished reading his long, repetitive paper, the women were deathly weary of him also.

Among other letters the following year, he wrote a long, angry one at priests, parents, and the hierarchy over the lack of formal religious training for the new generation. He seemed unaware that the new generation, as the children of immigrants had been called, was no more; a third generation, the grandchildren of the immigrants had appeared. He ended his letter: "After fifty years we enter church and leave and we have not catechized one boy or girl in the Eastern Orthodox dogma."

He had talked about this with the current priest, a tall, handsome man, just graduated from the seminary, and was assured that more would be done and that new literature was coming for the Sunday school classes. John liked the respectful, soft-spoken young priest exceedingly until his sermon relating the Turkish restrictions on the Patriarchate in Constantinople. Never would John, a Greek, call it Istanbul. There were further proscriptions on the dwindling Greek population there and in Smyrna, which John would not call by its Turkish name, Izmir. John thought the priest was lukewarm about the Turks: there was no fire in his voice. He sat up most of the night composing a letter to the priest suggesting that in his next sermon representatives from the church board, from the two general lodges, the American Hellenic Educational Progressive Association—the AHEPA—and the Greek American Progressive Association—the GAPA—and from the lodges representing provinces in Greece make an outcry to the American government about the Turkish tyranny.

The priest did not mention John's letter the following Sunday. Every Sunday from then on John sat angrily in his usual place, the second pew on the right side, and only made a pretense of kissing the priest's hand when he handed out the consecrated bread at the end of the liturgy. He felt vindicated when the priest was transferred to a California parish.

Then came a most feverish letter-writing period that left him sweating and forced him to change his clothing several times a day. President John F. Kennedy had been assassinated. The young man who had translated John's letters had long since moved to Chicago, so he bought a secondhand typewriter with English letters and typed the letter himself.

Honorable President,
Lyndon B. Johnson
Washington, D, C, November 30, 1963

After witnessing on television and reding in the news papers the description of the tragic events of last week I thought I in my humble way, might express to you my sendiments of my heart. History record this as one of the worst tragetes that has befallen nation. As a humble citizen of the United States may I thank you for paying such honor and tribute to our former president John Fitzgerald Kennedy, by renaming Cape Caraveral and the Misele station in his name, I thing that you would be doing our country a grate service if you could by proclamation change the name of our street where our beloved president was so tragically slain to John F. Kennedy St, and place in the center a memorial plague descriping the incedent and denouncing this act. As was custom in my native land Greece. Anathema.

With heartfeld Sincerity,

John G. Hagros

A year later the Archdiocese sent him a two-sentence letter: "Archbishop Iakovos and the Greek Orthodox Diocese wish to thank you for the copies of the letters that you sent to President Johnson, Governor Connally of Texas and Mrs. John F. Kennedy. We are glad to have this for our files." It was signed by the Director of Information, someone with the un-Greek name of Arthur Dore. John fumed over the letter. He had given up writing to the Archdiocese because no one had ever taken his letters seriously. The Archdiocese did not deserve to have his letter in its files.

For two years he wrote letters extolling President Kennedy, "the ever memorable martyr, bing the forerunner for peace and savior to all mankind." Unfortunately, there were devils in this world. "It would have been better this Lucifer Satan Lee Harvey Oswald not been born." "We glory in President Kennedy's name," he wrote, "we lay incense for his memory. His name will leve as a memory to humanity while the sun shines in the heavens." He ended his letter with the traditional Greek invocation for the dead, the words *eternal memory,* which John wrote in English as *internal memory.*

John's next writing enterprise was over the decision to build a church in the suburbs where many of the second generation had moved and where almost all of the third generation lived. This left the immigrant church one-fourth filled on Sundays. Angrily he berated the board for having to borrow money to build the church. Where did all the money from dues, from special trays, from the *horoesperidthes* go to? There was no excuse again to ask people to donate to a new church when money had flowed through the hands of the church boards for sixty-five years. Also, why should the new building cost seven-hundred-thousand dollars? There were four Greek builders in the parish; they could donate their services and save half of the money. John also brought out his twenty-year-old sickness and death plan which the "hard-hearted Greeks" had not put into practice. But it was not too late. Now he revised his figures to comply with present-day economics and showed how easily his plan could be implemented.

John was then living on Social Security. His godson Milt, nagged by his mother, had taken him to the government offices to fill out the forms. Regularly Milt took him to the University Medical Center for a variety of illnesses, mostly arthritis. No one had asked John to take a photograph in years. The coffeehouses and Stellios's restaurant on Second South had all closed. The old-timers, the bachelors who had frequented them, had died or were in nursing homes; a few like Stellios had gone back to Greece.

John now spent his days recycling his letters. On the corner from his apartment building a copying center had opened. When John realized his letters did not have to be copied in his spidery crooked writing—he had developed a slight palsy—he became a frequent customer. The plump, bustling woman there helped him along because he took so much time carefully placing the pages exactly between the green lines, slowly bringing the lid down, and gazing at the numbers to decide which one to punch while he thought of whom he wanted to receive copies. The list of people changed with each new church board and city administration.

After making the copies, he spent the entire day mailing the recycled letters and reading the Greek-language and local newspapers. He complained to his godson Milt that Greek life in America was doomed. The Greek pages of the Chicago and New York newspapers were shrinking and the English were gaining. "Yeah, yeah," Milt would answer. Milt took him to a *horoesperidha* in the adjoining memorial hall built to honor the soldiers who died in the Second World War. Aghast, John said in a loud voice, "What do these young people think they're doing? What kind of Greek dancing is this? They've spoiled the noble dances! And who allowed those *bouzouki* players in here? The *bouzoukia* are only good enough for the seaports, for scum!" Milt took him home.

Milt now had grandchildren of his own; he was training, or so he explained it to his wife, his sons and son-in-law to take over the business. After his mother died, Milt always invited John to Christmas, Easter, and Thanksgiving dinners, but he began to decline. "I can't stand the noise," he told Milt. In reality he was too busy thinking about World War III. It had come to him starkly one night. At first he thought it was a dream that had awakened him, but, no, he had not been asleep. He was sure of that. It was telepathy. Someone, God probably, showed him a massive onslaught of Russian tanks landing in New York, moving down the streets, many streets, not just one, as in a parade, and fluttering above each one was a Red flag with the hammer and sickle insignia.

He sat up, shocked. Then with great urgency, his heart palpitating, he sat down and wrote President Jimmy Carter that the Russians were coming! World War III was on the horizon! He waited a week for an answer. His heart strangling inside his thin chest, he went to Western Union and sent a telegram to the president. Again he waited and heard nothing. Then he realized that the tone in the newspapers had changed. Something was going on. The Russian ambassador had been asked to call on the president. The American ambassador to Russia was summoned to the White House and then returned to the Soviet Union. That's how it was, he realized. For security reasons the government could not draw attention to him and his letter. The triumph of it! John sat down and wrote a long letter explaining how he had thwarted World War III. He copied it and, using the church directory, mailed it to a long list of people.

He was perplexed. He met people on the street, in church—when his arthritis wasn't too painful—and no one mentioned his letter. "Did you get my letter?" he asked, and they nodded and smiled and someone told him to keep up the good work and turned from him with a smirk. He complained to Milt. Here he had performed a great service, and no one appreciated it. People were invited to the White House and given medals for doing nothing much, and he, who had saved the country, the world, from World War III didn't get even one letter of thanks. Milt's brother-in-law had even smirked. Well, maybe it wasn't a smirk, but it looked like it.

He would not let it go. Milt brought him a plate of feta cheese pastries one day, and after telling him about his troubles with his sons and son-in-law, talked about one of the last of the old-timers who had gone to Greece to live on his Social Security. "He sent a letter to his nephew that he wished he'd gone back sooner. His relatives treat him like a king." It was a lie. The old-timer congregated with other returnees in the Athens Astoria Bar and talked about America—how they wished they had stayed there, how much better people were there. In Athens you were treated like an upstart when you went into a store to buy something, were ignored. They didn't do this to tourists unless they were Greek-American. Then they looked at them with contempt. As for relatives, they conveniently forgot who sent them money for dowries, who helped them open a shop, who made it possible for sons to go to universities. When they found out that the only money they had was Social Security, they cooled immediately.

It began to take John longer to walk down the few steps of his apartment building; he had to stop several times on his way to the Broadway Store two blocks north to buy cheese, Kalamata olives, and sardines. Sometimes he ached so much he could not leave his apartment and drank coffee, ate stale bread, and hoped Milt would come by before he died of starvation.

One day he realized there was nothing left in the cupboard, only coffee. He crossed himself at the icon, cursed Milt for abandoning him, and begged the Virgin to send the Philoptochos church women with a basket. No one came. He used up all the coffee, searched in drawers for pastries that the church women brought and which he might have forgotten. He found nothing. He lay down on the cot, fully dressed, folded his arms, and waited for death, for Charon to come. He dozed. Suddenly he opened his eyes. Milt was standing over him. "You, you," he stammered, but he did not have the energy to finish calling him a devil. Milt insisted he had told him that he was going on a trip.

"You left me to starve," John whispered.

"Starve!" Milt opened the refrigerator. "Look!" There on the shelves were cheeses, olives, sliced ham, smoked fish, pickled vegetables, and cans of beer, which John did not drink, but which helped Milt pass the quarter-of-an-hour visits he felt obligated to spend with his godfather.

John stared at the open refrigerator. He hadn't looked inside. Then he knew something was very wrong with him. He had grown old, too old. Milt prepared a plate for him and he ate only a little of it. It was repulsive to him. "You know, Milt," he said, looking away with bloodshot eyes, "I better go to Greece, better go live with my niece's daughters." Milt quickly made the arrangements, packed John's bag, and took him to the airport. He never received a single letter from him.

A Mother's Curse

In a western cemetery a large polished granite stone stands over a double grave. Above the names of the young couple with their birth and death date—they died together—an oval glass frame encases their picture. They are young and handsome, the man with the sleek hair and the woman with a fluff of bangs of 1920s fashion. An ornamental iron fence encloses the grave. The grave is barren now, but for decades it had been tended by the man's mother and sisters; geraniums and basil grew about it, and a pink climbing rose made an arch over the top of the gravestone. The man's mother died; his sisters married, moved away, yet came back regularly to take care of the grave. When they died, nieces and nephews would not make the journey.

The bride's mother never visited the grave, nor did her three remaining daughters—they did not dare. The mother had pronounced her curse, it had taken effect, and she would never forgive the stain on her family's honor.

The dead couple's families, the Hatzimihalis and the Manolakis, had been neighbors in the western mining town. The daughters had visited back and forth since they were children to sit on each other's porches crocheting and embroidering their dowry linens. The Hatzimihalis's four daughters—they had no brothers—and the three Manolakis daughters were the only Greek girls in the mining town, in the entire county. The oldest daughters of each family had been properly married off. The second Hatzimihalis daughter Agape, barely seventeen, was engaged to a prosperous Cretan ten years older than she. He was a respected storeowner.

Other immigrants waited around for the younger two Hatzimihalis schoolgirls to become eligible for marriage because there was a problem with the Manolakis daughters. The youngest daughter's right arm was considerably shorter than the left and withered besides. On his deathbed the father had made the family take an oath that the middle daughter would not marry until a husband was found for the youngest. The shortage of Greek women in America did not spur anyone to accept her, and the two Manolakis daughters remained unmarried despite the efforts of their two remaining brothers. A third brother had been killed by a freight train while crossing the railroad tracks on a starless black night.

Whoever married into the Hatzimihalis family would be fortunate. The daughters were pretty and plump. The Hatzimihalis restaurant was also prosperous, the popular place to eat after mine shifts. The young men did not care that Mr. Hatzimihalis with the smiling blue eyes was not a first-rate cook and that sharp-eyed Mrs. Hatzimihalis (sensing her newfound importance) was even more sharp with her tongue.

Although both mothers were not yet fifty years of age, they wore black dresses, stockings, and caps edged in black lace for the dead of their clans in Crete, and Mrs. Manolakis, further, for her husband, who had died in America, and the son who had died on the railroad tracks. The mothers were on good terms—small, quiet Mrs. Manolakis never disagreed with Mrs. Hatzimihalis. They had mutual acquaintances back in their villages and behaved toward each other with the impelled politeness of people with marriageable children.

It was impossible, though, to overlook the obvious: there were times when Mrs. Hatzimihalis reminded the immigrants of her volatile father, who had led an uprising against the Turkish rulers in 1898. In contrast, people said Mrs. Manolakis was *glykia,* sweet. Sweet, people said whenever her name was mentioned. The two mothers spoke to each other while they hung up wash or watered their small gardens. Mrs. Hatzimihalis was more than civil to Mrs. Manolakis because she had lost one son and because her son Nikos, the gambler, had almost been lynched during World War I for giving an American girl a ride in his new red Packard. Calls had gone out to every coffeehouse in the surrounding mining camps, and a horde of Cretans came running with guns in their belts to save him.

Mrs. Hatzimihalis tsk-tsked over poor Mrs. Manolakis, whose youngest daughter had been given the bad fate of a withered arm. Certainly no one would marry her, and that would leave her and her older sister unmarried, a blot on the family's honor. The family was doomed to have four unmarried children. Custom would keep Mrs. Manolakis's two sons from marrying until their sisters had. The older son had worked in a coal mine and with his savings had established himself as a representative of a wholesale grocery distributor. The younger Nikos had never worked in a mine. He drove his red Packard from one mining camp to the other with passengers—"Nikos Hatzimihalis Stage." His real work was gambling.

The two families lived on a short lane behind the one street of the town. At one end of Main Street the small restaurant of the Hatzimihalis family stood next to the coffeehouse. The floor was bare, and oilcloth covered the tables. On the walls were maps and pictures of Cretan heroes of several revolts against the Turks. Wearing black breeches, fringed head kerchiefs, and bandoliers of bullets crossed over their chests, they challenged anyone to come nearer. Mrs. Hatzimihalis's father had a place of honor on the wall next to a potbellied stove. His Arabic eyes looked out fiercely, and the tips of his luxuriant mustache twisted upwards. Mrs. Hatzimihalis had his eyes. On the deep windowsill, gnarled rubber plants grew in large, square olive oil cans and in front of them potted basil plants for which the men pinched off sprigs for their lapels. Since the oldest daughter had married and moved to another mining town seven miles away, the second daughter, Agape, helped her father in the kitchen and waited on tables.

Agape was to be married on a Sunday but was still working in the restaurant on Thursday when her neighbor Nikos Hatzimihalis came in and sat at a table near the door. No one was in the restaurant. It was three o'clock; the mine whistles had just signaled the change of shifts from day to afternoon. It would be some time before the miners washed themselves, changed, and came to eat.

"So, Agape," Nikos said in a low voice with a glance toward the closed kitchen door, "you're going to marry Spirogiannis this Sunday."

"Yes," Agape said and sighed.

"Why don't you marry me instead? Spirogiannis isn't much of a man."

Agape took off her apron, and a few minutes later they were on their way to a justice of the peace in a neighboring mining camp. She made two telephone calls, one before the ceremony to Spirogiannis.

"Is the house ready?" she asked him.

"Yes, ready."

"Is the bed ready?"

"Ready."

"Find another woman to lie on it."

After the justice of the peace pronounced them man and wife, Agape made the second telephone call, this time to her mother. "Mama, Nikos Manolakis and I have married, and we're coming home."

"Dead you will come, alive never," her mother answered, slammed the receiver, and marched next door to the Manolakis house. Without knocking she barged into the kitchen and berated Mrs. Manolakis, who at the moment was making cheese pastries with her two unmarried daughters.

"That gambler son of yours! That worthless buyer of prostitutes, that miserable scum of the gutter!"

Mrs. Manolakis crossed her floured arms against her chest and shriveled. "What, what?" she whispered. Her daughters clapped their floured fingers against their mouths.

"He enticed Agape! They eloped! You knew it! You knew what was going on! You devil of a neighbor!"

"No, no. I knew nothing! How could I? He has two unmarried sisters to think of."

"You lie! Him and his honeyed words! And to think we treated that devil like a son because we were neighbors! Let them rot in Hell!" Mrs. Hatzimihalis ranted on as Mrs. Manolakis slumped onto a chair weeping softly. "He should have been killed along with his brother and found cut in two! He should have been hanged when he took that American girl for a ride! But no! His stupid countrymen went to his rescue! You wretch!" Mrs. Hatzimihalis shouted in parting.

She trudged to her husband's restaurant, swinging her arms like a soldier off to war. Mr. Hatzimihalis was at the stove pouring wine and sprinkling cloves onto a stew. He had knotted a handkerchief around his head to keep the sweat from dripping into the simmering meat. Mrs. Hatzimihalis shouted at him for not keeping an eye on his daughter, for being a happy-go-lucky man who saw no evil. Her husband stared at her out of startled blue eyes: he hadn't missed Agape; he thought she was cleaning the tables.

Mr. Hatzimihalis took the stew off the coal stove, locked the door, and went next door to the coffeehouse. There he found a cousin and two of his fellow villagers. Their eyes flashed at the news. They knew what to do. The cousin had a gun inside his belt, the villagers knives.

Mr. Hatzimihalis then walked to his house. His wife had telephoned their married daughter, and by the time the two younger daughters returned from grade school, she, her husband, and their baby were present at the table. While they waited the return of the cousin and friends, Mrs. Hatzimihalis glared at the younger girls and told them, "No more school for you. Before we know it, you'll bring us American husbands!" The girls bowed their heads and cried silently.

Mrs. Hatzimihalis condemned them all for not having seen what was coming. She hurled questions at the youngest daughters. "Didn't you see anything? Did you see something and not think to tell me? Were you in conspiracy with her, that slut, that *poutana*, that wretch who has blackened our name! How are we ever going to marry you now! See what you have done by being dumb and blind! You worthless daughters! That's what we get for bringing you to America for a better life!"

No one was exempt, not the married daughter trying to look innocent or her husband who protested, "How could we know what was going on? We live seven miles away."

"People talk! You must have heard something!"

"Nothing! We saw and heard nothing!"

The baby cried and was taken into a bedroom, where his mother nursed him. An hour passed, the family sitting at the table and waiting, Mrs. Hatzimihalis fuming on. At the rattle on the porch screen, they all stood up. The cousin and friends entered shaking their heads. "They got on a train going east," Mr. Hatzimihalis's cousin said.

"Go back and open the place," Mrs. Hatzimihalis said to her husband. "We lost a snake of a daughter; we can't lose our livelihood, too."

Apologetically and even fearfully, Greek Town women came to visit Mrs. Hatzimihalis. She served the traditional sweet and Turkish coffee and loudly castigated the Manolakis family, particularly Mrs. Manolakis. The women were afraid of Mrs. Hatzimihalis's wrath and were reluctant to visit Mrs. Manolakis, although several telephoned to ask about her health. Mrs. Manolakis's daughters began hanging up the wash at night when the Hatzimihalis house was dark, with only the faint glow of the icon light coming from one window.

Then the terrible news came. Agape and Nikos were dead. Their rented car had failed to take a curve and plummeted down a hillside and into a lake. One call said a sudden rainstorm obscured the road, another that Agape had grabbed at Nikos. Neither she nor Nikos could swim. From the Manolakis house cries and sobs came from the windows; black crepe hung from the front and back doors. No sound came from the Hatzimihalis house. Mrs. Hatzimihalis allowed no weeping. The waiter who had taken Agape's place said tears ran down Mr. Hatzimihalis' face even when he was not chopping onions.

It took ten days to recover the bodies. Mrs. Manolakis's remaining son, the grocery distributor, took a train to Chicago to bring the bodies back and made the funeral arrangements. The bodies were then brought to each family's living room for the women's laments. The keening lasted a few hours in the Hatzimihalis house. In the Manolakis house the keening went on all day and night before the funeral. The married daughter, the old maid, and the crippled sister took turns, but their mother would not leave the side of the closed casket. She had wanted it open, to see Nikos with the wedding crown on his head, but her son said it could not be, so many days in the water, no, she would have the terrible memory until she died. People went from the Manolakis house to the Hatzimihalis house to pay their respects at the closed caskets. Mrs. Hatzimihalis nodded, stony faced.

Blue incense rose before the icon screen in the small, flower-filled Byzantine church. The priest intoned beautifully. Mrs. Manolakis, her daughters, her son wept, wept, wept. Mrs. Hatzimihalis's husband and daughters wiped their eyes furtively. Neither in church nor in the graveyard did Mrs. Hatzimihalis shed a tear. Mrs. Manolakis fainted and was revived by her son and daughters; at the funeral dinner afterwards she ate only enough to satisfy the custom of farewell to the dead.

Mrs. Hatzimihalis followed all the traditional funeral rites, remained cloistered for forty days, prepared the memorial wheat forty days after burial, the boiled wheat mixed with raisins, nuts, parsley, and pomegranate seeds, had her daughter's name read by the priest along with those of her parents and other dead relatives on Saturday of the Souls. But it was said then and for years afterwards that she never shed a tear.

Mrs. Hatzimihalis gave the Manolakis family no peace. When the daughters quietly opened the door on their way to buy groceries, Mrs. Hatzimihalis hurried out to shout at them. Mrs. Manolakis never left the house except to visit the grave, clean it, and plant flowers, but Mrs. Hatzimihalis stood at the fence and shouted curses at her anyway: "I know you can hear me! Gypsy! Street woman!"

Then in the worst years of the thirties Depression, the youngest Manolakis daughter was married to a poor man, the owner of a shoe repair shop over a hundred miles north. A matchmaker then arranged a marriage for the older sister, in her mid-thirties, to an immigrant in his fifties, and she took her mother with her to Los Angeles. Regularly they sent money to keep the graves weeded and in flowers. Several times each decade they returned to care for it themselves.

"If," people said over and over again, year after year, "Nikos had followed tradition and not married until his sisters had, it would not have happened, but he was headstrong. In America he forgot his culture." "If Agape had been a proper daughter and married the man chosen for her, it would not have happened." "If Nikos had not come into the cafe when it was empty, it would not have happened." "If the Hatzimihalis had at least one brother to keep Agape in check, it would not have happened." "If Mr. Hatzimihalis had not been so carefree holed up in the kitchen." "If Mrs. Hatzimihalis had not been so proud."

Then they spoke the ancient words: "It was their fate," and the proverb followed: "A mother's curse is the worst curse of all."

Old Jim

In the 1980s no one was alive to have known the tragedy firsthand except an old man in his late nineties, living in a nursing home. He had never been certain of his age. Yet in his great old age, vestiges of the once handsome man he had been showed in his well-shaped head, unlined forehead, and straight nose. On holidays the Greek church women brought him baskets of toiletries that disappeared from his bedstand during the night and fruit and sweets, which he gave to the nurses and aids. Otherwise no one visited him. His friends had died, and he had never married: he had been afraid he had bad blood from visiting brothels.

All day he sat in a heavy reclining chair and sometimes stared across the hall into the four-bed ward. He would be moved there when his money ran out, and he would have to go on Medicaid. He could see one bed from where he sat; the old man curled up on it could not remember the names of the children and grandchildren who visited him.

The nurses and aids called him Old Jim. In the village he had been called by the diminutive "Dimitrakis," then after a few years in America "Dimitrios," then the American "James" or "Jim," and at last "Old Jim." Sitting in the chair left by the previous client, as the social worker called patients ("And how is my client today?"), Old Jim was beginning to forget the first ten years—more or less—of his life. When he and his young uncle left their Greek mountain village for America, his mother, father, the doddering midwife, and the priest who had neglected to record his baptismal date, all offered different dates. The exasperated mayor wrote down "ten" on his emigration papers.

Old Jim remembered more about his life in America and thought he should have lived his life differently, married, raised children, and, most importantly, kept away from brothels. He remembered as he sat in his cubicle the first time he had gone to one and the terrible beating his uncle had given him. He had been either fourteen, fifteen, or sixteen, and as fate would have it, his uncle, who should have been sleeping in preparation for the graveyard shift at the mine, was entering the brothel as he was leaving it.

Hardly a day passed, though, that he did not review a decades-old tragedy, speaking aloud to the bare wall ahead. He began with the same words and in Greek—the closer he came to the end, the fewer English words he spoke: "It would never have happened if a Greek woman had been there. But Yiannina and her husband didn't come until the next year, in 1902. If she had been there, she would have served us the fish dinner after the funeral. We would have sat around and talked about the forgiven one and passed the evening, but she hadn't come yet." Sometimes he would pause, forget his story, and dwell on Yiannina.

When Yiannina arrived in the mining town, the first Greek woman among two thousand men and a few boys, she had been angry at learning the laborers and waterboys on railroad gangs and in mines lived in tents and shacks. The men had built the shacks themselves out of blasting powder boxes. Neither the shacks nor the tents had water or privies, which did not bother her; they had neither in the village. She had walked a mile each day to bring back a jug balanced on her head, and bushes were the village privies. It was the lice in the clothes, in the boys' hair that she would not tolerate. She ordered the boys' relatives and villagers to throw clothes and bedding over her fence once a week. With a long stick, because they were crawling with lice, she dropped them into a large pot of water boiling over an outdoor fire. She lectured the older men about washing their hair, and cowed by a woman who was forgetting in America the subservience of women, they did. Once a week she had the boys line up in her backyard and used plenty of kerosene and soap on their heads. Old Jim, then called Dimitrakis, liked to be first in line. Afterwards she served them stews and sweets that were not luxuries in America. She never smiled.

Yiannina took charge of the boys while she gave birth to a child every year. New waterboys replaced the older ones, who then went to the railroad YMCA for showers. With a faint smile Old Jim gazed at the wall while he thought of Yiannina.

At other times he told the story straight through. In 1901 a steamship agent came to their village. He was dressed in store-bought clothes and a brown derby; he smoked thick cigars and had shaved off his mustache. Men and boys gathered on the village square to ask about America. There was not a question the agent could not answer. After being in America a few years, the men remembered some of his foolish answers. For one thing, he had said, yes, American women were also required to have dowries.

The labor agent's mission was to hire men to work in mines and on railroads in the American West. The agent worked for another Greek, he said, who knew all the mine and railroad managers there, and he would advance ship and railroad fares and deduct the cost from the men's wages after they got to the West. The first to sign up was Dimitrakis's young uncle. His three friends immediately followed. First Stavros, his special friend; they often spent weeks together on the mountainside tending their families' few sheep and goats that browsed among scree and holyoak. Villagers praised his voice, a wonder compared with the old chanter who croaked along and had done so even as a young man. Next, Evangelos laboriously wrote his name, although he was never called by it, but either Slavos because of his wide Slavic head or Squash, when he did something stupid, which was often. Last to sign was Nondas, the acclaimed dancer of the village. On feast days the villagers crowded about the square to watch him jump and twist while he shouted his joy.

Dimitrakis and other boys gazed longingly. Dimitrakis wondered if he would ever go to America. His uncle looked at him and smiled. "I'll send for you when I get settled," he said. Dimitrakis did not return the smile or nod. He'd heard villagers say too often that America swallowed up young men; they left and were never heard from again. Suddenly his uncle said to the agent, "Can I take my nephew with me?"

"Yes," the agent said, "he can work with you." With those words Dimitrakis, heart beating crazily, ran after his laughing uncle and friends down the mountainside, trudged to the seaport four days distance, vomited bile for three weeks in steerage, and rode a railroad coach over an endless land of prairies and mountains to the western mining camp.

The labor agent had accompanied them. Well-dressed, like the steamship agent, and with a diamond ring on his little finger, he had explained what the words *strikes* and *strikebreakers* were. He would send money orders to the village for them for a fee of a dollar, and he would show them where the red-light houses were.

In the camp tent Dimitrakis cried for his mother every night. He had to cry silently or be cuffed by his uncle. Most of the time it was too cold to undress. One morning he opened his eyes and saw a sheet of something moving from the bottom of the tent to the top. Lice.

At night he went to the coffeehouse with his uncle, Stavros, Squash, and Nondas. Two other boys his age were always there, and the *kafejiz* left them sit close to the big pot-bellied stove and gave them a pair of dice to play *barbout*. In their villages boys would not have been allowed to hear their elders telling ribald stories and forgetting their dignity, but in America the old rules were suddenly gone. Although the men had not yet seen gypsies in America, they were afraid to leave the boys alone. The gypsies had the cunning to find where they were and kidnap them. Also the Americans did not like immigrants, and who knew what they could do to the boys if they found them alone? And so while the phonograph creaked out old songs of heroes fighting the Turks and the men sang, danced, played cards, and sometimes fought, throwing chairs about and jumping on each other, the boys sat near the stove, pretending not to hear and see and told exaggerated stories about pranks they had played in their villages.

Two weeks after they arrived in the mining camp, a thunderous tremor riveted Dimitrakis inside a room of coal. Screams, scurryings, whistle-screechings sent him running over the rail tracks toward the mine entrance. Half-way there miners were lifting big pieces of coal and handing them to others who carried them off. Then their carbide lamps made diffused yellow circles on Nondas's mashed body. Dimitrakis's uncle, Squash, and Stavros shouted obscenities, railed against the saints, called down curses on the coal, on America, and on their country, whose poverty had forced them to leave it. His uncle led Dimitrakis out of the mine. Dimitrakis could not speak the rest of the day.

The labor agent appeared at the coffeehouse that night and told the men he had telephoned a priest from Chicago to come for the funeral. He also said he would write a letter to Nondas's family for a dollar. "No! I'll do it!" Dimitrakis's uncle shouted, and the labor agent, taken aback, lifted his pink palms in acquiescence.

The following night the men went to the station to meet the priest. He stepped off wearing black robes and tall priest's hat. The men led him to the miners' hall while men and women on the boardwalk turned to stare and boys followed snickering. Nondas lay with blackened face and flattened nose in the coffin. Because he was unmarried the men had done their best to follow custom and bury him as a bridegroom. Dimitrakis had gone with his uncle up a mountainside where they found white sego lilies at the base of a boulder. Tears wending down his face, his uncle placed these about Nondas's misshapen head in lieu of a wedding crown. In Nondas's lapel the coffeehouse owner had put a sprig of basil, and all the miners had contributed to a wedding band. The labor agent called in a Mormon photographer to take the final picture for Nondas's family.

In the barren hall the priest gave Dimitrakis the censer and told him to swing it; the acrid blue smoke made his throat swell, and he was in a panic that he would not be able to breathe. After the liturgy for the dead, the coffin was placed on a wagon drawn by two white horses with black plumes on their heads. Suspending their strike hostilities for the day, Italians wearing band uniforms led the procession while playing a dirge. A crowd of boys and a few girls followed at the side, grinning and looking at each other, saying something to Dimitrakis that he did not understand. He looked at them with hate.

At the open grave the lid of the coffin was lifted. The priest chanted the closing prayers, dripped three drops of consecrated oil and sprinkled three pinches of dirt over the body. The coffin was lowered, and the men shoveled rocky, alkaline dirt over the coffin. Dimitrakis shivered at the sound of rocks hitting the wooden casket. He kept swinging the smoking censer, although this evidently was not necessary because the priest took it from him. Then his uncle, Squash, and Stavros pounded a black wooden cross into the mound. Across the arm was Nondas's name in white Greek letters.

The men followed the priest to the coffeehouse. The *kafejiz* had prepared the funeral meal of dried codfish, dandelion greens he had gathered near a farm at the river bank, feta cheese, and Kalamata olives that were sent to him weekly from Salt Lake City by train. The priest had no time to drink a cup of Turkish coffee. He had another corpse to bury, another young man killed in a Gary, Indiana, steel mill accident.

The men put the priest on board a Denver & Rio Grande Western train and returned to the coffeehouse. They sat around the small round tables morosely. "*Patridha, patridha,*" someone cried—Fatherland, fatherland. Dimitrakis and the two boys sitting with him near the stove began to cry. The men wept, groaned, called out words that would be heard over other young men. To die young, to be buried in foreign earth, to die without women keening the laments, to be in a coffeehouse far from home, to leave sisters without dowries, parents destitute!

After their litany about the miseries of exile, the men talked about the mine accident. Again Squash related how he had been working next to Nondas in the room of coal when he heard a faint sound. "It was a sound like mice scurrying. I knew it was a sign! I stepped back, but Nondas kept swinging his pick. Then I hear this big creak, and Nondas looks up, and the coal falls on him! It was his fate that he didn't hear that first little sound. His days were used up."

Dimitrakis's uncle reached over the table and grabbed Squash by the lapels. "Why didn't you shout at him to run! You worthless donkey! Because you were scared shitless!"

Squash leaned back, afraid. The labor agent gently pushed the two apart, like the just and reasonable man he thought he was.

The men finished reliving the accident: how they came running and began lifting the heavy pieces of coal, how the foreman brought a pulley for the big piece, how they lifted the broken body onto a coal car drawn by a blind mule, how they followed outside, and how the doctor waved his hand without bothering to open his black bag.

Again the men were silent. A passenger train called as it disappeared through the narrow opening between the mountains. Inside the coffeehouse only the sound of water simmering on a portable coal stove could be heard. The silence went on. The labor agent sprang up.

"*Kafejiz!*" he called, "a round of *mastiha* for my friends. We'll drink in memory of Nondas for the last time."

The men began to talk and laugh, just as they would have, had they been in Nondas's village house to make his relatives forget their grief. Dimitrakis's uncle told the Peloponnesians and islanders about Nondas's dancing and his whistling that echoed across the valley. Then he related a humorous incident about Nondas as a boy tending goats on the mountainside. Nondas had fallen asleep, dreamed he was being chased by Turks, woke up, and ran down to the village square shouting, "The Turks are coming! The Turks are coming!" Squash told a story about him and Nondas being caught stealing cherries from the village witch's garden and being roundly beaten by the schoolteacher.

The men moved restlessly; something was missing and Squash, the dimwit, said it: "We should have sung at least one lament for him."

"I'll sing one," Stavros said, "the young shepherd who meets Charon near his sheepfold." The men nodded eagerly, and Stavros began the lament in a clear yet heavy voice. Charon tells the shepherd God has sent him to take his soul. The shepherd will not give it up so easily. They wrestle on the marble threshing floor until, exhausted, the shepherd pleads to Charon to let him go: his sheep are unsheared; his cheese is unweighed; his wife is young and should not be a widow; he has a son, and being an orphan would not become him. Charon will not listen.

The men hummed along and sighed deeply at the end of the lament. After a while, Squash said hesitantly, because talk of vampires was spoken in hushed tones, "Do you think *vrikolakes* exist in America?"

The men stared with fright. They leaned toward each other even though the labor agent said with an authoritative shake of his head, "No, no, not in America. Did Christ cross the ocean? No."

"Still," the coffeehouse owner said, "it could be. Vampires go everywhere. They don't have to cross on a steamship."

The men knew the supernatural could not be found in such a strange place as America, but a great relief came with arguing spiritedly. Would a vampire try to enter the grave and take possession of Nondas's body?

"There is one way to tell," the labor agent said, "but I'd be too afraid to do it."

"What?" Squash demanded. "Tell me. I'm not afraid of vampies or anything else."

Even to Dimitrakis this was something to laugh at; he whispered to those near him that at a village wedding, Squash had run up the mountain in terror and later said one of the gypsy fiddlers had put the evil eye on him.

"All right, I'll tell you, but only the bravest of men would dare do it."

"Just tell me!"

"Well, then, at midnight, go to the graveyard and see if vampires will try to enter the grave."

"I will!"

A little later Squash said he would go to the back yard to use the privy. Instead he went to his tent, took out his grandfather's pistol, and hid it inside his belt. While he was gone, Dimitrakis's uncle said one of them should be at the grave to frighten Squash when he got there. "That braggart! Too scared to tell Nondas to run." One man went off for a miner's cap with a carbide lamp, another, fortunate enough to live in a Slavic boardinghouse, smuggled a sheet off the bed. Then, who would go to the grave to do the job? Stavros said he would. "I've played tricks on him since we were children." He turned to the boys, each with a tentative smile on his face. "Now, if you give us away, I'll cut out your tongues!" Smiling still, but frightened, they shook their heads.

When Squash returned, the men kept up a banter of vampire stories. They laughed and leered at Squash. "Do you want to back down? You might fill your pants." Squash paled; sweat shone on his forehead. With his arms folded at his waist, he shook his head even more sharply each time. He did not notice when Stavros left by the back door. Near midnight he stood up, put his shoulders back, and said loudly, "I'm off."

"We'll be waiting for your report," the men called after him, among other good luck wishes and sallies.

Squash hurried to the graveyard as if something were chasing him. The sky was black with whitish clouds sweeping over it. He stood for a moment at the entrance and looked at the gray headstones and black crosses searching for the fresh mound. He approached it, his hand on his belt. Then slowly a white figure with a blinding yellow eye rose slowly from the new grave. "EEEeeeeee," the figure moaned. Squash fired at the eye, the figure dropped, and Squash ran all the way to the coffeehouse shouting, "There *are* vampires in America! I just killed one!"

Stavros lay in a coffin several days before the priest could return. He was buried next to Nondas, and the twin rocky mounds now had identical black crosses at their heads.

The men talked about Stavros's death nightly in the coffeehouse, in the dim mine. "Ach, ach," they groaned from time to time, blaming themselves, castigating themselves for acting like fools. Yes, Stavros would be alive working next to them if they hadn't been such donkey-heads! Dimitrakis's uncle was obsessed with it. He would recount the details of that night, hitting his fist on the table, to see if an overlooked detail would shed light on it, but he often stopped talking and stared as if he didn't know what he had just said. He would grab his head and moan, "We didn't bury him as a bridegroom. We didn't sing one lament."

Then they stopped blaming themselves. Dimitrakis's uncle ranted at Squash for taking a gun with him, but, the men, said, why shouldn't a man take a gun to protect himself against vampires? Yet wasn't it Squash who first brought up the subject of vampires? Also wasn't the *kafejiz* the one who said vampires could go anywhere; they didn't need steamships to cross the ocean? And the labor agent, hadn't he suggested someone go to the grave to see if vampires would attempt to enter it? The men began to look at the labor agent coldly. Dimitrakis's uncle despised himself for taking off his cap to him in the village when he signed up to come to America. He was hardly better educated than any of the laborers. And the diamond ring—bought with the bribes they had to pay him to keep their jobs. Someone should put a bullet through his chest.

Squash left tearfully with the labor agent, and no one was at the station to shake his hand. A few weeks later a wandering showman came to the coffeehouse with a puppet play and a painted woman who sang songs of hashish and forgetfulness. Dimitrakis and his friends were allowed to see the puppet play and laughed near hysteria over the vulgar dialogue. Then they were told to go back to their table, play *barbout,* and not look at the singer. The men told the showman about the two tragedies, and he laughed uproariously, offending them. When the painted woman passed around a tambourine, they grudgingly gave less than they otherwise would have. New immigrants who had not been in the coffeehouse the night of Nondas's wake also thought it a funny anecdote.

The men stopped telling the story. Dimitrakis's uncle decided to sign up on a railroad gang laying rails over the Sierras. "When I get settled, I'll send for you," he said. Months later he wrote Dimitrakis to come if he wanted. He did not order him. By then Yiannina had arrived in the mining town, and Dimitrakis put off joining his uncle. He would remain in the mining camp three more years until his uncle wrote him to come to Salt Lake City, where he had found work in the railyards and a restaurant job for Dimitrakis in Greek Town.

A few months before Old Jim died, he no longer thought about Nondas and Stavros and vampires. He thought of Yiannina all the time. He remembered her taking hot loaves of bread out of her outdoor earth oven; there in his cubicle he could smell its wonderful scent. He remembered her clean house and how once she had made him stay on a cot in the warm kitchen because he was feverish. She undid his shirt, had him lie on his stomach, and put hot glasses on his back to raise the flesh and take out the sickness in his blood. She brewed chamomile tea, heated wine with cloves, made chicken broth for him.

Old Jim was barely conscious when the priest came to give him communion for the last time. "Yiannina," he said to the uncomprehending young man.

The Greek Pioneers
of 1902

People went out of their way to catch a glimpse of the young couple. They had never seen a Greek before, and they passed the two-room frame house glancing from the corner of their eyes. The man was big with thick eyebrows and a mustache that twisted into vertical points. Straw bosses at the mine said he was enrolled as John Diamanti by a Greek interpreter from Salt Lake City. The interpreter explained the straw bosses' rules and orders to the Greek and left. Neighbors said the woman had heavy hair that was coiled on top of her head, no different from white women. People talked about them, wondering how he and his wife got to Utah, and surmised that they would get lonesome without any of their kind. They told each other they hoped the Greeks wouldn't stay and bring a string of other Greeks on their coattails, like what happened with the Italians and Austrian Slavs. After all, Americans, their folks, had pioneered the town.

But more Greeks did follow. Soon a few young unmarried Greek men arrived with tags tied to their lapels reading: To John Diamanti, Helper, Utah. Then a group of twenty-five was brought in to break a strike. Men continued coming, singly and in groups, mostly from the same mountain village, the ancestral home of the young couple. Four or five together, they rented small, unpainted houses in the same neighborhood and took turns cooking. The Americans called their neighborhood Greek Town.

Although the young husband was only a few years older than they, the later arrivals began calling him *Barba,* meaning "Uncle." This was a sign of respect because Barba was a folk healer and an honest man. He used linseed and onion poultices on leg wounds caused by picks the men used in the coal mines, and an array of remedies for lung problems, all of which contained plenty of whiskey; he nicked the string of flesh under the tongues of young children to cure lisping. He had one or more remedies for everything. If the sick could not come to him, Barba went to them. They said they felt better even if he merely sat by their beds and said nothing. He could tell, the Greeks said, when a patient had wrestled with Charon and lost. For such patients he prescribed water glasses filled with ouzo.

The men thought of his wife as being much older than they, although she was younger than most of them. They remembered she had given birth to a daughter in their mountain village who had died early. The men called her *Kyria,* Madame.

Almost immediately one of the young men opened a coffeehouse, and another a restaurant. Barba gave up the mine and began raising lambs for the restaurant, the Greek boardinghouses, and the bachelor houses. He began with a few lambs and ewes in the space between his backyard and the river and fed them on alfalfa. Whenever one of the bachelors was celebrating his name day, Barba brought him and his bachelor friends home to eat. If he saw a stranger on the town's single street who was obviously Greek, he brought him home also.

Year after year Kyria gave birth to boy babies. She both feared and was ashamed to have the mine company doctor deliver her and lay well covered with a sheet while Barba pulled out the babies. "It's no different from a ewe and a lamb," he said. Kyria was always either pregnant or had recently given birth when the immigrants began bringing over picture brides. Barba and his brother tacked on a leanto where the women lived until their weddings. The brides called Barba's wife by her given name, Efthimia. They knew Efthimia's history: she would never, they said, sadly shaking their heads, have the solace of a girl to care for her in her old age because she had cursed her mother-in-law back in the village.

Barba built a bigger house of red brick, and the little house became a washhouse where among Efthimia's tubs and scrubbing boards, Barba's brother slept on one cot and various sojourners slept on the other. Barba planted grass and fruit trees. While Efthimia cooked a wedding dinner and babies cried and toddlers hung on her skirts, Barba killed a lamb. He first made the sign of the cross three times and asked God to let his knife be quick to spare the lamb as much pain as possible. He cut off the pelt expertly, threw it on the chicken wire fence to dry, and emptied the entrails. Squatting, he on one end of the spit and his brother on the other, they turned the impaled lamb over hot gray ashes. Grease dropped and sizzled, blue fumes rose upwards, and Barba and his brother closed their eyes and sang the dark folk songs of the Greek revolt against the Turks. At their heels were glasses of wine, and under the sun, red, sparkling rays flashed on them. American boys leaned against the wire fence and looked on solemnly. Always a baby cried, screamed, while the songs went on and on. The brides looked out the window and said dreamily to Efthimia, who never smiled, "Barba is so good-natured. An honest man. I hope I have such good luck." Efthimia jiggled the baby on her hip.

The new house had a telephone. On the wall Barba had written the telephone number of the coffeehouse. He trained Efthimia to turn the handle and when the operator answered, she was to repeat the number in English. Efthimia spoke those numbers to the operator: nine gwon. When the *kafejis* answered, she told him to tell Barba it was necessary for him to come home. Sometimes it was for a sick baby, but more often a pregnant woman stood before him to get his prediction: would she give birth to a boy or a girl? Barba's face flamed with embarrassment for himself and for the woman's modesty as he gave her protusion a quick glance and looked away. He never made a mistake, the women said. Following custom, Efthimia had the visitors' tray ready with pastries, liqueurs, and Turkish coffee.

Both men and women came to have Barba interpret their dreams. Barba would put on his dime-store eyeglasses, open the dreambook he had ordered from the Atlas Company in New York, read what was written, pondered it, and then if he did not like the answer, gave his own interpretation. Efthimia brought out the tray, but usually did not have time to sit with the visitors. She was out chasing her older sons and jogging the youngest on her hip.

Efthimia washed until late at night, ironed, and tended sick babies, while in good weather Barba sat on the front porch, silver lace vines festooning it, and in winter in the small living room warmed by a potbellied stove. Listeners asked him to tell again the old, wonderful village sagas of miracles, revenge, and treachery, and the comic priest stories. Leisurely, his heavy voice resonating, he intoned, stopping between stories to call Efthimia to bring more wine and a *meze*, a snack.

Barba was especially busy during lambing in the spring and winemaking in the autumn. So many Greeks had been sent into the county by labor agents that Barba bought more sheep and moved them to a grassy plateau twenty miles beyond the town. Barba's sons looked on big-eyed when he waved goodbye and got into his Studebaker with his brother. A supply of food had been set on the backseat and in the trunk. Efthimia had been cooking and baking for a week. They drove off. Efthimia looked at the car moving down the dirt road; her sons whimpered because they would not have penny candy for a while.

Whenever Easter came early by the Orthodox calendar, Barba left his brother and sheepherders in charge of the shearing and drove back to town for the celebration. As the patriarch he was expected to foretell the coming year's events by examining the bumps and lines on the shoulder blade of the Easter lamb. When he arrived at the neighborhood festivities, he was hailed. The celebration could then begin in earnest. The women said he increased their joy at Christ's Resurrection. Children called him Uncle John and liked to sit near him.

In autumn Barba and all Greeks made wine for the coming year. Above Greek Town the sour-sweet scent of fermenting grapes floated. One autumn Efthimia, with her sons, the oldest, her interpreter in the stores, and the youngest in her arms, walked up a street behind the grade school where Americans lived. In a back yard an American wearing boots was stamping on grapes in a galvanized tub. Efthimia stopped a moment, looked at the boots, and walked on. Until then the only wine Efthimia had tasted was in the communion chalice. Even though men washed their feet when crushing grapes, Efthimia disdained the wine they made. Men were unclean. Efthimia told Barba about the rubber boots. He protested weakly. Efthimia raised her voice, and neighbors were not surprised that at the next wine-making Barba, his oldest son, and his brother wore rubber boots. All Greeks then followed Barba's example. They sneered at the Italians in Wop Town who crushed the grapes with their bare feet as even they, the Greeks, had done in the old country.

Barba also made *mastiha* liqueur from the *tsipouri*, the grape skins. Then he learned to make whiskey, which was unknown in Greece. He had tasted it for the first time when an American sheepman grazing his sheep on the same plateau called out to him to come over. The two sat on a step of the neighbor's sheep wagon, and Barba drank and liked what he drank. From then on he drank whiskey by the glassful but was never drunk.

This was a turning point in Barba's life. When Prohibition was voted in, Barba became known in the town, then in the county, then in the state as the best of all bootleggers. Doctors, lawyers, the newspaper editor all said it: "John Diamanti makes the best whiskey in the state. You can trust it. Never have to worry about going blind." The Great War, strikes, killings, the Ku Klux Klan, mine explosions came and went while Barba raised sheep and made whiskey.

The plateau was ideal for bootlegging, far enough from town to avoid the attention of the feds. Barba delivered the whiskey himself when gallons were ordered, and his sons delivered the quarts and pints wrapped in newspaper. Barba was doing well with his bootlegging, so well that neighbors tsk-tsked over Efthimia, who reportedly would not stoop to pick up pennies but swept them outside. No one really believed she did this, but said it anyway. For certain everyone knew that Efthimia scolded Barba for risking going to jail. "That's Greek mountain love," Barba said of her scoldings. Still she was compensated. On her way to town with the bootleg money in her purse, she said to ragged boys and girls around the grade school, "Come onee. I buy you shoes. You, I buy coat."

The feds came into town from time to time, and the first place they raided was Barba's house. Barba kept his whiskey in the cellar under the washhouse. The trapdoor over it was under one of the cots and covered with a tarp. The feds almost always found Efthimia in the washhouse using her new electric washing machine. Once in her attempt to appear nonchalant, she leaned too far forward and caught her breasts in the wringer. Efthimia had her sons move the machine into the kitchen.

It was inevitable that Barba would be caught, and he was, again and again. The third time he was arrested, he had a load of whiskey in the back of his two-ton truck destined for Salt Lake City. The judge, one of Barba's customers, was sorrowful. "Mr. Diamanti," he said, "I am taking into consideration your large family who needs you. If you promise not to make any more whiskey, I'll let you go."

Barba smoothed out his mustache, head bent, contemplating the judge's words. Slowly he raised his head, moved it from one side to the other, and said, "I don't know, Judge.", His attorney who had come from Salt Lake City to defend him, jumped up. "Your Honor, he misunderstood you. Let me explain to my client." Afterwards he told Barba he didn't have to be so damned honest.

Barba's life was not affected much. He still made whiskey, continued to be the patriarch, the folkhealer, and the interpreter of dreams, and read the markings on the shoulder blade of the Easter lamb. He still brought visitors home from the coffeehouse to eat, but not so often as in the first years because many had married by then. This greatly lessened Efthimia's burdens; with her sons older and needing less attention, and many women now in Greek Town to share the traditional hospitality responsibilities, she had some leisure. As the matriarch, the younger women came to her when American life was heavy for them, when their children wanted to be like the Americans. Efthimia was against most of the American ways, especially the women going around half-naked. Who knew, she said, what went on between men and women in their houses. "I never saw my man without his long underwear," she said proudly.

Whenever Barba heard that a visiting priest or bishop, a traveling newspaper man, or the Greek vice-consul was in town, he took him home to eat. He brought out bottles of whiskey from the state liquor store now that Prohibition had been repealed, while Efthimia furiously cooked for the unexpected guests.

On Mondays Efthimia pushed the washing machine into the dining room, where she had more room to work. Suddenly one Monday the front door opened and Efthimia looked up to see Barba standing there with the archbishop in his black robes, large silver pectoral cross, and his tall, rimless black hat. He held his staff of office in one hand.

"Old woman," Barba shouted as if Efthimia were far off, "I've brought the archbishop to eat."

"Why didn't you telephone me?" Efthimia screeched. "Look at me! Look at this house! What am I to cook?"

While the heavily bearded archbishop gazed with large brown eyes, Efthimia shouted on. Barba tried to get her attention, and when she stopped for breath, he put out his palms and said, "What's the fuss? He's only a man."

Efthimia's neighbors could not understand why Efthimia talked in a clipped, angry manner. Wasn't Barba a special man? Wasn't he good and honest? What more did she want? Why wasn't she satisfied that her sons had become businessmen, sheepmen, and owners of a small coal mine? And one of them had won the election for mayor; the sons and daughters of immigrants had banded together and voted him in. This amazed Barba: "In 1924 they put on sheets and burned crosses to scare us out of town." He was proud of his mayor son. The mayor, on the other hand, was exasperated with his father. The town had put up a semaphore on Main Street. "You've got to stop when the light is red," the mayor said. "You can't drive through when the light is red!"

"Well, I look to the right, I look to the left, and if no cars are coming I go on through."

"No! No! You've got to stop when the light is red! How does it look, me the mayor and my father breaks the law?"

Efthimia died, worn down but nagging Barba to the end. She was mourned not only by the women of Greek Town, but by the neighbors beyond. Barba went on doing exactly as he pleased in his quiet, honest way. One day it occurred to his son, the mayor, that he had not seen Barba for a few days, and a suspicious thought came to him. He got into his car, drove to the red brick house, walked quietly to the back and down the steps to the cellar. As he expected, his father and uncle had dusted off the old copper still and were fermenting grain. The mayor picked up a sledgehammer and smashed the still while Barba and his brother looked at the pieces in dismay, not paying any attention to the mayor's frenzied obscenities.

When Barba died in the late 1960s, the local newspaper called him a pioneer.

A Fine Marriage

Sophia had married Thanasis Sampalis in 1923 through the arrangements of a correspondent for the New York Greek Language newspaper, the *Atlantis*. A fine marriage, the correspondent had assured
her, and Sophia had been relieved that she would no longer be a
burden to her people. She was without a dowry: her family had lost its
property when the Turks expelled the Greeks from Asia Minor. After
the family had made its way to Athens and miserable poverty, a cousin
in New York sent Sophia ship's fare to America.

The cousin hurriedly sought out the correspondent, a man who
made marriage arrangements all over the United States as he traveled
in search of news and subscriptions. The correspondent sent Sophia's
picture to a labor agent in the West, a prosperous businessman who

wrote back that he was willing to marry her. Sophia responded to his letter by return mail and asked if within a few years it would be possible to return to Athens. She felt confident she could ask this because she had heard and read of the great number of unmarried Greeks in America wanting brides. Thanasis replied that, of course, all Greeks intended to return to the fatherland. Someday he would light a candle at his sainted mother's grave; he would return to the hallowed earth of the fatherland to celebrate holy Easter with his family. Achh, he was alone in this exile, he wrote in closing; just that day he had said goodbye to his only relative in America. Sophia was impressed with the fine penmanship in purist Greek.

Three men met Sophia at the depot. Two were in their late twenties, wearing gray, sharply pressed suits and straw hats slanted over their foreheads. They were not handsome men, but they were young. Sophia hoped one of them was Thanasis. The third man with a heavy gold chain across his stolid front reached out to shake her hand, and she knew he was the man she was to marry. Smiling, laughing, Thanasis introduced his groomsmen. Keeping up a light banter, he led the way to the nearby Greek church. This pacified Sophia's drum-beating heart. She had had enough of long faces and eyes full of pain.

Waiting inside the church was a small priest with blue eyes and a gray, pointed beard. In green brocade robes he stood before the central door of the altar screen, opened a silver embossed book, and married Sophia and Thanasis. Sophia stood alone, no woman at her side, while the priest's monotone echoed under the dome and a cold silence pressed against her back.

Afterwards Thanasis drove the four of them in his Hupmobile to the Athens Restaurant. Sophia sat on the front seat holding the wedding crowns in a glass box. Inside the restaurant several men rose to shake her hand. Throughout the dinner Thanasis smiled and laughed, lifted his wine glass to the men at the surrounding tables and called, "To your wedding crowns!" Thanasis spoke a dialect with a few pompous purist words thrown in. It was obvious to Sophia that someone else had written the letter to her, perhaps one of the groomsmen.

Sophia did not touch the roast lamb that suddenly looked repulsive to her and ate bread to assuage her hunger. Thanasis's cigar with thick gray ash lay on a plate, and the smell pinched her nostrils together. The strange country confused her—not one woman in the church, the priest not sitting with them at the wedding dinner.

The groomsmen left, and Thanasis talking volubly about his business, drove the Hupmobile to a finely furnished house with a colored glass chandelier. It was a distance from Greek Town, he said; no use everyone knowing their affairs. He showed her the electric washing machine on the porch before leading the way to the bedroom.

After the first few nights of sharing Thanasis's bed, Sophia waited until he fell asleep, then went into the adjoining bedroom. It was the only room in the house where cigar smoke had not penetrated; Sophia kept the window opened all day and the door closed. On the dresser she placed her mother's icon of the Virgin and said her prayers. She gazed at the profound suffering patience in the Virgin's eyes and agreed: yes, he chewed on gristle and put the remains on his plate, but he had saved her from the ignominy of spinsterhood. She thanked the Virgin that Thanasis did not care when she told him she finished sleeping in the next room because he snored. Thanasis did not snore, but he did not know this.

Sophia said she would prepare the customary dinner for the groomsmen, but they were gone, Thanasis told her. They never stayed in one place long. "And what work do they do? How do they live?" she asked. Thanasis burst into loud, appreciative laughter. "By their wits!"

Sophia never again saw the groomsmen. Immediately, though, a few young mothers visited her out of curiosity and duty. Sophia went through the ritual of hospitality, arranging the tray properly with liqueurs, sweets, demitasses of Turkish coffee, and hoped the visitors would not notice her reddened eyes. The women said nothing, asked nothing about her wedding. They talked about the leading members of the community, a doctor, two attorneys, and the newspaper editor. The women knew from which province in Greece they had come from, which notables stopped to visit with them on their way to the cities of the West and East, and if they were married, had children, or left families in Greece. Only one of them, an attorney, had a wife with him. They spoke her name with respect: she played the piano.

Sophia fantasized about having these educated people seated at her dining room table. Throughout the day she thought about the food she would serve them and changed the menu several times until she decided on fish soup, chicken *oreganon*, stuffed grape leaves with lemon sauce, feta cheese triangles, vegetables *Macedoine*, an array of honey-nut sweets with coffee, and then liqueurs. She would seat the guests at the table covered with the exquisite white embroidered linen cloth her family had managed to salvage in their flight from the Turks. Under the colored glass chandelier they would see she was a woman of culture, and this would make up for Thanasis's dialect and bluster. She had read in the Greek newspaper that in America Greeks of all classes were thrown together for their self-interest. Meanwhile, she gave Thanasis a list of ingredients she would need to make honey-nut delicacies. They would keep well until the day her guests sat at her table.

Sophia constantly thought about the attorney's wife who played the piano. She thought of the two of them visiting each other in the afternoons, discussing the poems published in the *Atlantis,* talking about their families, and unburdening their hearts in this lonely exile. The attorney's wife would become as close to her as her sister Katerini. They would cry together for their lost families, their lost country. Sophia would describe her Smyrna home to her, and in her memory the two-story, stuccoed house became larger, grander; the marble floors, worn lusterless from two hundred years of footsteps, were suddenly shiny and kept polished by the servant girl. An elderly distant relative who did a few tasks outside the house in return for meals became a gardener, and the small ordinary circle of grass and potted acacias enclosed by a high wall transformed itself into a paradise of flowering almond and lemon trees.

Sophia would tell the attorney's wife about the Catholic girls school she had attended. Better, she must remember to say, than the Greek schools, but she would leave out details like the horrible food served at midday, eggplant fried in the cheapest olive oil, the bread always stale. She would tell little anecdotes about the nuns, how strict they were, how they made her undo the embroidery on an entire dresser scarf and stood over her while she made new stitches. She could think of nothing to equal playing the piano. The nuns educated students to become housewives, and there were no musical instruments in the entire convent school. Then Sophia would weep; minutes passed and the weeping went on while she remembered her mother looking at her with folded arms, her big eyes suffering like the Virgin's. She thought of Katerini and their brother sitting side by side writing her a letter, telling her how much they missed her. The weeping exhausted her.

Yet two, then three months passed, and the attorney's wife had not paid Sophia a visit. Sophia hoped to see her in church and thought of the two of them coming down the steps at the same time, exchanging pleasantries, and then their friendship would begin.

Thanasis balked at Sophia's wanting to attend liturgy every Sunday. "You're overdoing it," he said. He drove her to the curb, then went off to the coffeehouses to attend to business. The first time he had done this, Sophia said, "Business on Sunday?" and he had shouted, "Yes, on Sunday! That's when the laborers are off work! Don't argue with me." Sophia hoped no one heard him. Thanasis would return and wait outside in the car until liturgy finished. The priest with his little face and pointed gray beard often droned on longer than usual. Then Thanasis would be fuming, but Sophia did not care because she was certain that on one of those Sundays the attorney's wife would be there and they would walk down the steps together. It happened.

On that Sunday only a few people were in the congregation to listen to the priest raise his fist and condemn those who were seduced by America's work and money and who forgot about coming to church, let alone contributing more than a dime when they did. Sophia was already seated on the women's side, the left, when the attorney's wife came in. At the end of liturgy, as the congregation filed down the aisle to receive the pieces of consecrated bread from the priest, it was easy for Sophia to make her way behind her. With stabbing heart, Sophia followed her out of the church and down the steps. Sophia gave her a tentative smile, and the woman nodded and went on down the steps, joined her husband, and disappeared.

Thanasis was standing on the sidewalk in front of the church smoking a cigar and talking loudly to a well-dressed man with a diamond on his little finger. The diamond glinted as he put a cigarette into his mouth. In the car Sophia dabbed at tears of disappointment. "What's eating you?" Thanasis asked. Sophia shook her head, but later hope returned. She remembered her mother's proverb: patience is the jewel of life.

While Sophia waited patiently, she entertained visitors from Greek Town. Two of the women, from the same village, came regularly, walking all the way from Greek Town six blocks west. Mrs. Kampanis brought her three children along, but they were well behaved. The two older ones sat on the floor and looked at the American comic newspapers they brought with them; the other, a baby, nursed continually, comfortably perched on his mother's mound of flesh. The other visitor, Mrs. Sourias, was childless and moaned about what the Virgin and God had done to her. "I don't know why He hasn't sent me children, and I pray to Her morning, noon, and night. We work hard. I worked in the fields from the time I could walk. I'm not ashamed of it! My man suffered in America! He wasn't one of those wastrels who live off other people, who cheat and steal, who never held a pick or shovel in America!" Mrs. Sourias spoke directly to Sophia. Her black, piercing eyes brought a twittering to Sophia's stomach. Mrs. Kampanis spoke a few platitudes and invariably gave the same advice: "Have faith and the little Mother of Christ will hear you."

Sophia was thankful that Mrs. Kampanis was quick to turn Mrs. Sourias away from her obsession with her childlessness. She was surprised that a woman would speak so openly about her feelings and showed her lack of proper manners with her disturbing talk about men cheating, living off others, and repeating it again and again. Sophia had been raised to keep complaints, disappointments, and bad thoughts toward others within the family, as cultured people did. Also she was better educated than Mrs. Kampanis, and Mrs. Sourias could neither read nor write Greek.

Speaking polite Greek while holding her demitasse close to her chest, Sophia told them about her family and that she would be returning to Greece within a few years. Her husband had agreed, she said. She was aware that the women were silent at this, but took it for envy. Mrs. Sourias said *she* would never return to Greece: in America she had water from a tap and an indoor bathroom and did not have to work in the fields. Sophia showed them a hat and a pair of shoes she was saving to take back with her.

"A man in a coal mine or on a railroad gang," Mrs. Sourias said "would have to work a week or two for this dress and shoes. Maybe longer, after paying the labor agent."

Sophia's backbone stiffened at the sarcastic tone in Mrs. Sourias's voice. She thought perhaps this village woman had forgotten Thanasis was a labor agent and, if not, that he was good enough to get laborers jobs. She wished Mrs. Kampanis would come alone to visit, but there were times when even she made Sophia uneasy. To fill a lull in conversation on one visit Sophia told the women that the past Sunday Thanasis had taken her for a ride in his automobile and pointed out his business properties. He couldn't take her inside because he didn't have the keys with him, but she could see enough from the outside. She was almost sure that the women glanced at each other with a slight rise of their eyebrows. When she mentioned this slyness to Thanasis, he laughed, calling the women jealous peasants, took out his billfold, and gave her money to buy a new dress. The next day they went to a department store and Sophia bought the dress. She hung it in the closet along with the hat and shoes.

Thanasis was often at home when the women visited. He sat in the kitchen and read Greek-language newspapers published in New York and California. During silences while the women thought of what they could say next, a pinging sound came from the kitchen. Thanasis had a great liking for Kalamata olives and spit the pits, one after the other, onto a plate. Sophia's eyes flicked at the sound, and it was just as well for her, she thought, that Thanasis did not come out to greet the women.

One quiet, sunny day visitors brought the dreaded news that the attorney and his wife had moved to California. Sophia went through the ritual hospitality and hardly heard a word of the women's gossip.

Sometimes Thanasis drove Sophia to Greek Town to repay visits while he tended to business. For two or three hours she was able to forget her homesickness and even Thanasis. As a labor agent for railroad gangs he did not keep regular hours. Almost every day he stopped in the managers' offices in the Denver & Rio Grande Western and the Union Pacific depots to see if men were needed in the railyards or on section gangs. If they were, he drove three blocks east to the coffeehouses and recruited the needed number of recent arrivals who spoke no English at all and were grateful for work. Besides being a labor agent, Thanasis sat in the coffeehouses and wrote letters for these men, who could barely write their own names in Greek. He also interpreted for the immigrants in court and went with them to the post office, where he made out postal money orders to Greece. He never charged fewer than five dollars. Men often called him "Tom," the American name he gave himself. The youngest among them, who easily picked up American slang, referred to him as "Five-Buck Tom."

It galled Mrs. Sourias's husband and other Greeks to see Thanasis sitting leisurely in the coffeehouses, talking to visiting clergy and newspaper men from California, Chicago, and New York, and visiting the red-light district. He, himself, had never gone to those places, Mr. Sourias told his wife. When he was about thirteen, his mother had made him take an oath while holding the family icon of the Virgin and Child, and he had kept the sacred vow. Mr. Sourias was galled by

Thanasis Sampalis's wealth, and Mrs. Sourias was galled by Sophia's
not knowing how he got it.

Of the women in Greek Town, Sophia visited Mrs. Sourias only on
her husband's name day. Mrs. Sourias was an enemy. Sophia did not
know why, and she thought perhaps it was because she was pregnant
and Mrs. Sourias was not. She could not know that Mrs. Sourias had
another obsession besides her childlessness, an obsession to tell Sophia
that for all her airs, everyone knew Thanasis Sampalis and how he got
her the fine house with the colored glass chandelier. Mr. Sourias had
come on the same Italian ship as Thanasis in 1907, except that Thanasis had a second-class berth and Mr. Sourias and the other Greeks
came in steerage. Thanasis would come down to talk with them and
sing along the old songs of the struggle for freedom and hate for the
Turks.

On the ship Thanasis Sampalis had been friendly with a group of
Greeks from his provincial town in the central Greek mountains. He
had been a jailer there. He boasted of his money, enough to keep him
from working in factories or on railroad gangs on the prairies and the
sagebrushed West, enough to keep him out of coal mines in West Virginia, Colorado, Utah, and Wyoming, where the rest of the men were
destined to go. The men joked enviously about Thanasis's wealth; it
was no secret. As a jailer he had ruled, but benevolently, over his prisoners, most of them locked away for vendettas, for killing seducers of
sisters and cousins, and for stealing goats and sheep. Thanasis had told
the men he would free them for a sum of money. Relatives scraped together enough drachmas to satisfy him, and one night he unlocked the
cells and with the men walked over the mountains to Nafpaktos,
where accomplices had made arrangements and bribed boatmen to
row them across the bay. From there they walked to Patras, took a
boat to Naples, and boarded an ocean liner before the empty prison
was discovered.

In New York the prisoners scattered to Chicago, Saint Louis, wherever they had relatives or fellow villagers to help them. Thanasis Sampalis, a cousin of Mr. Sourias wrote him, remained in New York
holding sway in coffeehouses, playing cards, learning a few words of
English from a pocket dictionary, and regaling men off work with his
exploits. One day an editorial in the *Atlantis* rebuked criminals who
came to America and blackened the name of hard-working Greeks
who took their responsibilities seriously, as all honorable Greeks

should. As an example, the editor wrote, the worst among us is a jailer who . . . . Thanasis came west immediately.

Mrs. Sourias's husband saw him again in Salt Lake City in the Open Heart Coffeehouse. Thanasis had stopped there on his travels between Montana to New Mexico, gambling with miners on paydays. His memory was uncanny, and he won regularly. Mr. Sourias next read in the local Greek paper *The Worker* that Thanasis had joined in a partnership with an Idaho labor agent to supply men for railroad gangs. A most satisfactory position for him, Mr. Sourias told his wife. It could not be called work. All his partner had to do was give a manager in the Pocatello railroad yards one-fourth the money he and Thanasis Sampalis forced the Greek workers to pay for their jobs. Then to let them keep the jobs, they extracted an additional two dollars monthly from each worker and kept it for themselves. Thanasis made Salt Lake City his headquarters and signed up the newest immigrants in coffeehouses.

To see Sophia sitting with the demitasse held close to her chest and that naive innocence on her face was too much for Mrs. Sourias. For Sophia, the Greek Town visits gave her a sad respite from Thanasis and her fine house—except for her first Saint Demetrios feast day in America. On that day Sophia visited Mrs. Kampanis to pay respects to her husband on his name day, and a frightening episode took place. When she entered the house, the women, all talking angrily at once stopped suddenly, and while she was in the bedroom taking off her coat and hat, shrill whispers went on in the living room. She stood for a few moments with her heart beating fast, wishing she could walk through the kitchen and out and away. The women stopped whispering when she took her seat.

"We were just talking about a horrible happening," Mrs. Sourias said, looking at her with a dark stare. Sophia glanced away and caught Mrs. Kampanis looking fixedly at Mrs. Sourias, but she went on. "This man," she said, her lips thinned over small cat teeth, "no, a devil, not a man. . . . " "We don't know his name," Mrs. Kampanis said quickly. Mrs. Sourias waved a silencing palm at Mrs. Kampanis and went on, "This horned devil destroyed a family, his own sister's family! His sister's husband came to America, worked on railroad gangs, and gave his wages to his inhuman brother-in-law for safekeeping. He was working to go back and set up a shop and educate his sons. After six years out on the desert, *six* years, with a pick and sledgehammer, he asks this devil of a brother-in-law for his money. And *he* gives him a check to cash in Athens, and when he gets there, he finds it's worthless!"

"Six years lost," one of the women said, swaying from side to side. "Back into poverty. No education for his sons."

"The poor, miserable man has written to Stagopoulos," Mrs. Kampanis said of the Greek vice-consul, "to the priest, the bishop, but that donkey denies it! Said he paid his brother-in-law in full before he left. Ach, men forget their honor once they come to America."

"And that devil," Mrs. Sourias burst out again, her face alive with fury, "mixed up with prostitutes. Takes their bribes to the *seriff* in a paper bag. He and the *seriff* are like this." Mrs. Sourias crossed a middle finger over an index finger. "The *seriff* tells him when they will make *bootlek* raids, and that devil collects money from the *bootlekkers* to leave them alone!"

At home again Sophia decided she would say nothing to Thanasis: he might tell her to stay away from gossips, and she was lonely. Why she became afraid of the women's talk and whispering she could not understand. She had no one to talk to. If the attorney's wife had remained in the city, she knew they eventually would have become friends, and she would have been able to tell her everything—almost. There was no use, she had learned, trying to talk with Thanasis. He was interested only in what groceries and meats she needed for preparing meals. She had learned nothing about him. He never spoke about his parents, his family, or how many sisters and brothers he had. She never saw him write a letter to the fatherland. She had asked him the day after their wedding what he had done before coming to America, and he had snorted and said, "What everyone else did, raised a few goats." There was something in his voice that kept her from asking more questions. She and Thanasis had nothing to talk about.

Wiping away tears, Sophia often wished she lived in Greek Town along with her visitors. They had so much to say to each other: church, priests, Greek school, and Americans who didn't feed their children properly. She would have liked to shop by herself in the Greek stores and breathe in the scents of baking bread, pick out cheeses and various kinds of olives in big barrels, choose sweets, *loukoum* and chocolates, and just look at everything on the shelves.

Shopping in the Greek Town stores would have taken up her time. As it was she spent her days keeping her house in order, cooking, and reading the local Greek newspaper. Sometimes Thanasis forgot to bring it home, and Sophia missed the stories and poems in it. Thanasis would say airly that he lent it or forgotten it in a restaurant. She thought of asking Mrs. Kampanis, who could read somewhat, for the newspapers Thanasis forgot, but she was certain that they had been thrown away. Mrs. Sourias at times brought her a loaf of warm bread wrapped in a newspaper. The bread did not please Sophia, but the newspaper did. The newspapers were issues Thanasis had lent or forgotten. On the front page of one she read about a court case in Idaho: railroad gang workers had sued a Pocatello labor agent for peonage. She had never met the labor agent, but he telephoned Thanasis often. Sophia clasped her hands a few times before asking Thanasis about the labor agent. "Isn't he your partner?" Thanasis smiled broadly, his face flushing a pleased bright red. "I never sign my name to anything," he answered as if talking to himself.

Almost once a week with Thanasis out of the house Sophia opened all the windows to air the house of cigar smoke. Then she sat at the kitchen table and wrote long letters to her family. On the wooden drainboard was a brown earthenware pot in which Thanasis kept coins and bills to pay for ice and deliveries. Whenever it filled up and Thanasis would not miss it, Sophia took out a five-dollar bill and enclosed it with the letters. She did not know why she did not ask him outright to send a money order to her family once in a while. She could not bring herself to do it, even though she wondered if her letters were opened in the post office and the money taken. Her family sometimes wrote "Thank you for your remembrance," and Thanasis never questioned what this meant. She had to remind him when the earthenware pot was almost empty, but he did not always fill it immediately, and she lived in fear of the iceman.

One morning while cleaning Thanasis's bedroom, Sophia found a small Greek-English dictionary. She gazed at the worn black leather cover, and it occurred to her that she could learn enough English to go to department stores and buy what she wanted without Thanasis hovering nearby. Women in America went everywhere without their husbands.

Sophia was too busy to go to department stores for a few months. She gave birth to a son in a Catholic hospital where nuns in white were also nurses. Ten days later she returned home with the baby. She knew nothing about babies and did not know how to quiet hers when he cried. She became fatigued with getting up at night to nurse him. If she had been in Greece, she would think angrily, she could have a village servant girl live with her for a pittance. For a few days Thanasis brought food from a Greek restaurant. Sophia began apologetically telephoning Mrs. Kampanis for advice.

When the baby was baptized three months later—the godfather another of those friends of Thanasis who never stayed in one place long—he was christened Constantine, and Sophia knew at last the name of Thanasis's father. By then the baby had learned to sleep through the night, and Sophia put him in a carriage and went shopping again. Two months later the smell of food and tobacco sent her running to the bathroom to vomit, and in despair knew she was pregnant again. When she was ready to deliver this time, she could hardly bear thinking of Constantine crying for her, screaming at the folk healer Thanasis brought to take care of him. "He's not crying at all," Thanasis told her after the baby, a little girl, was born. "He's quiet all the time." The midwife was putting a few drops of whiskey in Constantine's milk bottles while Sophia lay on the hospital bed wondering why she was not a good mother, and why she had not been able to keep Constantine from crying. The new baby, Maria, named after Thanasis's mother, was a docile child, and soon Sophia was putting both children in the carriage and visiting stores again.

"When will we go back to Greece?" she asked Thanasis when Maria was two years old. Maria would learn to play the piano in Greece, Sophia would think, looking at the round, sweet face.

"In a few years we can go back with enough money to buy a mansion," he said. "This is a good time to make money in America." He gave Sophia a handful of silver dollars that were as heavy in her purse as Maria in the crook of her arm. Sophia put Maria in the baby carriage, and with Constantine trotting at her side—he had become so stubborn he refused to ride in the carriage no matter how tired he was—they went shopping. Constantine, ready to cry, hung onto her skirt as she bought two dresses, a pair of shoes, and another hat to add to those already in the closet.

Sophia would not wear any of her special purchases. She kept her growing collection covered with bed sheets except when she showed it to her visitors. On one Saint Athanasios feast day, she was impatient for her visitors to finish their liqueurs and sweets so that she could bring out the dresses, shoes, and hats. Some were already going out of style. The women were not impressed, gossiping instead about a bootlegger who had been caught making whiskey in an empty warehouse near the church. They moaned over what would happen to Mrs. Papasimeon and her four children. "And of course," Mrs. Sourias, still childless, who would never go back to Greece because she had an indoor bathroom, said snidely, "his partner is walking the street like an army general with his head up and smoking big cigars."

Sophia had wanted to ask who the partner was, but her mother had dinned it into her children that such questions were gypsy talk. Thanasis said he did not know who the partner was either. In the evening when men came to pay their respects to Thanasis, she listened to their talk as she served them cheese pastries and honey-and-nut sweets. "Poor old Papasimeon," someone snickered, and another guffawed, "We won't have him to play barbout with for a while."

Sophia returned to the kitchen wondering why only coffeehouse idlers and laborers came on Thanasis's name day, why men with families did not come, why the doctor, the attorney, the newspaper editor had never paid a courtesy visit, and why Thanasis avoided going with her on name-day visiting.

Laborers came at other times, also. Then Thanasis sat at the dining room table under the colored glass chandelier and with flourishes wrote letters in English for the men. Sophia hoped Thanasis's English was better than his Greek. Another of his kindnesses was helping men get their citizenship papers, and it was true because she read his advertisements in the local Greek-language newspaper: GET YOUR AMERICAN CITIZENSHIP SO THAT YOU CAN GO ANYWHERE IN AMERICA FREELY. Once she heard Thanasis tell a woebegone laborer who could neither read nor write Greek, let alone English, "Don't worry, patrioti, I'll just give the judge a gallon of whiskey, and the papers are yours." "Thenk you, Tom," the laborer said with shiny gratitude in his big eyes. Sophia smiled at Thanasis's good heart.

Sophia also became a citizen. Thanasis drilled her on two questions and answers, although Sophia saw no need to become an American citizen. Why? she asked Thanasis, seeing that they would be returning to Greece. "The Americans hold it against us if we don't" he answered in the exasperated tone he used whenever she questioned him. "Besides, the women who came after the laws were changed, like you, will hear that you have your papers, and it will be good for business." Thanasis took her before a judge who asked her two questions, the name of the president of the United States and whether she forsook her country for allegiance to the United States.

Sophia wondered if the attorney's wife had her citizenship papers. Whenever she thought of her and became melancholy, Sophia had only to open the closet door and look at the sheet-covered dresses and the coat with a fur collar, the hatboxes on the shelf, and the shoes in a row on the floor. She would lapse into a reverie of herself and the children seated at a table of an outdoor Athens sweetshop dressed in finery. Her mother, brother, and sister sat about her in new clothes bought with Thanasis's American money. How they would look at her gratefully. Thanasis never appeared in her daydreams.

Thanasis bought a new Hudson. "But why?" Sophia asked. "If we are going back, you'll lose money when you sell it."

"We will take it on the ship with us." Thanasis, looking more prosperous than ever, portly, a little gray in his hair, smiled at Sophia, whose mouth opened in awe.

The very day he drove into the driveway in the new car, the telephone rang and an angry voice said, "Mrs. Sampalis, your husband please."

Her heart fluttered. The tone of the voice was like that of the Turks who had herded them out of their house, and the "please" curled with sarcasm. Thanasis came to the telephone and spoke soothingly, but Sophia could hear the man shouting obscenities and then slamming the receiver. "What is it?" she whispered.

"Ach, this old villager. Thinks I owe him money. I paid him. But he's a little"—Thanasis twirled his forefinger at his temple—"crazy."

"You borrowed money from him?" Sophia asked cautiously.

"Not really borrowed. Don't get involved in men's affairs!"

The closet was becoming crowded, but Sophia solved this by putting two and three dresses on one hanger and stacking the shoe and hatboxes. By then, near the end of the 1920s, Thanasis had to give up being a labor agent. Sophia read in the newspaper that America had passed a law in 1924 that cut off the great number of Greeks coming to the country. Mrs. Sourias folded her arms across her long, drooping breasts and sniffed. "Why do the men still in the mines and railroad *gengs*, need those leeches anyway?" As if, it seemed to Sophia again, she did not know Thanasis was a labor agent. Mrs. Sourias snorted, "They've learned how to bribe managers and *bossis* without those devil labor agents."

Sophia feared they might not return to Greece, but it was a minor setback. Thanasis turned to selling shares in Nevada gold mines. The mines had never produced even an ounce of fool's gold, but Sophia did not know this. Mr. Sourias himself came one night and bought some shares, and afterwards Thanasis told Sophia not to say a word to his wife. "What goes on in this house should not be repeated to outsiders." Sophia agreed.

Little by little she became diffident with visitors. Families were leaving Greek Town for newer houses farther east. Mrs. Kampanis moved to a large, six-room brick house near the Liberty Park. It had a breakfast nook and a bay window where her oldest daughters sat at an upright piano and practiced scales. "Tell your father you want to learn to play the piano, Maria. Tell him to buy you a piano." Maria shook her head and said she would rather play the gypsy tambourine she was given for the fourth-grade orchestra.

Then something terrible happened, something called the Depression. Thanasis moved his family out of the fine house with the colored glass chandelier; he explained he had sold it and bought another. They moved periodically. Some houses were equally as good as the previous one; at other times they needed paint and their porches sagged. Several of the old houses were in Greek Town near the church and railyards. Now at least Sophia could attend liturgies as often as she wished, but she was afraid to hang up the wash in the backyard. Laborers walked down the alley to and from work and looked at her with steady curiosity. Some actually scowled at her. The furniture began to look worn, but Sophia was not concerned because once they were back in Greece they would buy everything new. Yet it seemed to Sophia that other women were progressing and she was left where they had once been.

Thanasis went into another venture. He showed Sophia and the children his newly acquired houses, empty, of smoke-smudged red brick no longer sharp at the edges, and with small, tacked-on porches. They had been built during pioneer days. Their owners, he said, had sold them to him before leaving for California to look for work, and when the Depression ended, he would sell them at a good profit. Thanasis rented the houses out to newcomers also looking for work and charged them from five to ten dollars a month. When they could no longer pay, he took Constantine with him, and they removed the doors. After the people moved out, Thanasis replaced the doors and again nailed up the FOR RENT signs with his penciled telephone number.

One afternoon while Mrs. Sourias and Mrs. Kampanis with her six children were visiting, they mentioned that the priest had asked for help: a destitute traveling family needed a house until relatives sent money from California to repair their car. Sophia said, "Perhaps Thanasis has an empty house," but Mrs. Sourias did not let her finish, "He doesn't own *any* houses," she said with such venom that Sophia was speechless. "He just takes them over." Sophia was humiliated. She said nothing to Thanasis, but to Constantine, then ten years old and intelligent for his age, she related the conversation. Constantine gave her a long look that forced her to glance away.

Nor did shopping in the Greek stores give the satisfaction Sophia had anticipated. It was all because of an incident that happened during Lent. One afternoon Mrs. Kampanis, who had been visiting a sick woman in the neighborhood, passed by Sophia's house with her younger children. Sophia was putting a coat on Maria, who had run out to play in the cool April morning. Mrs. Kampanis said she was on her way to the Vasilopoulos store to buy Lenten food. "I'll come too," Sophia said and ran to get her coat. Constantine refused to go with them, but Maria eagerly took hold of Mrs. Kampanis's youngest daughter's hand.

At the store they bought halva, chick-peas, olives, and canned crab and shrimp. Mr. Vasilopoulos was friendly to Mrs. Kampanis but hardly looked at Sophia. When he tallied her bill, she said, "Charge it, please." Mr. Vasilopoulos's pencil lifted from the pad, and his head remained bent as if he were thinking it over. After a few miserable seconds he finished writing and handed Sophia the paper sack without smiling. Sophia barely spoke to Mrs. Kampanis on the way home, and when she told Thanasis about Mr. Vasilopoulos, he said she had misunderstood what had happened. Sophia, though, never stepped into the Vasilopoulos store again.

Sometimes Sophia wondered if Mrs. Sourias was right: Thanasis might not really own the houses. Whenever she had such thoughts, she unlocked her closet door to look at her clothing, took it outside to air on the clothesline, brushed the hats, and dusted the shoes. She kept the key to the door in her pocket. Maria and neighboring children liked to hide from each other, and she could not take the chance that they would dirty her clothes, and, also, a burglar would not want to take the time to break down a locked door.

"Shouldn't we go back to Greece now?" she asked Thanasis.

"What are you saying, woman? If times are bad here, what are they like back there?"

Sophia cried and Thanasis said irritably, "As soon as the Depresh is over we'll go back."

The Depression went on. Thanasis complained she spent too much money. Sophia economized on food, but not so Thanasis would notice. He loved food and she was fortunate he liked stews. Now she bought her dresses, shoes, and hats at sales. She went by herself. The children were then thirteen and fifteen and could stay by themselves. It was a relief not to have them complaining that they were tired and wanted to go home. Constantine was causing her other problems; he didn't want to attend Greek school any longer. "They tease me. They say things."

"What things? What could they possibly say?"

Constantine glanced at his father, who chewed on his cigar. "People are jealous," Thanasis said. "Don't believe gossip."

"Of course you have to go," Sophia lectured. "How will you get along in Greece if you don't know your lessons?"

One day Constantine screamed, "I won't go to Greece! I was born here!"

Sophia felt faint at his words, as though an icicle had stabbed her bare back. Constantine was out of the house before she could say more, but she thought, of course he would go. How could he stay in America by himself? Thank the Virgin, Maria never gave her any trouble. Another year or two in America would be better; she would lose that childish fat, and maybe her looks would improve.

"You see," Sophia said sternly, when Constantine ran in one afternoon, sweating, his clothes disheveled after throwing rocks at two boys, "In Greece boys are well-behaved. They wouldn't tease you."

Constantine went into his room and slammed the door. For a few seconds the two boys stood on the sidewalk outside the house shouting, "Five-Buck-Tom! Five-Buck-Tom!" Sophia wished she knew English better to understand what the rude boys were shouting.

In two years war had started in Europe. There was no hope of going back to Greece until it ended. On the day the United States entered the war, Thanasis died of a stroke. It had happened in the coffeehouse, the last remaining one in what had been Greek Town.

Sophia was surprised at the number of people who came for the funeral, especially men she had seen over the years in church but who had never come to her house. She was relieved that the children would see these businessmen and lawyers. There were American men in the church she had never seen before, except for the judge who had signed her citizenship papers. She stared at Thanasis in his casket, now bald with sagging cheeks, closely shaved and powdered, an icon on his chest, Thanasis who went to church on Great Friday and Saturday only. She knew now with black certainty she would never go back to Greece to live.

Men filed by the casket to make the sign of the cross and kiss the icon. They had come to follow the dictates of the church to forgive a monstrous man. Outside the church people shook Sophia's hand and spoke the traditional "Life is the Word." Maria cried and insisted with each condolence, "He was a wonderful father, a wonderful man. He helped everyone, no matter how poor. People loved him." Constantine waited in the funeral limousine, took out a cigarette, thought better of it, and put it away.

A year after Thanasis's death Constantine left wearing a United States army uniform, and when the war ended he used the G.I. Bill to get a college degree in business. He married an American woman who came to the house once a year on Mother's Day with the two disgruntled children, who whined because they couldn't understand *her* when she tried to talk to them. Constantine's name appeared in the paper, but no one said anything to Sophia. It had something to do with his selling uranium mining stock and having to appear before the Securities Exchange Commission. Sophia often looked at him and saw how much he had come to resemble Thanasis.

Maria came every day, scolded, cleaned, took Sophia to doctors and dentists, had her children read their Greek lessons to their grandmother, told them she wished they could have known their wonderful grandfather. In her younger years she had been friendly with Mrs. Kampanis's daughters, but her friends now were bustling women like her, overweight, wearing clothes that Sophia thought common. Mrs. Kampanis's daughters had all learned to play the piano, and the youngest had graduated from the university. Three of her sons and two sons-in-law had businesses of their own, and the daughter who had gone to college had married an attorney. Maria had married a butcher who blew his nose at the dinner table.

Sophia lived another forty years. Her eyelids closed half-way over her eyes and gave them a hooded look. She sat in front of the television set, gazing at it, but not following what she was seeing. She was thinking instead of Smyrna, her family house, her parents, her brother, and sister Katerini. For an hour or two she would sit in reverie, and she resented the ring of the telephone or the doorbell that took her away from it. Then she could go on another day.

Sophia seldom left her house. Mrs. Kampanis hardly ever visited her; she was too busy with her children, grandchildren, and a great grandchild. Mrs. Sourias, her black, hard eyes rimmed about the iris with gray, came often and spoke gibberish about a devil who preyed on the uneducated, sent them to certain doctors, lawyers, and when they died to morticians, and got a percentage of their fees. This devil, she said, who bought groceries, clothing for the whole family, and signed other people's names to charge accounts. "Oh, that big-nosed priest, he would go right into the coffeehouses and call *him* names and tell *him* he was going to the devil!"

Sophia listened patiently, waiting for Mrs. Sourias to leave. "You know," Mrs. Sourias said one day, shaking her head slowly, trying to fathom what she was saying, "my man never touched me once after the wedding night." Sophia's eyes widened at Mrs. Sourias's unburdening herself after all these years. A feeling, faint, somehow familiar to her, but quickly gone, brought her eyelids back to their natural state.

In those forty years, sitting in her silent house in the black dress of mourning to satisfy custom, when she was not immersed in reveries of Smyrna, Sophia thought and recalled, thought and recalled. When she died, her children cleaned out her house, could not find the key to the locked door, and had a locksmith make one. They took out the dusty boxes, shoes, and sheet-covered dresses and coats. The granddaughters tried on the old-fashioned dresses, shoes, big veiled hats, and head-hugging cloches and screamed that they would be great for Halloween.

The Coffeehouse Election
of 1922

In each of the two coffeehouses in the mining town, three pictures were nailed to a wall painted the sky blue of the Greek flag. King Constantine looked out from one of the frames, bald, mustache twisted upward, his bemedaled uniform embroidered with braided bronze. He was seated holding a white plumed helmet. The picture next to his was of Premier Venizelos, white hair fringing his bald head, small metal-rimmed eyeglasses, a white mustache and goatee. The men's cheeks were tinted a bright pink and their lips a red-black. Off to one side was President Warren Harding's picture, cut out of a Greek-language newspaper. Above the pictures, American and Greek flags came to a point, with wooden dowel tips touching.

For some weeks the leisurely sipping of Turkish coffee, reading

Greek newspapers, and playing *barbout* had been suspended in the cof-feehouses. Old-timers—miners and ranchers—said they had never seen anything like it. Oh, every once in a while there had been a killing, something about the Greeks getting even with other Greeks over some-thing that happened in the old country and, of course, assaults. But what could you expect when ninety-nine out of a hundred of those Greeks were young and hot-headed? Like Judge Christensen said, he'd never seen so many Greeks brought into his court for assault as he had in the last few months. And of all things, because of the elections that were coming up in *Greece*, not in the good old USA, but in *Greece.* You'd think they were still in the old country, the way they took the politics back there so seriously. You'd think now that they were in America and making good money in the mines, they'd stop speaking Greek on the streets and stop sending their money back to the old country. They acted like they were still in Greece. Crazy. Crazy. Here the United Mine Workers were talking about calling a strike, and in-stead of saving up for God-knows-what's-to-come, those goddamn Greeks were acting like wild animals. They'd never be real, red-blooded Americans. They ought to go back where they come from. Like oil and water, they just don't mix.

The Greeks had no idea that the Americans had noticed them at all. They divided into the same factions as they would have in Greece. The Cretans and a few miners from Mani upheld Venizelos, the liberal Cretan; the Peloponnesian and central Greek miners favored King Constantine's party. In the poorly lighted tunnels and rooms of coal, they shouted at each other, "You'll see! You'll see!" and muttered obscenities, but not loud enough to provoke fights that would bring straw bosses to fire them. They swung sledges against the boulders of coal, shoveled the glossy black chunks into the waiting cars, all the while listening for the whistles that would end their shifts. Then they hurried to their boardinghouses, quickly washed themselves of coal dust, and marched into the coffeehouses to continue the arguments begun in the mine.

When the union called its meetings, the Greeks went, squirmed on the rickety chairs, preoccupied, and ran back to the coffeehouses as soon as they heard the words: "The meeting is adjourned." There in the blue haze of tobacco smoke, newspapers and coffee cups littering the scarred tables, the men got up to orate against the backdrop of pic-tures and flags. The Cretans expounded on their longer bondage under the Venetians and Turks, their greater sufferings, their great heroes: Venizelos was the hope of Greece. The royalists brought forth their own great heroes under Turkish rule and refuted the greater sufferings of the Cretans: the royalists under King Constantine knew how to govern Greece best. Men pulled down their mouths: their own history was the epic one.

One night in the coffeehouse north of town a Venizelist shot and killed a royalist and left a bullet hole in the wooden floor. The mayor and councilmen closed the coffeehouse. The Greeks buried the royalist and continued their fight in the Acropolis coffeehouse at the other end of town. The men divided the room, royalists on the right, Venizelists on the left, and a no-man's land down the center, where the coffeehouse owner, the big-bellied *kafezis*, walked up and down with trays of demitasse filled with Turkish coffee.

The strikers lamented the closing of the other coffeehouse, and each side talked of going to the Greek businessmen to ask them to intercede with the mayor. Then the Venizelists could meet in one coffeehouse and the royalists in another and not have to put up with each other. Nothing came of it: the businessmen did not like the coffeehouses either. They gave a bad impression, they said, to the Americans, who were certain the demitasse contained whiskey, not coffee, and some Americans believed the men were Bolsheviks.

Within a week, when the United Mine Workers came closer to calling a strike, two men became the leaders of the rival Greek political parties. Mihaêl Louloudhakis headed the Cretans and Maniots, a tall, dark man, handsome, with a finely hooked nose. Stavros Monyios for the Peloponnesians and central Greeks was stocky yet agile, already a favorite because he played the *santouri* at weddings and baptisms. The two men had been competitors from the moment they met in the mining town and vied in the church basement over their dancing skills.

The strike was called. An hour later strikers and deputies fired at each other outside a mine portal. A guard was wounded in the leg; a Greek was shot in the arm, and another was hit in the chest. Immediately guards and deputies forced the strikers out of the mine company houses. The United Mine Workers set up a tent town just beyond the city limits on a barren, dusty field. Miners brought their possessions in old trucks and cars; tubs, scrubbing boards, coal stoves, mismatched chairs, cots, and beds. Clotheslines were strung between poles, and immediately women and boys carried water from the river. The women washed and hung up the laundry; they cooked outside, some on stoves, others over open fires. Children ran chasing each other around the tents, down to the river and back again, shrieking their adventure. The smells of grease, lye, and kerosene hung with pungent thickness over the tent town.

The Greeks had no women with them. Except for two of them who had left wives in Crete, they were unmarried. They slept on cots, ate bread, cheese, olives, and onions, and it did not occur to them to wash their clothing. They had the elections to think of.

Stavros knew English better than most of the Greeks because he had come young and learned quickly. He met with the strike leaders, and later at night in the tent colony the Greeks gathered around kerosene lamps to hear him repeat the strategies they were to use. The men listened, but moved around in their seats, looked about, and yawned. Mihaêl turned one of his shoes on its side and scraped it back and forth. "Who's that squash-head making so much noise?" Stavros demanded. "No squash-heads here," Mihaêl said mockingly, while the Cretans laughed. Stavros let it go. He was eager to get the meeting over with and talk about the election. Until midnight, while babies cried and a woman screamed in labor, they called from tent to tent, quarreled, and shouted, all trying to convince their opponents that they were wrong. Strikers of many nationalities yelled at them to let them get sleep for the next day's fight.

Strikers and strikebreakers caught each other and used fists, brass knuckles, and two-by-fours. "Don't go anywhere alone," Stavros told them. "That's what the bosses say. Go in groups."

One morning a runner brought the news that a deputy sheriff was trying to start his stalled car at the north end of town, outside an Italian farm. Mihaêl and another Cretan put guns in their belts and ran to accost the deputy. Mihaêl's friend fired at the deputy, who shot back and killed him. A great commotion rose among the Greeks in the tent colony and in the town. Four hundred men, women, and children dressed in black and holding small Greek flags followed the hearse to the graveyard. The Americans watched at the side of the road and shook their heads. After two days of fury, vows of revenge, unspeakable curses, the men met in the Acropolis at the end of each day's strike duties and again began talking about the coming elections. Groups walked the mile to the postoffice to get their Greek-language newspapers. The royalists subscribed to the *Atlantis*, and the Venizelists to the *National Herald*. Each editor was as volatile as the miners. The men waved the newspapers at each other, shouting, "Have you read this? Read it. Then talk to me!"

In the daytime the Greek miners harrassed strikebreakers and beat those foolish enough to venture out alone. At night Cretans in the surrounding mining camps walked over the mountains and brought them guns and ammunition. One morning, hearing that a train was bringing in strikebreakers, they took positions among boulders, sagebrush, and junipers. In the crossfire of sheriffs and strikers, a deputy and a Cretan were wounded. Five friends carried the Cretan to a town doctor and pointed guns at him while he sewed the man's gashed arm. They then placed him on the back floor of a car, covered him, and drove fifty miles to the Ute Indian Reservation. They left him there with a homesteading Greek, returned to the coffeehouse, reported to Stavros and Mihaêl, and asked about the latest election news from Greece. Then a brawl broke out.

The National Guard marched in. The soldiers, fingers on triggers, forced the men out of the tents to the schoolyard, where they lined them up. A mine manager who had been on the train looked at one man after another. He chose fifteen—fourteen Greeks and one Italian—as men who had fired on the train; they were immediately taken to the county jail to await trial. The Greeks sat up late at night around bonfires cursing the American bosses and especially the mine manager. He had picked out men who had not been hiding among the boulders and sagebrush and passed over miners who had, like Stavros and Mihaêl. A week went by, and the men began talking and quarreling again over the elections in Greece.

The National Guard patrolled the alleys and streets of the mining towns, searched boardinghouses, and closed Greek poolhalls and coffeehouses. The commander then sent soldiers to gather the strikers in a field near the tent colony and lectured them on the meaning of martial law and demanded that they give up their guns. Stavros interpreted the commander's words, and the Greeks could hardly keep from smiling. Mihaêl had brought a handmade gun with him from Crete; it had killed many Turks. "Let them try to take my mistress," he said, "and I'll slit their throats." He also had a beautiful knife with a silver-chased handle.

Stavros knew an Italian who farmed on the riverbanks. When a spy came running with the news that the guard was coming to search the tents, he gathered up the guns, including Mihaêl's, and took them to the Italian for safekeeping.

The National Guard succeeded in curtailing strike activities. In the daytime the Greeks attended the trials of the fourteen Greeks and one Italian and watched as one after another was given a long prison term. Now that they had plenty of leisure—with the National Guard patrolling the street and strikebreakers mining the coal—they had more time to fight over the elections. As the day neared, chairs flew, glasses and cups splintered, and Stavros and Mihaêl fought a historic fight that ended with both bloodied and exhausted.

Someone broached the subject of casting their own ballots on the same day that Greece held its election. The men became frenzied. Mihaêl and Stavros campaigned until late at night to make certain of each Greek's loyalty. They offered ouzo, took men they were uncertain of to the Paradise Cafe for dinner, and hinted they would bring over sisters and cousins at their own expense for marriages. When they met in the coffeehouse or passed each other on the street, the rivals no longer gave the two-fingered Greek salute. "You'll see," Stavros would say, "You'll see. The royalists will win," and Mihaêl would retort, "No, *you'll* see, the Venizelists will win." A hot triumph buoyed the innocuous words.

Americans stopped each other on Main Street and discussed the commotion among the Greek strikers. Something bad was going on. Didn't everyone know that their lodges took orders from the old country? And see, they have two lodges right here, probably representing different political sides in their country. Each side is fighting to get the upper hand in Greece. Don't think those Greeks are here to stay. Remember how they weren't too eager about joining the army in the Great War? On a moment's notice they'll hightail it back to Greece and be treated like heroes. They're out to undermine the United States Government. Just look at them—getting good wages in America and they turn around and send it to the old country. And why do they send it to the old country? I'll tell you why. They're Communists. They're supporting people back in Greece who want to get hold of the government. It's a conspiracy with Russia.

The mayor and councilmen asked the Greek businessmen what was going on. What was it all about? People were saying the Greek strikers were Communists. The businessmen denied it, and when the strikers came into their groceries, dry goods stores, and restaurants, told them they were giving the rest of the Greeks a bad name. Pretty soon, the businessmen said, the Americans would stop coming into their stores. Affronted, the strikers told them they were not real Greeks anymore, they were only interested in money. They had lost their honor, their *filotimo*. The strikers solved the problem by buying at the Miners Mercantile.

The Greek businessmen asked the Greek vice-consul for Utah to talk to the strikers. He went to the tent town and with the United Miners' permission asked all the Greeks to meet in the big meeting tent. The strikers hailed the short, big-stomached, bald man: he was an educated man who did not look down on them, who always spoke the demotic, not the purist. The men produced a bottle of ouzo, which the vice-consul took phantom sips of—he was fastidious and suspected it had been made under dirty conditions. For all his careful, diplomatic advice in the demotic, the men looked at him from under black frowning eyebrows and said not a word.

Next the businessmen sent the priest, who immediately forgot his mission and berated the men for spending their Sundays in the coffeehouse instead of in church.

The businessmen thought of one last messenger, the pioneer among the Greeks, who was called Uncle or *Barba*. He had befriended the men as they came from Greece. A folk healer, he had tended their wounds and illnesses, and he had been generous about lending money. Barba was dispatched to the tent town and because he was hospitable, took a gallon of his bootleg whiskey with him. Until late at night, the men sat in the warm light of kerosene lamps, on camp stools, boxes, and upturned galvanized tubs and listened to Barba give his philosophy in proverbs. He interspersed the proverbs with swallows of whiskey. "Yes, boys, as we say in our sweet country 'Buy shoes from your own country, even if they are patched.' " The strikers nodded as he spoke more platitudes upholding their passion for Greece and then slowly in his sonorous, unhurried voice, repeated proverbs of self-destruction: "Whoever pees in the ocean, will taste it in the salt" and yet again, "Whoever spits upwards gets it in his face."

A few more proverbs and Barba, by then well warmed both outside and inside, began on anecdotes to illustrate the errors of splitting into factions when more important goals were present. With embellishments, branching off and coming back to his subject, with long pauses given to drinking glassfuls of whiskey, he told of two generals, related by marriage, who delayed an important battle with the Turks by quarreling over the bride's dowry. Instead of becoming sober at the moralizing tale, the men burst out laughing. Barba laughed too and slid into entertaining the men with his complete collection of priest and bishop stories. Barba left at dawn with the men calling out *Yia sou!*—Long life. The Greek businessmen gave up.

Rumors began. Stavros gleefully told his men that from his count, the royalists would win. Mihaêl wanted the election to include all of the Greeks in the surrounding mining camps. "How can you do that with soldiers all over the place?" Stavros asked with a sly, knowing look.

"They can come over the mountains like they did when they brought us guns and bullets," Mihaêl reminded them.

Even his Cretan followers knew it was impossible and, even more so, dangerous: they would be deported, and all their parents' hopes would be lost. The day of the election came. The few men who owned cars parked them on a side street, afraid their windows would be smashed following the counting of the ballots. One of the men had hammered together a crude ballot box out of an apple crate, and at seven o'clock hundreds of excited men began voting. Stavros glanced at the door with a perplexed look. At nine o'clock, the time for the end of balloting, Mihaêl had not yet appeared. Stavros asked a Cretan, "Where's Mihaêl?"

He shook his head. "He's been after us to be here on time."

Suddenly the door opened. Mihaêl ran in, picked up the ballot box, and streaked out to a waiting car. With a surge, like a giant gust of wind, the men leaped up and ran after him. They got only a glimpse of the getaway car speeding off into the night. Stavros looked about, eyes bulging, and shouted, "Someone drive me after them!"

"Come on!" one of the men yelled. Minutes passed by the time Stavros and the driver ran to the man's car and drove down the narrow road into the blackness. They could see no sign of the fleeing car. "Maybe they're parked behind a barn, hiding," Stavros said, staring hard into the night shadows. They sped on until there was hardly any gas left in the tank.

Mihaêl and his driver were never seen again. Long after the National Guard left the mining town, people found pieces of paper written with foreign letters in alfalfa fields, on the river banks, and on the side of the dirt road leading west. The Cretans and Maniots laughed, but furtively, because Stavros had gone to church and before the icon of the Virgin and Child vowed to get revenge.

When the Ku Klux Klan marched through town two years later, burned crosses on the mountain slopes, and painted the letters KKK on their countrymen's stores, the Greeks could not understand why they hid their faces behind hoods.

Crying Kostas

She had been no more than five years old. At the last moment her brother Bill, ready to ride off on the brown and white pinto pony Danny Boy, had looked down on her. Their mother handed Bill a flour sack stacked with tin plates of food, which he tied to the saddle horn. "I'll take the baby with me," he said to their mother, who looked worried. "It's not far. Kostas has already reached the pines."

Their mother lifted Athena behind Bill. "Hold on tight," she said, "and you, Vasili, careful. Your eyes four."

Danny Boy trotted up the dirt road that led from the white frame house in the clearing. The last crop of alfalfa was at one side ready for cutting; a few old ewes and a limping lamb were grazing in a pen of weathered horizontal poles. Athena was excited, clutching Bill's waist, feeling grown-up.

For a short distance they followed the irrigation stream at the side of the road; on the other side dusty sunflowers and Indian paintbrush bobbed as they passed. Then Danny Boy left the road and followed a path through meadow grass glistening with dew, and they were into the pines, cool and still. Danny Boy's hooves crunched on dry pine needles until they came to a grassy plateau where hundreds of sheep grazed. Kostas's black sheepdog rushed barking toward them. Kostas whistled and the dog was silent.

Bill turned in the saddle and carefully lifted Athena to the ground. Kostas was sitting on the step of the sheep wagon whittling a twig into a fine point. He watched them approach, probing and cleaning his teeth, spitting and probing. Even sitting, his back was straight, shoulders back, his nose large and mustache curved like a British officer in a movie about India they had seen in Grand Junction. Bill had driven Athena and her older sisters there for supplies. When the officer appeared on the screen, Athena had thought he was Kostas and got excited. "That's not Kostas. Be quiet," her sisters hissed.

"Eh, my lad," Kostas said in heavy central Greek dialect as they stood before him, "and you, Athinoula bebé." That was his greeting.

"Mama sent you some spinach pita and some *koulourakia.*"

"Tell her may she live long. I get tired of my own cooking. Eh, sit on that log." Kostas got up and climbed the three wooden steps into the wagon. Its dingy canvas was stained with rust over the arched staves. He returned with a box of chocolate-covered cherries and held it out to Athena and Bill. The bottoms of the cherries were pushed in. Athena ate her piece and tasted its staleness. She shook her head when Kostas offered her another chocolate, but he pressed the box toward her. She took one and ate it quickly to get it over with.

Although their mother had told Bill to return immediately, he leaned forward and began a leisurely, mostly one-sided conversation with Kostas. He spoke in Greek to him, as did everyone. Kostas learned little English. "Yes," Kostas said or, "Hmmm." Then Bill asked a question, and Kostas began talking about an autumn when he was bringing the sheep down from the mountains to trail them over the Colorado border to their winter grounds on the eastern Utah desert. He spoke slowly with a measured cadence, and even though Athena could have played at the side of the sheep wagon where pine cones and desiccated white shells of snails lay, she listened, in a spell, though not understanding all the story then.

Kostas went on describing the descent down the mountain, other flocks joining, and then on the road west, herders from other outfits he met. Kostas repeated every dialogue fully, but when he came to their leaving the hamlet of Rifle, his voice took on a heavy urgency, and he told of a scent in the air, signs on the ground, early winter warnings.

They got to the border and a blizzard hit them. His voice broke as he told of the horror, of the blinding, swirling snow, the howling wind, his dog Leon whining, scratching on the door until he opened it. The two of them nearly frozen inside the sheep wagon, he making the sign of the cross at the shelf he had made to hold a small icon of the Virgin and Infant Christ, crying because he was helpless. Two days later the wind subsided, and he went out to count the frozen sheep strewn as far as he could see.

He went on, for there was more: he met other herders and owners in the corrals at the Jensen water stop where sheep were loaded onto railroad cars. No one had enough sheep to take to Kansas City. All of them sold on the spot to a sheep broker who took the remnants east. Some herders had to go out and work in towns for strangers. He wasn't the only one who could not go into a town store that autumn, slit the laces of his hightops with a knife, have the clerk throw the boots away, and walk out with a new pair.

"Your poor mother," Kostas said, "she had to feed you, put clothes on you, send you to school with only pennies in her purse." He cried fresh tears, wiped his eyes, and the saga ended.

When they returned, their mother lectured Bill for staying away so long, but Athena could see she was not really angry. "Poor man, out there with his holy book and the sheep. He cried, of course."

"Of course."

"Poor Crying Kostas. Big happenings, little happenings, and he cries just the same."

From that day Athena became aware of this crying—silent, yet wholehearted, tears streaming down the craggy face, never-ending tears. When other sheepherders came to the house, they asked about Crying Kostas, looked at each other, and laughed. Once when all the sheepherders were gathered at the table, her mother told Athena and Bill to sit on the empty chairs on either side of Kostas. Athena felt sorry for him; she saw how others avoided him.

The next time she went to his sheep camp, she was ten years old. She had gone with her father, who had brought a box of supplies, flour, canned beans, bacon, and a roll of Greek newspapers, the *Atlantis* from New York. Athena and her father, a finicky man who ate at none of his herders' camps except Kostas's, sat in the shade of the sheep wagon and ate beans and biscuits on tin plates. Kostas apologized, "I never cook meat on Wednesdays and Fridays in memory of our Lord Jesus Christ."

Even more finicky than her father, Athena only pretended to eat. While her father walked into the pines and beyond to a grassy plain among the sheep, Kostas told her in his thick Roumeliot accent how he had come to work for her father. Athena was miserable that a grown person was talking to her as an equal. "The Boss," the American sheepherders called her father. The "*Bossis*" Kostas called him. "I was thirty-seven years old when I came to America. It took that long to save the money along with the little pension I got from the War of 1912. That's how long it took to save the twenty dollars for the ship's fare. In the summer I made charcoal, and in the winter I took other people's sheep and goats and drove them as far as Mesolonghi for pasture. When I hurt my leg in the coal mine, a patriotis sent me to the *Bossis*. Out there in the sheep *cemp*, I taught myself how to read and write our renowned language. For that alone I thank God and our little Christ for sending me to America. There was a reason America was my fate.

"I worked for the *Bossis* ten years, then my leg got worse. I could only do the work of an ordinary man, so I hired out to an *Amerikanos*. After two years I got better and I came back to the *Bossis*. Look." He took out two medals pinned inside his shirt pocket. "I got these in the war against the Turks, in 1912. And it was for this reason."

Kostas began a long story about his army unit caught in a hollow not far from Thessaloníki. Throughout the night the Turks had climbed up a surrounding ridge. Kostas cupped his left palm, blacklined, to lay out the terrain, then walked his right fingers over the ridge of fingers. He broke off and began talking about a young lieutenant. "A handsome, manly leventis! He had two children. Once when I was sent south as a runner, he gave me little gifts to bring them. The telephone wires had been cut." Tears flowed down his sunburnished, deep-lined face, and he tried to go on. He chewed on his lips; his strong yellow teeth clicked, but no words came. "Ach, Kosta," her father said when he returned, "still crying? 'Even God tires of too much Kyrie, eleison.' " As they drove off in her father's half-ton truck, Kostas watched them, his lips moving, telling them something.

"Why does he always cry?" Athena asked her mother when she returned home.

"Who knows? People from his village say he was like everybody else until he went to war. Then he came back crying at the least little thing."

At intervals Athena saw him, and the story was always the same, except that the time he had spent working for the *Bossis* changed from ten years to fifteen, to twenty, until it was forty-seven. Kostas was eighty-two when Athena's father sold his sheep and died soon after. Kostas moved to the city, to a rooming house near the church and the one remaining store in old Greek Town.

For years someone in the family, but mostly Athena, brought him to their mother's house for Thanksgiving, Christmas, Easter, and the Dormition of the Virgin. On the feast day of Saints Constantine and Helen, her mother prepared a large box of pastries for Kostas to give out to the other elderly roomers.

Kostas had been named after Saint Constantine, he said, weeping, because the saint had saved his life. He had been born in the 1880s when northern Greece was still under Turkish control. A Turkish officer had been ambushed and killed on the outskirts of the village, and his soldiers were searching the mountains looking for the fleeing villagers. Kostas's mother gave birth to him behind a boulder, and his father ripped off a shirt sleeve to wrap him in. The villagers wanted him killed to keep his cries from attracting the soldiers, but his mother placed him under the altar of a wilderness chapel dedicated to Saints Constantine and Helen. Three days later when the soldiers had gone, his mother returned and found him alive. He was baptized in the chapel and named after the saint.

Kostas attended every liturgy and always sat on the first row of a side pew, facing the icon of Saints Constantine and Helen. He was proud, he solemnly told Athena, to be named after the Byzantine emperor who established Christianity in the Greek world and proud, too, of his mother, the Empress Helen, who searched the Holy Land until she found the True Cross. "Out in the desert, nothing out there, except a green basil plant growing. 'Dig there,' she said. They dug and there was the True Cross."

After liturgy, old gaunt Kostas would be waiting for Athena at the bottom of the steps with a letter from Social Security or a piece of junk mail he wanted her to translate into Greek. She would insist on taking him to the rooming house and help him into his room. He began to refuse to come to the family dinners: he couldn't eat the rich food, he said, and besides, her mother was dead. The young people didn't need him around. Athena sensed he wanted to be alone with his church books and some memory that she knew could tell her why he was called "Crying Kostas."

There in the rooming house he would begin the same old story, and his eyes would lose their far-seeing gaze and become frantic, hypnotic. He would not hear her excuses, see her attempts to get away. The tears would spill over his hollowed cheeks, and he never finished the story. It never varied. He would begin by talking about his village and began crying when he came to the War of 1912 and the dead lieutenant. His gray eyebrows bristled; his craggy face turned red; his mouth twisted. He leaned forward trying to bring out words.

"What is it, Mr. Kosta? Say it. Please try to say it."

Yet on a scorching August day, there he was at her door, leaning on his shepherd's crook, a taxi driving away. "Mr. Kosta! What if I weren't here? Then what would you do? No, you couldn't wait outside. I could be gone for days. I'll give you the money for the *taxi*, but you must never do this again. Where would you telephone for a *taxi* if I weren't here?" She thought of her neighbors' not letting him inside. "Please don't ever do this again."

Kostas leaned his crook against a chair and sat on the edge of the living room sofa, furious. He had just read in a Greek-language newspaper that priests were beginning to use English in the liturgy. "Anathema! I learned the Greek tongue at my mother's breast! If we lose our language, we lose our religion! We lose Christ!" For several minutes he went on, pronouncing curses on the archbishop in New York, on bishops, on priests.

Athena controlled her annoyance, then anger at Kostas and his obsession with the Greek lanaguage. She said, "Mr. Kosta, we live in America . . . "

Kostas raised his thick gray eyebrows, shut his eyes, and lifted the palms of his veined old hands. "Sst," he said, that old Greek admonition that brooked no dissent. Then he was off again talking about the Greek language, the language of the Bible, the language of Christ (Athena did not bother to refute him), the language of the great philosophers. Alexandra stood up. "I'll make some coffee," she said and escaped into the kitchen. She took out the *brik,* the long-handled small brass pan her mother had given her when she married, and made Turkish coffee.

While she placed a shot glass of ouzo, the demitasse of coffee, and a honey-nut sweet on a tray, Kostas kept up a harangue in the living room. He refused the ouzo because a doctor in the clinic told him alcohol wasn't good for him and pushed the sweet away. "Have you forgotten I have sugar?" he said. "You know I only eat boiled apples and boiled eggs." Of course she knew it; it had occurred to her when she took the sweet out of the container that he would not eat it but might feel slighted if it were not there on the traditional hospitality tray. Kostas blew on the coffee, sipped noisily, and then began again on the imminent loss of the Greek language in America. Suddenly he was talking about his village. He cried when he came to the War of 1912 and the dead lieutenant. He could not go on.

Athena said the familiar words: "What is it, Mr. Kosta? Say it. Please try to say it."

His mouth stilled. He cried until his red bandana was wet. Athena drove him back to the city. She gave him a sideways glance: he sat straight, not leaning against the back of the seat, in a world silent to her, teeming to him.

By winter of that year pain had hardened on his old face. Then, although she lived closer to the new suburban church, Athena most often attended the old immigrant church to see if Kostas were there. No, he would not let her pick him up. "This is the way I have to go," he said. Once when she commiserated over his arthritis, he waved her words away. "Pain is good for people," he said.

Walking the two blocks to the church, Kostas would stop to rest, leaning on his shepherd's crook, then went on slowly through the old immigrant district. Giant service stations for diesel trucks, moving van warehouses, and factories dwarfed the last of the old houses and decrepit apartment buildings. On a corner stood the Greek church, stolid, impervious to the noise, its rust-colored brick smoke-tinged, its three copper domes rising against the skies. Near the railyards in a small park homeless men and a few women congregated. Athena sometimes thought of Kostas being accosted and raising his shepherd's crook.

One Mother's Day Athena climbed the church steps, newly redone but the cement already chipped. A member of the church board, a contractor, had replaced the old ones "just for the cost of the materials."

Kostas had railed that old people were going to fall down them. He didn't like the contractor, called him a donkey and that old American epithet "big shot." He was becoming more irascible.

Athena opened the heavy doors and stepped into the narthex. Only a few candles burned before the icon of the Trinity. She exchanged a smile with the old man tending the collection basket. "Yes," Kostas had said, "there wasn't a prostitute he hadn't gone to in the whole state, and now he comes to church every Sunday with a pious look on his face." Athena had been surprised when he had said this; he was careful with his language around her; he was a Greek puritan, if there could be such a person.

She placed a dollar bill in the basket, lighted a candle, and crossed herself before the icon. She stepped to the glass door on the left. The narrow-faced, sad-eyed Virgin and the Infant, a miniature adult in her arms, thumb and third finger touched in blessing, gazed out at her. "Forgive me," she said vaguely and opened the glass door leading to the nave.

For Mother's Day a large bouquet of red carnations had been placed at the right of the central door of the icon screen under the icon of Christ in bishop's robes and miter, and another on the left of it under the icon of the Virgin and the Child Christ. Athena sat on an empty pew toward the back. The choir and priest were chanting supplications for seasonable weather, for the safety of travelers—when she was a child the words were travelers on sea and land, now the word *air* had been added. Athena glanced toward the right front where Kostas always sat, but the Corinthian column painted to resemble marble blocked her view. She hoped that he was mercifully dead, ninety-three years of age, dead in his sleep, his six-foot-four body stretched out, his ancient profile serene, a dignified patriarch if a person didn't know him.

Her face relaxed. Fresh incense clouded the icon screen as the chanter, an officious new immigrant, noisily clinked the censer before the icon of the gently smiling Christ in golden bishop's robes. Trying to take care of both the chanting and the altar boy duties because the boys were late, he broke in before the priest finished the long drawn-out *We beseech Thee's* with his nasal *Kyrie eleison's*. Kostas thought he had a good voice, "like the chanter in my village."

Then Athena knew Kostas had not died. Something was wrong that he was not in church wiping his eyes. Little ice points pricked her arms. She thought of him lying on the bed, unable to move, his mouth opening and closing with no sounds coming out, no one hearing him, the occupants of the old rooming house, aged, bent, shuffling past his door and not knowing of the struggle beyond the bolted door.

She moved forward to leave, to drive the two blocks to his rooming house, but she slid back: it was only his bad leg, more painful than usual with the sudden cold. The liturgy wore on. Again Athena decided to leave, but then she would not have the *andithoro,* the consecrated bread, for Kostas. She glanced at her watch, another fifteen minutes at least. The priest, who should have known better—he had been born in America and had a university degree before entering seminary, began his sermon, repeating that old ridiculous story. She had heard it from immigrant priests from the time she was a girl. Here she was, seventy years old, and she was still hearing it: "And he was so madly in love with this beautiful evil woman that when she said 'Prove your love. Bring me your mother's heart,' he ran to do her bidding. Then, holding the bloody heart in his hands, he hurried to his lover. On the way he stumbled and fell, and the heart said, 'Have you hurt yourself, my son?' That, dear parishoners, is mother love."

The priest was still droning on about mother love. He was a generation younger than she, raised by American-born parents, and had taken on some of that sentimentality Americans spouted when talking about "values."

She stayed, sitting there among her people, and gazed at the icons she had known since a child. The icons, the domes, and the arches were lovingly familiar to her now. She knew she would never become used to the new church in the suburbs, away from the drunks, from the diesels, from the immigrant past. A cold building, it looked like a California mortuary outside, and inside like almost any Protestant church, with the addition of a few biblical mosaic figures in a see-through grill to represent an icon screen.

The liturgy ended, and Athena stood in line to receive the consecrated bread. She thought of asking the priest about Kostas. She had written his name on Kostas's government documents to be called in emergencies, because she might not be in the city. It could be the priest had admitted him to a nursing home, that hell Kostas feared and ranted against. An eighty-year-old Greek Kostas knew had gone back to Greece and brought back a fifty-year-old spinster. When Athena had tsk-tsked, Kostas bristled. "Why shouldn't he? He wasn't interested in making babies. He wanted a woman to take care of him in his old age so he wouldn't end up in those devil nursa homes. And for her to come to this country and live off his Sosha Secure and the little money he saved, she was well off. You were born rich in this country. You don't know the poverty back there! Do you know what kind of a life a spinster lives back there, too poor to have a dowry to marry? She's a slave to every member of the clan, trying to earn her bread. And they beat her besides. I know. My oldest sister lived that way. I was too young to help her," and he commenced crying.

The priest was giving out the small squares of bread and having his hand kissed in return. For some reason he was speaking Greek, "My dear countrymen, I was in McGill, Nevada, this past Friday to bury an old patriotis. You are fortunate. Those poor people in that desert have been without a priest for twelve years. You're indeed fortunate, fortunate people."

"Why don't you add that you're fortunate also to be here and not there?" a tall, white-haired man said.

Everyone laughed, and the priest sheepishly along with them. Athena enjoyed the repartee; she would have something of interest to tell Kostas. She decided not to interrupt the easy goodwill by asking the priest about him. The priest dropped several pieces of bread into her palm and smilingly wished her a happy Mother's Day. At the door an altar boy handed her a red carnation and also wished her a happy Mother's Day.

As she hurried to the parking lot, she looked for transient drunks. A freight train had left a layer of raw smoke under the sky. While she drove to Kostas's rooming house, she ate a piece of the consecrated bread. It stayed like a hard little mass in her stomach. She parked the car in front of the dilapidated one-story building; its brick had been painted a dark dingy red after a fire. Two old men shuffled down the long, dark hall. The cool smoky air was shut out, and she stood in a stale warmth outside Kostas's door.

A muffled sound came from the other side of it. She rapped sharply and listened. The muffled sound went on. She knocked harder. "Mr. Kosta," she said in Greek, in a loud whisper, hoping not to attract the old men behind their doors, afraid they would line the hall and watch her, the old men living on old-age pensions and Social Security who had no families or who abandoned them or been abandoned. Once a year during Holy Week Kostas made a truce with them; he dyed eggs a dark red with dye from a Greek importing store. American dye was not, he said, the true dye of the Resurrection. He presented an egg to each of the old men telling them "Christ He risen."

Alexandra knocked, called, hoped now that someone would appear so that she would not be alone with what was behind the door. Down the hall two indistinct figures stood in doorways watching. "Have you seen Mr. Haliris?" she asked.

"Why, yes," one of the men said and limped as quickly as he could toward her. The other man followed more slowly, hands folded meekly at his waist. Eager, filmed eyes, mouth twisting about false teeth: "He's there. He was a-pounding in there all morning."

"Mr. Kosta! Mr. Kosta!"

"Eh?" The voice was strong and clear.

"Open, please, Mr. Kosta. I'm Athena"

The two men waited with Athena in silence. A bolt pushed out of a slot, a chain link fell against wood, and a key shook for several seconds around and then into the keyhole. Athena shook her head: how many times had she told him that if there were a fire, he would never get the door unlocked in time?

The door opened and he stood straight, head back, looking down at her with the far peer of sheepherders. He moved his head slowly to scowl at the old men. "Go way. Go way," he said in English. "Come in Athena. Come in, Athinoula." He made way for her and began to cry.

The room was brightly lighted by a large dangling light globe. On worn brown linoleum all of Kostas's belongings were heaped: stacks of the Greek newspapers *Atlantis,* tied with knotted string; a few cans of green beans; empty egg cartons; rolled-up long underwear; a double-breasted, wide-shouldered suit he had bought decades ago to wear to church; his shepherd's crook; three small wooden boxes he had made out of scrap lumber, each one secured with two big locks. Inside the boxes were church bulletins, letters, and form notices sent to him over the years: Dear Social Security Client, new payment for . . . ; Dear Member of our Senior Citizens, the Salvation Army invites you to be its guest at the annual Thanksgiving . . . ; Dear Householder. . . .

"I should be ashamed to bring you into this mess. I've been searching since yesterday. I went—pardon me for saying this—to the toilet, and when I came back my medals were gone, stolen! Stolen! My med-

als from the Balkan War, and the one was the King's medal, the medal
I got when we were caught outside Thessaloniki and . . . ''

Alexandra breathed rapidly to get some air in the closed-up room.
She burst out, "Mr. Kosta, how could that be? You always have them
pinned on you. And you always lock your door. They're here. Remember the time you thought you had lost your Saint Constantine
medal and we found it in you coat lining?"

"Look! Look!" Crying he held out his long, lined palms, the pads
of the fingertips a pattern of vertical, parallel wrinkles, the hands of
the very old. "I've been searching since yesterday. I haven't left one bit
of space undone!"

Alexandra looked about the room. The white metal bed had been
meticulously made with the burlap covering Kostas had sewed out of
gunny sacks and pinned to blankets. He did all his own sewing.
"Don't tell the Greek women," he had said the first time she entered
the room, "they'd laugh. But who was going to sew buttons and rips
in the sheep cemp?"

The sink was clean, a rag hung dry in the curved pipe under it.
"Haven't you eaten this morning?"

"I ate a piece of bread."

"Did you take your medicine?"

"Yes, I took it! I'm not ready to die yet." Fresh tears ran down his
cheeks. His head dropped toward his thin chest. "I'm not ready, but
He Who knows all . . . ''

On the dresser two apples and a knife lay on a newspaper next to a
hotplate. A board under the hotplate had a deep charred spot. 'He'll
burn the whole place down," the priest had told Athena.

"And look!" Kostas pointed a hooked finger at a nail hole and a
surrounding oblong space lighter than the dingy wall. "My mother's
picture! Gone. I took it to the church secretary. I told her to wrap it up
and mail it to my grandniece back in the village so they wouldn't steal
it. Now I can't look at her picture anymore. My sainted mother who
gave birth to me in a ravine when our villagers were running from the
Turks. My holy mother!"

"Oh, Mr. Kosta, you shouldn't have given the picture away. Who
would take it?"

"Who? These animals, that's who! Last week I found a scorpion in
a little glass bottle in my pocket. They bring insects and push them
under my door. Beasts! Not a Christian among them! I try to remind

them of Christ with Easter eggs, but it's all in vain." Suddenly he was shouting, calling the roomers "whorelickers," "fuckers of mothers and sisters" and other names she did not know. His old hand clutched the knife by the hotplate, and he lifted his arm to strike out. Athena's heart beat frantically at this unknown Kostas. She looked at the bolted door. Then he saw her and put the knife down as if nothing had happened.

Still frightened, Athena looked at the pile of belongings. Kostas pinched his dripping nose. "Mr. Kosta," she said in a fluttery voice, "you lie down, and I'll straighten out the room. And I'll peel and boil your apples. You've had too much strain."

"No! You stay where you are! I'll rest and search again after you've gone."

"Here's a piece of andithoron."

"What! Was there liturgy today?"

"It's Sunday . . . "

"Ach. Ach. I was so wrought up I forgot." Kostas made the sign of the cross, looked at the church calendar nailed near the barren oblong space. "Yes. How did I forget it? Old age. Old age." He knocked the side of his head with his knuckles.

"Have you any letters for me to read?" She wanted desperately to get out of the little room.

Kostas lifted his hands impatiently. "It was Fate that made you come today. I was going to take a *texi* and come to your house."

"Mr. Kosta! Please. Just go to the church office and have Mrs. Markakis dial for you and you can tell me what you want."

Tears coursed down the rivulets of his sunken cheeks. He pinched his nose and sniffed. "No, what I'm going to tell you I have kept inside me, locked in my heart, since the War of 1912. *I must tell it!* I never wanted to tell it to a priest. I love our church, but I hate priests!" He gasped for breath.

"The young lieutenant I told you about, the palikar, with the nice wife and two small children. Orphans all these years!" Kostas made the sign of the cross and turned his head stiffly from Athena. He hesitated. "When we were in the hollow at night and the Turks came up on the ridge, the captain got excited. I was standing by the lieutenant. I was his orderly. The captain wanted the men to wait until dawn and storm the ridge. The lieutenant said we should follow a soldier who came from those parts out of the hollow. There was no moon, but the soldier knew the way.

"The captain went crazy when the lieutenant argued with him. The lieutenant kept trying to convince him. Then the captain! The captain! The captain put his pistol against the lieutenant's head and fired! The liutenant fell dead, and because of the shot we had to follow the captain up the ridge at dawn.

"The few of us who came out alive got medals. King Constantine himself pinned them on us. And I never told anyone about the lieutenant. The poor young lieutenant! Never! Who would listen to me, a charcoal maker, a sheepherder who didn't have a pair of shoes of his own until he went to the army? Who couldn't write his own name? Who would have paid attention?

"A young man in his prime! A young widow, two orphan children! The captain fat and prosperous! And I never said it to anyone. Right after the war, I came to America. I learned to write, but I never wrote anyone about it. I wanted to tell the *bossis,* but, good man though your father was, he wouldn't have done anything. 'The priest's shoes are none of your business,' he'd say."

Tears were in her eyes, but Kostas had stopped crying. He mumbled and looked at his clasped hands. "It was seventy years ago, Mr. Kosta. God understands." Her voice weakened as she spoke the platitude. "Don't blame yourself. Maybe no one would have listened." She gazed at his bowed head: if he had known town ways, been able to read and write then, go to a newspaper. If he'd been a different kind of man.

"Forgive me, Athena, but I better lie down."

Kostas followed Athena to the door. She shook his old hand tightly and put her other around his bony shoulder. She stepped into the hall and heard the bolt being pushed into place, the chain clinking, the key rattling.

Two days later he telephoned her; they were taking him to a nursing home, and he begged her to come to see him for the last time. "Where are they taking you? I can't hear you. Where?" He didn't know, he said, his voice thin, frantic, but "come for the last time." She said she would and went back to preparing dinner for her visiting children and grandchildren. She thought she would call his rooming house the next morning to ask where he had been taken, but she could not remember its name; it was English. She repeated words: Lancaster, Devonshire, but the word *Bristol* eluded her. She took the grandchildren to the zoo the following day and thought she would go by the rooming house afterwards, but the children were tired, quarreling and hitting each other. She would call the church office then in the morning; the priest might know. The next morning she read his obituary. She would wonder later if it had been longer than two days, perhaps a week, and the days had gone by so fast during the children's visit while old Kostas had been dying.

Fifteen years later she was in church; it was the feast day of Saints Constantine and Helen. She lighted a votive candle for Kostas, crossed herself, and while the priest's voice receded into a void, she gazed at the icon of Saint Constantine until it blurred.

Mother and Son

It was six in the morning. The stout woman Tula and her old husband had always been early risers. Even now, when his illness interrupted their sleep, they still woke up before the newspaper thumped on the front porch. Thinking her short gray hair askew, she rearranged the hairnet over it; she had no time to look in mirrors. Then she gazed at him, Gus, sitting on a worn sofa across from her. The metal walker, which he used only to help him get to the bathroom, was set in front of his feet. Tula smiled at it. Their CPA son had bought it. Such good sons, all of them. She frowned, thinking of the oldest, Sam. Now Gus's freckled, almost hairless head dropped lower, his eyes half-closed. The Darvon she had given him half an hour ago was taking effect.

She thought it would be a relief to sit where she was and rest. She was so tired; she knew now what people meant when they said they were so tired their bones ached. Gus took all her energy. He didn't want to be a burden to her, he'd said before he had descended into this almost permanent, drugged stupor. "Put me in a nursing home," he told his sons when he emerged from it for a few moments at a time, but "not yet" she would tell them.

It would be so good to just sit there, but she had that duty, maybe not a duty, but that something she had to do. She got up heavily from the straight-backed chair—she could not get up from a comfortable easy chair any longer—and turned on the record player. Shuffling in black felt house slippers, she walked toward the door to the strains of an old Greek folk song: "Woman of Samos, when will you return? I'll send a boat with golden sails for you. Roses I'll strew on the seashore." It was Gus's favorite song. He no longer cared much about anything. Even the remembrances of his boyhood in Greece and his early years in America had stopped. Maybe he had sensed she was not really listening, but she knew it was not so. It was old age, long, long old age; he was ninety-four, twenty years older than she.

At the door of the family room she stopped, turned, and looked at him. She breathed in deeply: she would gladly listen now to those tired memories—his mother, her black kerchief loosened, crying and shrilling at the same time for him to hurry to America to make money for his sisters' dowries. For their *prika, prika* and "I heard the word everywhere I went in those wild mountains. It was 1910. I was fifteen. My mother had tied some bread and cheese and a few clothes in a black goat's hair rug. I looked up at the village for the last time, so afraid."

At first he told the rest of the story straight through: in New York shining shoes for an older second cousin who took all his tips; on freight cars riding with other Greeks, looking out for railroad detectives; on a Midwestern plain, a water boy running with a bucket on either side of a pole across his shoulders, running to each command of young Greeks laying rails; in a Chicago coffeehouse giving a handsome labor agent all his savings and being sent into an eastern Utah coal mine, he and a new friend building a shack out of blasting powder boxes.

He had remembered every place he had been, hamlets, water stops, mining camps all over the Midwest and West, gone, never to be seen again. In coffeehouses, Greek restaurants, in railroad camps, black-robed priests, Greek newspaper reporters, Greek government officials telling them to save their money and go back to poor Greece that needed their earnings. On Saturday nights to the YMCA for a shower.

His eyes had always brightened when he told of becoming a businessman. Wearing black protectors over his white shirtsleeves in his fruit and vegetable stand in Salt Lake City's west side Greek Town. Sleeping on a cot in the dark, musty back room, eating feta cheese and bread from the bakery down the street. At four in the morning in every kind of weather driving an old Ford Model A pickup to the wholesale stalls a few blocks away. Bringing back fruits and vegetables, arranging them in pyramids on gondolas, but the Japanese next door doing his better, nicer looking. Then both of them on the lookout for American boys who ran down the sidewalk with sticks outstretched, knocking over the pyramids, squealing as apples and oranges rolled into the street. One of them Jack Dempsey the fighter's brother. Killed in a fight with a Greek.

Then a real businessman, leasing space in the growers' market, delivering to Greek and American restaurants and grocery stores; buying this house from a dentist who had lost all his money in the stock market crash of 1929; marrying Tula—"You was pretty good lookin' girl, joost right for the house, six rooms, then made family room after Second World War for the kids to play in."

His remembering usually stopped there, but after a while he jumbled everything up. Sometimes he inserted dreams as if they were happenings: dancing on the village square with the schoolmaster and teacher who had "their noses in the air. Too good for us"; Andreas his best friend in America, killed when a railroad car fell on him, yet leaping, twirling as if he were still alive.

Gus's head now rested on his chest; his breathing came deep with an added sound, a kind of low whistle. Tula sighed. She then began a ritual that had started a few months past and had gone on for a while before she realized it had become a daily necessity. Slowly she walked through her immaculate kitchen of white, glass-fronted cabinets and hexagonal-tiled drainboard. She glanced about to see that nothing was out of place—no cannister, spice box, or implement on the stove or drainboard.

On the table near the window she had earlier placed a black laquered tray, a gift of her insurance son's wife, and on it two small dishes of twisted sweet *koulourakia,* two cups, each with a pink packet of artificial sugar on the saucers—the only concession to health she and the visitor she was expecting made. She had covered the tray with plastic to keep nonexistent dust and flies off it. She frowned guiltily at the folded paper napkins on the tray next to the dishes, as if her dead mother were watching her. It would be the first time she would use paper instead of linen napkins when serving a visitor, but then anger took the place of guilt. If Connie didn't think they were good enough for her, then too bad. *She* didn't have a ninety-four-year-old husband who needed constant attention. *Her* husband had died ten years ago at the kitchen table stuffing his fat stomach with bacon and eggs. And what a vain woman! If something made her miss her weekly hair appointment, she acted like the world was coming to an end. It never occurred to Connie she could wash her own hair. Her mother had spoiled her, didn't have any sons so she spoiled Connie. She wouldn't trade her life for Connie's any day—her kids didn't turn out so hot. Tula folded her arms under her big bosom and with a smug smile thought: I've got the best sons imaginable—except for Sam, of course, but as Gus used to say, 'What the householder knows, the visitor doesn't.' ''

Tula looked at the coffeemaker. She had filled the paper liner with coffee and the glass pot with water. All she had to do was pour the water into the slot at a quarter of ten. The corners of her mouth turned down as she thought of Connie's routine the day of her hair appointment. First she stopped at Tula's for a cup of coffee, next to the hairdresser, then lunch and cards with her bridge group, and afterwards wandering through malls to see if there was something she could want. Sometimes she telephoned Tula in the evening to tell her a bit of gossip she had heard at bridge. She'd yawn into the telephone and say, "I'm worn out. I've chased all day." Chased what? Tula wanted to say. Tula breathed in long and deeply; she wanted Connie to visit to bring some change into the house, even though she was gloomy and left an unpleasantness behind, but Gus might need attention. And she was so tired.

Tula sighed and walked into the living room. Her felt house slippers made a swishing sound. She looked at everything carefully. The sofa and two matching club chairs were covered with green fringed cloth bought at KMart. On the end tables at either side of the sofa were costly vases, blue gray Llardo figurines, and cut-glass bowls, accumulated gifts from her sons and their wives. The rose silk lamp shades on the tables were protected with plastic strips. She peered at the lamps. She had bought them when the Auerbach department store closed, oh, many years past. Her sister May had asked a few days ago if she were waiting for the plastic to curl up and fly off by itself. Yes, the edges were curled.

On the spindly coffee table a pink shepherdess figurine was surrounded by several empty china boxes. For years she had dusted them and put them back exactly in the same place. The shepherdess had been given to her by her son Sam's first wife. After the divorce she had been tempted to give it to the church festival for their knickknack booth, but it was so pretty. His second wife had never given her anything, and she was glad of that.

The telephone rang, startling her. Her heart beating uncomfortably fast, she hurried to the kitchen even though she knew Gus was too drugged to be awakened by the ring. "Oh, it's you, Sam. How come you're calling so early?"

"I know you're up by now. I haven't gone home yet. I was . . . "

The word *home* annoyed Tula. To call that apartment a home! She interrupted, "What do you mean you haven't gone home yet?" Were you partying? she wanted to ask and to be told yes, so she would have more anger, more dissatisfaction with him.

"I took some leftover food down to the homeless shelter." His weary voice mollified Tula.

"Well, how long did that take? You closed the bar at one. I don't like you going down there on the west side like that at night. It's bad enough in the daytime. Everyday on the tv they talk about stabbings and beatings down there."

"Mama, I'm fifty-five years old."

He was the only one of her three sons who still called her "Mama"; the others called her "Mom." Not always, but at times hearing the "Mama" brought a yearning for his boyhood. She thought of him then with chubby legs stooping over to look at an insect on the sidewalk. Angrily she said, "Those derelicts you've gone and got yourself involved with!"

"Yeah, it's okay when you go around helping people out, but not okay for me to do it."

"Well, as long as you insist on going down there you can have that dark gray suit of Pa's for one of them. Your dad will never wear it again." She had thought of having him buried in it, but no, she must buy a new one. She went on hurriedly, "And it's not old at all. It's in very good condition. It's already cleaned. I was going to give it to that old man, the one who came from Greece after the Second World War. From the same village as your dad. Didn't have no family, no one. But he died."

"Yeah, I know. You told me. I'll come by some time today. Anything I can do for Pa?"

Anything I can do for Pa? As if you haven't done plenty to him. Aloud she said, "Not a thing."

Sam did not answer for a few seconds; then he said, "Okay. See you."

Not even, "See you, Mama," just "See you." Her mother had drilled her and she had drilled her children to add the person's name when greeting and when leaving, but that's what comes from being around lowlifes. Then she remembered her visitor Connie and that Sam might come at the same time. Maybe that day he wouldn't go home to sleep. That sleeping in the daytime! She didn't want Connie to see Sam. She thought of calling him back and reached for the receiver, but what could she say? He knew she would not leave the house. She could have said a white lie, something like "Come after eleven. I'll be through with my wash by then." Now she didn't know if he would go to his apartment to sleep or come for the suit first.

Tula went back to the living room, disgruntled that her ritual had been broken. She looked at the fireplace, of the same purple brick as the outside of the house. On the mantel was a mahogany clock, a wedding gift from her godfather. On either side were photographs and snapshots of children, grandchildren, and the three great grandchildren at various ages: in baptismal dress, in cap and gown, in wedding attire. As she gazed, a tear from each eye fell down her doughy cheeks.

In between the pictures were two small vases with colored straw flowers and several ornaments bought on a trip to Greece: a girl doll in ethnic dress, a boy doll in white pleated *foustanella,* a blue dish with an indistinct Parthenon painted on it, and a miniature hookah, a water pipe. She looked again at each picture and with a deep sigh went into the adjoining dining room. She realized she had sighed. She must stop it. Her MBA son Dan said she sighed all the time. She looked out the window hoping to see Sam's car. He could come and get the suit, have a cup of coffee, and be gone by the time Connie came, but there was no car at the curb.

She passed her hand over the beige crocheted cloth that covered the massive oak table. Her mother had crocheted the cloth for her trousseau. She thought of crying. In the center of the table was a cut-glass bowl jammed with past Easter and Christmas cards. Every year fewer cards came; friends were dying; people, even godchildren, were forgetting them. She gazed at the table with melancholy satisfaction. With added leaves it could stretch out to seat eighteen people comfortably. Ahh, she sighed, what dinners she had given all those years. Then, in the past ten years or so, the only ones that mattered were those for the family, all of them, children, grandchildren clustered around the table laughing, eating the Greek foods even the American daughters-in-law liked. The number at the table had begun to dwindle; the grandchildren had other things to do; no one had liked Sam's wives. She had overheard one of the daughters-in-law say there was too much togetherness.

Tula turned to face the china closet. It was filled with glass decanters, long-stemmed wine and water goblets, and white dessert plates from China embossed with raised golden dragons, a fifty-six-year-old wedding present. How she had loved to use the sparkling glassware and china when she was young, the house clean-smelling, the visitors talking in high spirits, and she going from one to the other carrying a silver tray with liqueur glasses of Metaxa and honey-and-nut pastries on the golden dragon dishes. The tray had held her wedding crowns. She had intended to make a list leaving the china and crystal to her granddaughters, but it had come to her lately that they were completely uninterested in her possessions. It had hurt. She had treasured the china and glassware, but the girls never looked into the closet, and Dan's and Jim's daughters once made fun of the dragon dishes.

With a long sigh she looked at the buffet where her family pictures stood, all in various sizes in plain and decorative gilt frames. Her parents' wedding picture was in the center, her mother small, unsmiling in a simple white dress, her tall father looking self-conscious in a store-new black suit, the short pant cuffs showing side-button shoes. When she had replaced the cardboard picture frames with gilt ones, she had written on a corner of the picture the wedding date, 1914, knowing she would always remember but not her children, grandchildren, and great grandchildren. (Why didn't you smile, Mama?

Brides aren't supposed to smile.) Under both sides of her jawbone a familiar pain lodged; she swallowed several times before it left. In one corner of the frame she had tucked a small card, a miniature icon of the Virgin and Child, and in front of it a whiskey glass holding a few white alyssum and violets, the first of spring. She made the sign of the cross.

She made the sign of the cross again looking at her brother John in air force uniform, his cap cocked to one side. The picture had been taken just before he was killed in a bombing mission over Berlin. An identical icon card was in the frame, with a diminutive bouquet before it. She would have to replace the cards with new ones; they no longer looked crisp. She gazed again into the bright, smiling eyes. In her later years her mother had kept a snapshot of John in her purse and took it out whenever she forgot what he looked like.

At the left of her parents' wedding picture was her own, she slim, pretty, at the side of Gus, oh, how extremely handsome. She shook her head in amazement and pride at the young woman she had been. She had been seventeen and Gus thirty-seven when they married. The first time she saw him she was only six or seven with a big red satin bow tied around the braid that already reached down her back. It was in the church basement, a celebration. The clarinet peeled, the *lyra* sang, and Gus was leading the circle dance, jumping high, coming down to a squat, hitting his ankles with a hissing sound between his teeth, then jumping up with a cry *"Hopa!"* He and her father, next in line, each held one end of a handkerchief that twisted as Gus twirled to the whistles and shouts of the crowd. She thought he was even more handsome than that Rudolph Valentino the older girls at school moaned over. In her senior year in high school a village friend came to her father to represent Gus. She was hot, uncomfortable, trying to keep her joy from showing when her parents asked her about the proposal.

They were married in the small church filled with the mingled scent of incense and lambs roasting in a nearby backyard. Afterwards they ate at long tables in the church basement while Gus's friends played the clarinet and stringed instruments they had brought from their villages.

Looking earnestly at the picture, Tula spoke aloud to Gus, "You was good to me, not like some of my friends married to old-country Greeks. We had some good times when the boys was little. We had a good life, except for Sam."

Her gaze passed over other family wedding pictures to an Easter picture taken in her parents' backyard against a grapevine trellis. Her parents were seated in the center, flanked by their teenage children. Tula spent several seconds examining the long silk dress her father had bought her in Kansas City. His lambs had brought a good price that year. The dress had been too big, but she and her mother had taken it in.

To the side of the picture was another taken a few years later, in the center their parents, seated again. Their mother was in black for John killed in the war. How patiently she looked into the camera eye. Their father was also in black, his hands spread on his knees, an unnatural smile on his whitened, sun-parched lips.

At the back of the buffet were four large pictures of her sons. Tula slid over the picture of Sam and looked at each of the other three in their university caps and gowns, all good boys, Dan the CPA, Steve the MBA with the Litton Company, Jim the insurance executive. How proud she and Gus were when their names were mentioned. All three at one time or another had had their names in the newspaper; Steve's picture was in twice. She looked back at Sam and whispered vehemently, "How could you turned out to be such a bum? Hurting your father and me. We sent you to the university to be a lawyer, and you drop out and end up owning a bar. We didn't even know you weren't going to classes. And you stayed there in that bar. You coulda got out. But you liked that lowlife, those floozies hanging around. Bad enough you married one; then you had to go marry another even worse. And your three kids. The first one took the two kids to California. They grew up and got married and had kids. I don't even get thank-you cards from them. And the other, Billy, we've got to bribe every inch of the way so he can stop off once in a while to say hello. And you, living in that awful, dark apartment, not even a picture or a single knicknack to show a person lived there. How could you turned out so rotten?"

Tula folded her arms over her breasts and looked at her angry face in the oblong mirror above the buffet. Flowers and garlands were etched in one corner. On one side of the mirror was a large picture of her father's mother sitting on a kitchen chair, her work-thickened hands spread on a full black skirt. A black kerchief was bound over her head, but a few wisps of white hair had escaped it. On the other side of the mirror was a picture of her father's father standing, wearing a tasseled fez, *foustanella,* and pompon shoes, his big moustache twisted into points. The features of the old people were hazy; the pictures had been enlarged from postcard originals and fitted into dark oval frames with concave glass.

"Look!" Tula hissed again at Sam, "your grandparents never got the opportunity to be nothing but poor farmers raising a few goats, but you, my wonderful Saloon Son, you coulda been a lawyer, you coulda been somebody, but no, you didn't have no ambition. How could you done it to your poor old dad? Came to this country when he was fourteen years old. Worked in a shoeshine parlor for his cousin who stole his tips. Worked on a railroad gang and in a mine. Oh, why, why?" She glared, breathing heavily.

She couldn't understand how he could have married that first simpering woman with lipstick on her teeth, but that second one! All he had to do was take one look at the family she came from, the men with a bunch of keys hanging from their belts and their trucks with a shotgun in the rear window and a dog in the back, the kind of truck parked in front of beer joints that had those go-go girls or whatever you call them showing their behinds and whatnots. And down the street their wives waiting on tables and their kids farmed out or left home with an older kid to watch them. And don't tell me your beer joint is high class!

She shook her head slowly. She had read all those articles in magazines at the grocery checkout counter, those psychology articles about children, but finally gave up. Not a single one gave her a clue as to why Sam ended up owning a saloon and living in an apartment that looked like a motel room.

She had been in his apartment only once. He had a bad chest cold, they told her at his bar when she called to tell him a letter had come to her house by mistake. She telephoned Sam that she was coming—to give the live-in time to get out. He protested, but she thought she heard something in his voice, like when he was a little boy sick in bed and she brought him soups and Jello, kind of like giving himself over to her, trusting her to make him well. In a paper bag she put the makings for mustard plasters: a jar of egg whites, another with flour, a can of powdered mustard, rags, and a spoon; in another bag a quart jar of hot soup.

Nothing, nothing in the apartment, except a blue glass ashtray filled with cigarette butts. If she opened the refrigerator or a closet she thought she might see some evidence of people living like they should, but it wouldn't be the right thing to do. She quickly made the plasters and pressed them on Sam's chest and back. He didn't resist. After he had eaten the soup, he fell asleep and she looked down on him. Even unshaven, he had the peaceful look of a child at rest after he had hurt himself.

She began to cry softly: Oh, Sammy, Sammy. You were such a nice little boy. Those big brown eyes. The first grandchild in the family. Everyone doted on you, brought you presents. And you were so good with the little kids. Never teased them, and you felt bad when one of them got hurt. And how they followed you, like your shadow. If only you had done like them, joined a fraternity, finished college, not pulled away like you did. Sammy, Sammy.

She hugged her arms; under the nylon sleeves, her skin was cold. Maybe if she had been nicer to that first one, the hippie, Sam would be a family man today, have his children and grandchildren around him. Maybe she shouldn't have been so critical of her sloppy ways, dirty dishes every place you looked, the floor sticky, mold in the refrigerator, the kids' bed sheets stained with food and nose drippings. But she tried! She tried! She kept the children all the time, had cribs and cots for them. When she went over to babysit, she cleaned the refrigerator, mopped the floor, gave the children baths, and changed their sheets. But the hippie made fun of her and sometimes even got annoyed and snapped at her. It was the marijuana. She knew what that smell was. When she was a little girl living close to the railyards before her father made enough money to move to the eastside, the Mexicans on the track gangs smoked it. Everyone looked down on them for doing it. Now it was the thing to do. Her arms dropped.

The record player had stopped. She looked around the dining room, the living room, the door to the kitchen. How still it was, and when Gus was gone, she would be in the house all alone in the quiet. That's why her mother had kept the television or radio on all day after her father died. So the house would not be so still. All day her poor mother had circled the house wringing her hands, wanting only to work, to work, tired of the television, tired of sitting, wanting only to work. It was going to happen to her too. It had already begun.

That's how it was; everyone had a turn. Her mother and father—born, married, struggled, raised children, knew health and sorrow, finished living, and died. Gus was nearly finished living himself, and she was behind him, walking into old age. That's how it was; everyone had a turn, her parents giving way to her and Gus, and they giving way to their sons, their sons already beginning to give way to their children, and then their children would give way to their children. That's how life was.

It had crept up on her. She could see it now. For the first time, last fall, Gus hadn't wanted to go to Wendover with the church's senior citizens to play the slot machines. He'd always headed for the crap tables after putting exactly ten dollars and no more in the slot machines, even if he was on a winning streak. The past Christmas he wouldn't go to his lodge party. He complained—everybody cooped up, those *bouzouki* players from the old country splitting his ears with their electric shit, and those college girls or whatever they were dancing that same old belly dancing that wasn't even Greek. No, he wouldn't go. She could go with her friends, but he wouldn't go anymore. Since when, she'd said, did women who had husbands go with their women friends? Then he said he didn't want to have the Easter dinner at their house. He couldn't stand the noise; if they went to one of their sons' houses, they could get up and go after they'd eaten. The noise was too much. And so what did she do? Cooked most of the food and had Jim pick it up and take it to his house for his first-time family Easter dinner.

He's failing, she whispered, *failing,* the word she'd avoided. And she might live on for years, alone in the silent house with her photographs and knicknacks. Suddenly she threw her shoulders back with a shiver, as if someone had run a cold knife blade down her bare back. She thought of Sam, stooped like Gus, wandering through his barren apartment. She shivered convulsively, then wanted to cry but couldn't. She walked over to the sofa and sat down, crossing her thick ankles primly. She wanted to think. Maybe she wasn't so bad, the live-in. She did look sad that one day she saw her at KMart. They knew who the other was. The live-in had looked away quickly. She was like women who dye their hair and put on too much makeup, women who don't have a real home. Maybe she wants a real home; maybe she tried to look young hoping someone like Sam will marry her.

Tula became aware of a pounding on the front door. As she walked toward it, she glanced out the window and saw Connie's new Cadillac. She had forgotten her. She opened the door. "I saw you through the window," Connie said, frowning. Her yellow-dyed hair, her white skin, and the bright lipsticked mouth with the wrinkles radiating about it looked almost, well, cheap to Tula. She decided she would no longer let Connie make her feel old-fashioned because she did not dye her hair or wear makeup.

"Did you ring the bell? I didn't hear it."

"Well, I could hear it all the way out here on the porch."

"Oh, I forgot to pour the water in the coffeemaker! It'll only take a minute. Sit down, Connie."

Connie followed Tula into the kitchen. "How's Gus?"

"The same, well, not too good."

Connie sat at the table. "Let's have our coffee here," she said, looking at Tula as if she would be contradicted. "Make things easy for yourself."

Tula hesitated. She had served her friends in the dining room or living room from the time Gus began to spend most of the day in the family room. She hadn't wanted voices to distract him from the television newscasts. Those were the only times he had become angry—when the news was interfered with.

Tula removed the plastic from the tray and set out the dishes, cups, and saucers on the table. "God, Tula, I can't believe you. Even in the kitchen you use tablecloths."

"It's a no-iron cloth," Tula said. She had practiced what she would say to Connie some day: "Connie, you're so critical. You make people feel like you're always looking to find something to criticize." She didn't say it. Connie had a bad mouth, but they'd been friends for so many years.

Tula poured the coffee. "Did you hear about Pete and Ann?" Connie said, dipping a *koulouraki* into her coffee cup. "Their daughter Hilary—what a name to give a girl!" (Tula wondered if she should remind Connie that Hilary had been named after her great-grandmother Hariklea, but she didn't care enough.) "Anyway, Hilary left that goofy guy she married three months ago, and Pete's hit the ceiling. He said he spent twenty-five thousand on her wedding. He's ready to kill her."

"That must be really hard on Ann."

"Oh, her," Connie, flapped her hand, "she's so dumb. And so is that Pete. They got just what they deserve, the way they raised their kids."

"No matter how you look at it, Connie, divorce is bad. I know."

Connie, whose three children had all been divorced at least once, shook her head at Pete and Ann's foibles, "How blind could they have been? Even a moron could see that marriage wouldn't last. But like my mother used to say this village proverb, 'The rolling cover finds the pan.' You know, people who are alike end up together."

Tula tried to think of something neutral to say that would not anger Connie. "The way things are nowadays it doesn't pay to spend a lot of money on weddings."

Connie looked out of the window darkly, "Yes, people spend so much money raising kids, educating them, giving them big weddings, then they hardly ever see them."

Tula was used to Connie's making general statements that were meant to mean other people's children, never hers. It was hard to be her friend: she hid whatever was bothering her, even acted as if she had a loving family, sometimes extolled one of the children or grandchildren when something bad leaked out. On television one day her oldest son was mentioned as being involved in a stock scam. Connie called her after the late-night newscast when Tula was already half-asleep. "It was all a misunderstanding. It had nothing to do with Mark. It was his partner. Mark had no idea what was happening. He's going to sue the station."

Keep talking, Connie, Tula had thought. You think people believe what you say. Tula never brought up the subject of whether Mark had sued the station or not. She had not seen him or his brother or sister in years. She knew that they all drove Cadillacs because Connie had told her so. "We're a Cadillac family," Connie had said. Tula could have said, "Except for Sam and his Chevrolet, my sons drive BMWs," but she didn't. She disapproved of how much money they spent: big houses, probably with big mortgages, those expensive BMWs, ski vacations, fancy clothes, children sent to big schools back east—as if schools in the city weren't good enough for them. She used to tell Gus, "It's not good. What if another Depression comes? We ought to talk to them when their wives aren't around." " 'Sit on your eggs,' " Gus said. "It's not your money."

She had to remember what Connie had said—oh yes: children who didn't give parents a thought after all they had done for them. "My kids are pretty good; they're considerate. They're good kids," she said. Then, afraid Connie might think she meant hers were good and Connie's weren't, she added, "Of course, they're all so busy with their work. They drop in." *Drop in*—that's exactly the right word for those quick visits. She was about to say other things, like their nagging her to get someone to live in the house with them, preferably someone with a car to buy the groceries. Instead she said, "Yesterday my CPA son brought Gus a box of figs."

"I know your CPA son's name," Connie snapped. "His name's Dan."

Tula looked at Connie questioningly; then she continued, "I didn't have the heart to tell him his dad couldn't eat anything with seeds anymore. He . . ."

Connie stood up. "You haven't finished your coffee," Tula said and knew instantly by the pursed look on Connie's face that something she had said had, as people said of Connie, "rubbed her the wrong way."

"I'm finished," Connie said and walked fast on her muscular, skinny legs to the front door and opened it. Tula, lumbering behind, wasn't even sure she had said goodbye. Tula lifted her arms and let them drop. She was too tired to figure out what she might have said, and she did not care. At least she had gone before Sam arrived. She went back to the kitchen, poured herself another cup of coffee, and drank it slowly.

Tula leaned forward. A sound came from the family room, a sound like a thump. With her heart fluttering, she pulled herself up and called in Greek, "I'm coming. I'm coming." For some time they had not spoken any English, only Greek. It seemed it took her longer than usual to get up because she was excited.

Gus had fallen; the walker was on its side. Tula tugged at him, as she had countless times before, but although he groaned, he could not move. She pulled the straight-back chair close to him and coaxed, "Get hold the rung," she kept saying.

She stood up, looking about, not knowing what to do. Then suddenly she walked to the telephone, picked up the receiver, and began to dial her son Dan. She hung up and picked up the receiver again and resolutely dialed Sam's number.

A female voice answered sullenly. "What is it?"

"Let me talk to Sam."

"Just a minute. I think he's asleep."

"Wake him up!"

Tula heard the voice say, "I think it's your mother."

"Mama? What's wrong?" His voice was strong, alert.

"I can't get your father off the floor."

"I'll be right over."

Tula was relieved he did not sound annoyed, and she went back to tugging at Gus until her arm tired and her swollen hands pulsed with pain. She sat on the useless chair and looked at Gus lying with one arm over his head as if he were protecting himself. A streak of pain ran from her right elbow to her fingers as she reached down to touch his head. "Oh," she said and unshed tears stung her eyes. She had done it again; it was that tendonitis the doctor told her came from all that tugging at Gus. The last time her elbow was in a sling for three weeks. To make it worse, it was her right hand. She was afraid: how could she take care of Gus? He was dead weight now.

The doorbell rang; she walked heavily to the front door and unlocked it. Sam stood there, black smudges under his eyes, his fleshy cheeks sagging (oh, oh, he's getting on, too), hair uncombed, a coat over his pajamas and robe. Wordlessly he went straight to the family room and straining, dragged his father down the hall and onto his bed. He put one arm around his father's shoulders and carefully eased him down.

Tula gasped. "Look at that big bruise on his cheek."

"Papa, Papa," Sam said, leaning over and speaking in a low voice as if to awaken him from sleep without alarming him. "Papa, Papa. Mama, wet some towels with cold water."

Tula sighed at being given orders. Sammy was in charge. She let the bathroom tap run until the water was as cold as it could get, wet a face towel, and wrung it out while pain burst through her elbow. When she returned to the bedroom, Gus's eyes were opened a little. "You fell, Papa," Sam said in Greek.

"Oh," Gus said, as if he had been told something unusual.

"We have to keep his head elevated, Mama. Give me the towel and you get two more pillows." Sam pressed the wet towel on his father's face. Tula brought the pillows, and Sam arranged them to keep his father almost in a sitting position. "You remember that's what the doctor said when Billy was little and had that concussion."

Tula pursed her lips: she remembered that concussion. It was suspicious to her. She had even said to Sam at the time, "I wouldn't be surprised if his mother didn't do it."

"I'll make some coffee, Sam."

"Good idea."

Tula went into her immaculate kitchen and prepared a perculator of coffee. She and Gus had been drinking decaffeinated coffee for several years, but as if it were a holiday of sorts, she took out a can of regular coffee. She thought of Sam gently putting his father down on the bed. Oh, Sam, you were a good boy. What happened to you?

She sniffed as she set out cups and saucers, opened a cupboard and supporting her elbow against her hip, used her free hand to take out a large white cannister. She knew it was her fault, too, and Gus's, the whole family's. He had been the first grandchild and a boy, petted, spoiled like Greeks do their oldest sons especially. Even when he brought home bad report cards, she scolded him, but never really forced him to do better. Maybe she shouldn't have paid so much attention to the house and the cooking and spent more time helping with his homework, like they said mothers should do in those home magazines—the odd way he wrote letters backwards. And they got him a car too early. She took out several braided cookies and sliced toasted sweet bread and placed them on a platter. We didn't do him no good, she decided, but that was no reason for him to end up running a beer joint and living in an apartment that looked like a motel room.

She looked through the kitchen doorway to the dim living room. She thought of herself standing there in deathly silence, Gus gone, his Greek song gone, she, alone, standing and gazing at her life's possessions, her photographs, her knickknacks. Again the image came of Sam, stooped like Gus, wandering through his barren apartment.

Sam came to the door. "Dad just wants coffee. I turned on the cable news for him."

"He doesn't care about the news anymore. Just turn on the tape recorder." The newscasters' voices brought a nausea to her; until a few weeks ago, Gus kept the news channel turned on all through the day, and the same news went on and on. "Here," she said, "take his coffee to him, and we'll have ours in here unless you think we should keep him company." Tula did not want to drink coffee and eat cookies in the bedroom; it smelled of urine even though she constantly used water and vinegar on the dribbles Gus left. She forced him to sit in the kitchen or the family room while she aired his room.

"He'll be okay," Sam said.

Tula put blue linen placemats on the table, set it, and waited self-consciously for Sam's return. She had thought for a moment to have them sit in the dining room, but then it would seem as if Sam was a guest, and that would be worse. She looked at the table, the battle-ground of countless arguments, recriminations, dire predictions. Sam came back and sat in the same chair he had squirmed on for years while his parents shouted at him until they saw the futility of it and let sarcasm take its place.

"*Koulourkia* and *paximadia*," Sam exclaimed, also self-conscious, and immediately dipped a braided cookie into his coffee.

"Oh, I forgot to light the *kandili*," Tula said, and with her hands on the table for support, got up and went to the icon alcove at the end of the hall. She removed the burnt taper, put it in a child's play dish, and poured olive oil into the glass of water. The oil rose in drops and formed a golden layer. She placed a small taper on a floating cork and lighted it, then made the sign of the cross three times and said the Lord's Prayer silently. She heard Sam behind her, and when she finished and turned, he was making the sign of the cross. She almost said, "Oh, you still know how to make the cross, do you?" but checked herself in time.

As soon as he sat down, Sam said in a quiet voice with a nod to-ward the door, a signal that they should speak softly, "This can't go on. You've got to put Dad in a nursing home."

"Never! Never! I won't go through what I did with my mother and father in Saint Joseph's. No, I won't."

"Well," Sam drew out the word while tapping his right palm on the table, "the time came when they had to go, and the time's come for Papa."

"Never. Never. I'll get visiting nurses. I'll get extra help." She clutched her elbow with her left hand.

Sam placed a hand over his face and pulled down his whiskered cheeks. "He won't let nurses give him baths, and a nursing home like Saint Joseph's has male nurses."

"I can't do that to him." Tula looked through the door to the dark-ened living and dining rooms.

"Sammy," Gus called in a thin voice.

Sam picked up his cup and saucer and walked into the bedroom with Tula following. "What's that ps-psi-ing going on in the kitchen? 'The ringing bell makes a noise.' I'm a man. I'm not a corpse yet. What plans do you think you're making for me?"

Sam looked into his cup and then above the bed at the framed needlepoint bouquet of flowers his mother had done when he was a child. "We're just talking about what we should do," he paused, still not looking at his father, "to help you."

"I'll tell you how you can help me!" Gus's red-rimmed eyes opened wide in anger. "You can put me in a nursing home like everyone else who comes to the point he can't take care of himself."

"No! No! What will people think? You've got a house! You're not homeless." Tula rubbed her paining elbow frantically.

"Don't listen to her," Gus said to Sam. "What the devil do I care what people think. I won't have my woman bringing me bedpans and giving me baths like I was a baby."

Tula was mumbling, "No, no, you can't go. You're not ready."

"I was ready months ago, but we fooled ourselves. We kept thinking I'd get better. *I'm too old. Understand?* Put it in your inner brain and stop fighting with fate."

Tula hurried into the kitchen and cried silently, sitting and facing the door to the living room. I can't, she kept saying to herself, I can't. Sam came in and put his hands on her shoulders. She reached up for them. "I don't like it either," he said, "but look at you. You're sick yourself. You'll go first at this rate."

"I can't, Sammy, I can't."

"That's what you said about *Papou* and *Yiayia*. You can not lift a dead weight like Papa."

She was pleased at his using the Greek words for grandparents, but she said, "*Papou* and *Yiayia* were much older when they went into Saint Joseph's."

"No, they weren't."

Tula put her hands on her face and sobbed. Sam carefully closed the door to the hall. He stroked her back. When she dried her eyes, he said, "I'll go back to my apartment, take a shower, and get dressed." She saw he wanted her to know he would look presentable. "I'll go down to Saint Joseph's and make the arrangements. If they can't take him right away, I'll be here every day to help you."

"I hoped I'd never see the inside of Saint Joseph's again. I hoped we'd die in our sleep."

Sam sat down and poured himself another cup of coffee. "Drink your coffee, Mama. It's probably lukewarm. I'll throw it out."

"No, I like it lukewarm," a lie, but she sipped to give Sam permission to enjoy his. Politely she asked about his three children and their children. She nodded as he enumerated what was happening in their lives, but at the moment she did not care about them. "How are you getting along, Sam?"

"Okay."

With great effort, Tula said the words: "How is she? You know."

"You mean the live-in?" His eyes were either amused or sarcastic, Tula didn't know which. "Her name's Donna. She's okay." They looked at each other while Tula nodded, not knowing what else to say.

When Sam left, she cried again, alone in the kitchen, a long steady crying while the Greek folk song on the tape recorder went on and on.

The Kamari
of the Village

From the time he was a baby, Zacharias was called the *kamari*, the pride, of the village. Under finely arched eyebrows, his large brown eyes shone with joy; thick, dark curls covered his head; and his well-formed body gave promise of his becoming a *leventis*, a handsome, brave man. When he was caught in mischief, like slashing the squash Widow Benaris had tended to get her through winter, no one, mother, priest, or schoolteacher, thought to beat him. Instead they shook their fingers at him. Smaller children followed him about. Zack chortled over their antics and sometimes watched them while their mothers hoed the rocky earth.

Even more, the villagers knew Zacharias would be a leader with brains. Still a boy, he had won every game of dice and cards from older schoolmates. Then he demanded that his godfather and his parents' cousins play *koltsina* with him. After he began winning regularly, they showed him off on the village square, bringing out a table and chairs because he was too young to enter the coffeehouse. The patriarchs nodded, watched each hand of cards carefully, and dragged travelers off their donkeys to see this phenomenon—little Zacharias beating grown men at cards.

When Zacharias was ten years old, in 1907, he badgered his mother to let him go to America with three older cousins. His mother put her palms against her kerchiefed head and would not listen, even though her daughters were without dowries and her husband was in prison. Zacharias's father had killed a man in a vendetta that had begun three generations previously when two families feuded over a sheep theft. On a winter night his father heard a noise outside his house and with Zacharias, an infant in his arms, opened the door and looked out. In the shadows a man darted. His father threw Zacharias onto a snowbank and shot and killed the man.

Zacharias begged his mother, pleading "I'll go to America and send back money for my sisters' dowries." His mother kept her palms pressed against her head.

One moonless night Zacharias crawled out the window and marched with his cousins, Lambros, Demetrios, and Elias, over the mountains and down to the seaport of Patras. Three weeks later they followed the directions to West Virginia sent them by a fellow villager. There Zacharias worked as his cousins' helper in a coal mine. They lived in a shack; streams of sewage and water for drinking ran parallel down the hill. Lambros, the oldest of the cousins, did the cooking on open fires outside. Lice spread through the shack, on their clothes, on their bodies. Elias and Demetrios washed the clothes in the stream and threw kerosene on the walls of the shack. They were ashamed they had no sisters to take care of them. Dry-eyed at night, Zacharias longed for his mother and sisters' pampering. He relived in his thoughts their saving sparse saints' days' delicacies for him, letting him roam the wild mountains while they hoed their rocky plot, sheared their few sheep, carded and dyed the wool with black walnuts, and wove it into clothing for him. He had eagerly put on the little jacket and pants whenever a saint's day was being celebrated on the village square. Now in the daytime he was frightened of the blackness, of not being able to get enough air into his lungs, of the creak of coal above, and after a few days he would not go down into the mine again.

The cousins took a freight train to Chicago, where they had heard labor agents spent their time in Halsted Street coffeehouses. They found an agent who sent them to a Grand Rapids furniture factory. Zacharias shrieked at the noise. Only the arguments among the immigrants that flared up inside the factory and were settled with fistfights after work made it bearable. He jumped and shouted as Serbs and Croats pummeled each other; when mainland and Cretan Greeks put up their bare fists; when Poles and almost any other immigrant group fought, staggered, rolled in the dust.

The men first took off their shirts to avoid tearing them. They faced each other, glaring, with their ready, powerful fists, thick veins wending over bulging muscles, sweat glistening on the hair of their massive chests. It began, the marathon, knuckle-slamming against flesh and bone. At every wince following a blow Zacharias and other immigrant boys shouted, their eyes shiny, avid. They screamed when one of the men lost his balance, laughed when the men danced a jig. And when one of the men, wiry with sinewy arms, pitted against a fighter of rock muscle, remained on his feet, persisted, endured, and stood victorious, Zacharias and the boys cheered and shouted until they were hoarse.

The four cousins were not, though, making enough money for their sisters' dowries. They returned to the Chicago labor agent, who gave them directions to an ally in Salt Lake City. After three days in a freight car, they arrived, found the labor agent, and for several months worked in a copper smelter west of the city. Catholic nuns there held night school in a company meeting hall for the immigrants. His cousins sent Zacharias to the nuns while they relaxed in a coffeehouse down the road. The nuns told Zacharias to call himself "Zack."

The smelter went on strike, but the cousins could not wait for a settlement: they had their sisters' dowries to consider. Again they returned to the labor agent, again paid him exorbitant fees, and took a freight to a McGill, Nevada, copper mine. It was an open pit, better than the coal mine, the factory, and the smelter. Zach did not like the work any better and annoyed his cousins with his frenzy over boxing matches. Regularly promoters brought young men from other mining camps to box each other. The matches were held in a smoke-filled hall, a wooden building where occasionally motion pictures were shown. A raised platform was put up in the center and a square roped off. The fighters wore shorts and boxing gloves like the men in the movie newsreels. Zack was not tall enough to look over the men around him and climbed to the window sills. Once he fell in his excitement but climbed back up to glory in the two fighters, hitting, hitting, with the men roaring at each deadly blow. He did not answer his mother's pleading letters. How could the village compare with this?

Between boxing matches, Zack, then about twelve, played cards with his cousins and their new friends and won more often than not. With a cigarette in his mouth, his right eye winking against the rising blue smoke, he expertly shuffled and dealt cards. His cousins pitted him against smirking, doubting gamblers who came into town during paydays, and Zack gazed at their American adornment, hand-tailored suits, silk shirts, diamond stickpins in their neckties, and flashing rings on their little fingers.

By the time he was fourteen he was tall enough to pass for a man. Each night he wet his head and tightly wound a towel about his hair to take the curl out. His hair then looked sleek like that of the movie idols he admired at the company hall movies. While his cousins sat around coffeehouses after work, he sidled into pool halls and watched Americans play cards. Looking over their shoulders, Zack learned all about poker.

Whenever a boxing match was slated, he hurried after work to the pool halls to hear talk of famous fights. Standing around the pool tables, drinking a soft drink, he longed to have watched the great Jeffries-Sharkey fight. Twenty-five rounds, an old man said, who had been there in Coney Island. "Broke two of Sharkey's ribs. Never seen anything like it." The men talked about the black Jack Johnson and the white hope Jess Willard. The fight would take place in Havana, Cuba. Zack wanted to go. His cousins told him he was crazy. They knew Cuba was far off, but they did not have a map to show him. Zack begged and shouted, and his cousins had no peace until Lambros, now called "Louis," went to the company store and bought a map. Zack saw he could never get to Cuba in time for the fight. The Americans in the pool hall celebrated when Willard won. One of them asked Zack if he were a foreigner but bought him a root beer anyway.

The next year, when he was fifteen years old, two slender, natty gamblers from his own northern Greek mountains arrived on a payday. They were twenty years old, and already each wore a diamond on his little finger. One of them boasted that he was the grandson of the bandit Karayoryis who, with several others of his clan, kidnapped three Englishmen traveling in their isolated mountains, held them for ransom, and when the money failed to come, killed them. The other was called "Fafoutis," a nickname used so often no one remembered the family name. Fafoutis talked fast, as had all the men in his family descended from a toothless grandfather whose rapid-fire words came out *faf-faf-faf*. The two belonged to a string of gamblers staked by the master gambler, Nick the Greek. "Come with us," they said. "We'll send a telegram, and he'll put you on." Zack left his cousins, smiling at Louis's demands that he stay and at his dire warnings of what America would do to him.

On the train going east to Salt Lake City, they talked about Skliris, the hated labor agent no one could best. Zack said he would be the one to do it; Karayoryis and Fafoutis bet him he couldn't. In the depot restroom Zack changed from his Sunday pants and white shirt to work clothes and walked the two blocks to Skliris's office. A young, squat Peloponnesian guarded the labor agent's door since the day he had escaped the bullet of an infuriated Cretan. Zack held his cap in his hands obsequiously and asked for work. "You can take the fee out of my first wages," he said. "I don't have any money." The Peloponnesian jumped up, went into the office, and returned with a note to an American straw boss in the Bingham copper mine twenty miles west of the city. "Can I buy a few things at the store? I need work gloves and a few things," Zack asked. The Peloponnesian wrote out a note. Zack went next door to Skliris's store, bought a pair of work gloves to allay the clerk's suspicions, a Stetson, a white silk shirt, a pair of Florsheim shoes, and a box of the most expensive Cuban cigars in the case. He almost ran to the Olympia Coffeehouse to show Karayoryis and Fafoutis the note and his purchases.

Laughing, Karayoryis said, "You better hide out for a few weeks, because when Skliris finds you didn't take the job, his soldiers will be looking for you." Zack took a train to Pueblo, Colorado, luckily just in time for the steel mill's payday.

In no time Zack owned plenty of the American finery he had coveted. With Karayoryis and Fafoutis he traveled from New Mexico and Arizona, through Colorado, Utah, Nevada, Wyoming, to Montana, and back. He knew every mine, mill, and smelter, and also every coffeehouse and pool hall on the way. In four mining towns the three of them formed partnerships with American sheriffs and became owners of brothels. Zack showed no remorse over the men he cheated. "They're free, white, and twenty-one," he laughed, an American expression he savored.

Zack could not believe his good fate. He smiled constantly, showing his small, even white teeth. Every day he read the sports pages of American newspapers to find where boxing matches were to be held. Sometimes Karayoryis and Fafoutis went with him, but more often he traveled alone. When he couldn't arrive in time for a fight, he broke something in the hotel room, a wash bowl, a pitcher, a chair. He was always able, though, to get to Salt Lake City and Reno, Nevada, to place his bets. In Salt Lake City he met a fighter named Jack Dempsey who had swept floors in Greek coffeehouses while learning to box. Zack always bet on him.

Zack saw Karayoryis and Fafoutis less often. When he did, they had raucous reunions, recounting their travels, talking about Greeks they had met, about escapades, one step ahead of the law. Fafoutis traveled with a prostitute called Omaha and after barely escaping prison under the Mann Act, married her to protect himself. Omaha was taller than Fafoutis. She had thick, light brown hair coiled on top of her head and stood up straight with a dignity that surprised Zack, considering how she made money for herself and Fafoutis. Karayoryis liked big cities and took his payday winnings regularly back to Chicago and New York.

In 1917 when Zack was about nineteen and America had entered the war against the Germans, he heard that the Butte, Montana, copper mines were working at full capacity and people were flocking there. He had been in America ten years. In his breast pocket he kept several Liberty bonds to prove to sheriffs and anyone else who accosted him for being a foreigner that he was not un-American. He drove a shiny dark blue Buick sedan; in the trunk were two new leather suitcases filled with the most expensive clothes sold at a Denver Hart, Shaffner and Marx store. He would remember for years what clothes he was wearing during certain incidents. Besides the car, he had bought the suitcases and their contents, the Florsheim shoes, the dark blue suit and the silk shirt, the diamond stickpin, and the sealskin fedora he was wearing with the three-thousand-dollar savings he had won from a Japanese laborer. The Japanese was on his way back to Japan after fifteen years working on Idaho railroad gangs.

Zack always looked after the Japanese and Chinese. There were fewer Chinese by the time he came to America because of the Yellow Peril hysteria, but there were many Japanese, fervid gamblers. To find them he sauntered past restaurants with "Whites Only" signs in their windows and walked into the seedier, rundown districts and into noodle houses. All he had to do was ruffle a pack of cards or shake dice nonchalantly and at least one, preferably only one—he did not want to contend with more of them after he had taken their money— followed him to his hotel. Preparatory to using loaded dice, he would place a magnet under the carpet of his room. Before the stunned loser came to his senses, Zack took his packed bags and was gone. The three thousand dollars had been his biggest take at one time, and with his usual precaution he wrote the name of the Pocatello, Idaho, hotel in a little black notebook to make certain he would never return to it.

When he told Karayoryis and Fafoutis about the three thousand he had won from the Japanese, he said, "He should have known better. He was free, white, and twenty-one." He then smiled sardonically. "Well, maybe not white."

Along the way to Butte, Zack had heard in coffeehouses that a second cousin was in Pocatello, a foreman on a railroad gang. He could not remember this cousin Markos because he had seen him only once, when he was not yet a year old. Markos, thirteen at the time, had walked over the Agrapha Mountains with his father, a self-taught lawyer, to represent Zack's father in court. The case was lost, and Zack's father was left to die in prison.

Throughout his ten years in the village, Zack had heard about Markos from people who had seen him walking over mountain paths to provincial towns in search of work. He was tall, they said, well-built, a handsome man. Zack was glad of that; all his people were good-looking. Then, just before Zack climbed through the window for America, a traveler had brought back news that people in Markos's village had looked down the crooked path to the valley floor, and when he crossed the river and they were certain he was really on his way to America, they danced wildly on the square in celebration: he had beaten up almost every man in the village. Zack was glad of that also; he had come from a clan with guts, *guts,* the American word he had picked up.

Zack was excited about seeing Markos—their fathers had been first cousins—and parked outside a coffeehouse to ask about him. It was a cold night, and the coffeehouse was filled with men between shifts at the railyards wearing heavy work pants and cotton shirts. Several men—like him with diamonds on their little fingers—were also in the coffeehouse. Zack gave them the two-fingered Greek salute, and the men—laborers and gamblers alike, several who knew him—jumped out of their lethargy and called out, "*Ti hambaria*, Zack?"—What do you know? He told them the latest news: two Greeks had nearly been lynched in Utah for having been seen with American girls; the editor of the Greek-language newspaper in Salt Lake City had been beaten badly after exposing a corrupt labor agent. He had more mundane news about picture brides, laughing as he described a former gambler who had been sent an ugly woman. The picture he had received did not look like the woman who stepped down from the train.

Zack asked about his cousin Markos. The men knew him. He was in town for the two months that it was too cold to work on the railroad gangs; snow was already brushing over the sagebrush plains. With several of his railroad gang he had rented the kitchen of a defunct restaurant, where they ate and slept. Zack followed the men's directions and walked down a dark alley to the back door of the restaurant. He was wearing a gray coat with a black seal collar over his suit and knew he would make a good impression. He pounded on the door several times while loud voices inside contended with the cold wind wailing past his ears. The door opened, and a tall man stood silhouetted against a dimly lighted room. "Who are you?" the man said. "Your cousin," Zack answered. The man stepped aside, and Zack walked into the dark kitchen that smelled of grease and food. A group of men were seated in a half-circle around a large open oven door. The men looked at him eagerly, blankets over their shoulders. On upright crates were spoons in tin plates with the residue of lentil soup. Zack glanced at the plates with a slight curl of his lips. One of the men stood up and brought a wooden folding chair for him.

Markos sat across from Zack, stared into his eyes, looked at his hands, asked how old he was, asked if he were a pimp and a gambler. Zack, afraid, said, "I'm a gambler." Markos, now called "Mark," gave him a clout on the ear. "You're not going to disgrace the name of our clan! You stay here with us, and when the weather warms, I'll put you on my labor gang." Zack said he would come in the morning and bring his clothes from the hotel. The next morning he got into his car and drove north toward the Butte Anaconda copper mines, looking over his shoulder from time to time.

He did not go as far as he expected. Autumn had given way too quickly to winter. Wind blew dust over the dirt roads, snow flurries forced him to keep one hand cranking the window wiper, and by late afternoon he had to stop in a small town for the night. After registering in the one hotel, a two-story, plastered-over adobe building, he ate in the cafe on the first floor. The waitress would not take her eyes off him, and he smiled encouragingly at her. He was used to women fawning over him. The cook, an old man with a drooping mustache, yanked the waitress into the kitchen and brought the check himself.

Zack lighted a cigar and walked up the town's single street. It was cold. Outside a weathered frame building, marked as a movie theater by a row of blinking light globes above the door, he stopped. Several wagons and two mud-splattered automobiles were parked on the dirt road in front of it. He bought a ticket, smiling at the young woman with red hair, her mouth open as she counted the change. She turned her head to watch him disappear. A clammy mustiness permeated the barren theater. Zack sat down on a wooden chair. In his wool suit and seal-collared coat he was warm. Farmers and their wives looked at him, the women incongruously wearing sunbonnets. Zack put his cigar under the seat. He was in Mormon territory, odd people to him who abstained from tobacco and liquor. The men and women surrounding him muttered to each other. When the newsreel came on showing American soldiers lying dead and wounded in the mud of France, he was suddenly pounced on, dragged by shouting men out of the movie house and down the street to a tree. "Hang the foreigner!" the men shouted, the women screamed, while he yelled, "Look in my pockets! I have Liberty Bonds in my pocket!" Slowly the hands loosened while men pushed and kicked him. "Git out of town and don't step foot here again, you dirty wop dago kike!"

Zack ran to his car, jumped in, and drove into the wind and snow. Although his heart was pounding, his only thought was that he was lucky he had taken only the overnight suitcase and not his bags into the hotel room. Twice he stopped on the way to Butte when great numbers of sheep blocked the road on their way down from the mountains to lower winter grounds. Sheepherders whistled orders to the dogs to keep the flock bunched together and moving. Zack got out of the car, smiling, watching the lambs trotting at the side of their big mothers, baaing, hurrying on their thin little legs to keep up.

Zack stayed in Butte until spring, living in one of the brothels in which he had an interest. All winter long men gambled away their savings, and he won a good portion. Then as he was ready to make the circuit of paydays southward, he lost everything he had to a drawling, innocuous-looking sheepman. The next day he put a silver watch chain in one pocket and a platinum chain in the other. He had devised a trick that came to his rescue when he was down on his luck. He walked into a jewelry store, took out the platinum chain, and asked how much he would get for it. The jeweler looked at it judiciously and said, "Twenty-five dollars." Zack shook his head, walked to the door, stopped as if thinking about it, and turned back. He said he would take the offer and took out the silver chain. No sooner had he left the store with his platinum chain intact, a twenty-dollar bill in his wallet, and five silver dollars in his pocket than the jeweler came running after him, screaming, "Come back! Thief! Come back!" Laughing, Zack hurried to his car and drove to Bozeman, where he had heard Mark was putting in a branch rail line for the Great Northern Railroad.

Zack's escapades were relayed from coffeehouse to coffeehouse, and Mark already knew of the latest one. After castigating him for blackening the clan's name, Mark took him out into the plains and immediately fired him when he found him drinking whiskey with the line boss in the foreman's shack. Zack drove on to Kansas City and for a year worked the Midwestern railroad gangs. One morning he found his car banged into a mass of dented metal. He did not know which one of the men who had played cards with him the previous night had done it, but knew it was time to leave, and in a hurry.

He boarded a Pullman with a ticket to McGill, Nevada. He had not written his cousins for almost a year and had the urge to see them, dour Louis, handsome Elias, and Demetrios, now called "Jim." While the plains of wheat and prairie moved with amazing speed past the window, he changed his plans. He would stop first in Pocatello to pay his respects to Mark as head of the clan. Karayoryis told him Mark was clearing sagebrush and planting wheat. When he reached the town he found there was no way to reach Mark's homestead except by walking the six miles' distance. He waited in a coffeehouse next door to a Greek grocery store, knowing Mark would eventually have to come into town for supplies. At first he enjoyed exchanging stories with the men, playing the dice game *barbout,* and watching a puppet show. The wandering puppeteer put up a bedsheet and behind it manipulated his puppets, the wily, hunchbacked Greek villager Karagiozis making a fool of pompous Turks. A few days in the coffeehouse and Zack sat slumpd in boredom. Then the *kafejiz* called out, "Your cousin's here." Zack hurried out to greet Mark as he stepped down from the buckboard. "Hiding out again," Mark said when he saw him. "Where's the fancy Buick?" Zack put his suitcases in the back of the buckboard. "This time," Mark said, "you're going to stay here and work like a man." Zack looked at the piercing eyes and was afraid. For the first time in his life his hands developed calluses.

On a November day Zack and Mark were driving the buckboard to town for supplies. Ducks were flying down to a pond, and Zack picked up the gun from the back of the wagon and shot a duck. Immediately the sheriff came out of his hiding place and arrested them for shooting ducks out of season. At the point of a rifle, he forced them into his wagon. "When we come to the curve," Zack said in Greek to Mark, "let's jump and hide in the bushes." "Stay where you are," Mark hissed, but at the curve Zack jumped, hid, could not be found. Mark was driven to the justice of the peace, lost his shotgun, and was fined ten dollars. A few days later a gambler came to the homestead and showed Mark a letter from Zack. He was to give the gambler Zack's suitcases to send on to Great Falls, Montana. "I'll beat him until the donkey looks like a priest to him!" Mark said.

In Great Falls Zack caught the worldwide influenza. He would not stay in bed, afraid he would die if he did. All day, shivering, bundled up, he walked the streets thinking of his mother, her folk cures, and especially the ritual of cupping. At intervals he sat in coffeehouses to gather strength. He ate fistfuls of garlic, drank bottles of whiskey, and lived.

For several years after the war Zack traveled, gambled, and took his take from the brothels, but the days of the gambler were waning. Laborers were marrying, becoming respectable businessmen, and the immigration restriction laws had cut down the Greek quota to a trickle. He saw too well that times had changed. Pool halls and coffeehouses were no longer crowded. He pondered what he should do. Louis still worked in the McGill copper mine; Elias had been killed by a runaway ore car; Jim had lost a leg and with three hundred dollars compensation from the company hobbled to a train and went back to Greece.

Zack learned that Mark had sold his farm and was living in the coal mining district of eastern Utah, where he had opened a grocery store. The Ku Klux Klan had rampaged through the town's main street and forced American girls working for Greeks in cafes and stores to go home. Zack wondered how Mark was faring. He had four little girls. Zack put a gun inside his belt and drove to the mining town. Each morning he followed the girls to school at a distance, and when the last bell rang he watched until they returned to their house.

Grudgingly, with warnings and obscenities, Mark gave Zack a job as a clerk. Zack's world collapsed. The work was hard; he had to mop floors, stack shelves, and wait on customers. Soon the entire counter was decorated with a row of charred vertical marks from cigarettes he left on the edge while he wrote orders and bagged groceries. Although the Ku Klux Klan burned crosses in the foothills and the railyards to frighten the immigrants, American women took their time at the shelves until he was free to wait on them.

In the evenings Zack showered, dressed, and walked down the steps of his hotel. On Saturdays he stood for a few minutes on the sidewalk, smiling, a cigarette in his brown-stained fingers. A vibrant noise hovered over the town: freight trains groaned as they moved out of the rail yards and whistled warningly at the edge of town; phonograph music swept out of pool halls and candy stores. On both sides of the street cars from the surrounding coal camps were parked. Miners and their families went in and out of stores holding packages they quickly locked in dusty cars speckled with coal dust. Their children looked about warily for mine managers out to catch them buying in town instead of at the company store.

He then crossed the single street to a candy store. He always sat on a stool at the counter and looked into the mirrored wall. Glass shelves in front of the mirror held clear, etched bowls of fruit and glasses of all kinds, tall for ice cream sodas, round and fluted for sundaes, and oblong for banana splits. Zack looked between the shelves into the mirror at this slender, incredibly handsome man who was himself. Women wearing the new short skirts came to sit next to him.

Several thousand Greeks lived in the county and had built a small Byzantine church. Zack never stepped into the church, not even on his name day. He often dropped by at the celebrations held in its basement, smoked, smiled, and watched the men twist and jump to the old traditional dances but never joined them. On Saturday nights he went to the Rainbow Gardens and danced with American women.

Zack was almost thirty years old when a town dentist, born in Greece but educated in the United States, came to see Mark. He said his cousin was coming to America because she was without a dowry and asked Mark about making a match with Zack, the last promising Greek bachelor in town. "I won't vouch for him," Mark said, and to Zack, "It's about time you married a respectable woman and settled down. Are you going to live in hotels all your life?"

Zack looked at the photograph of a pretty woman, but remembering the gambler who married an ugly picture bride, he said he would wait until he saw her in person. With his first look at her sitting demurely in Mark's living room, a woman with fair skin, light brown hair, blue eyes, and a nicely slender body, he turned to Mark and said, "Tell him yes." The next day the dentist came into the grocery store during the noon hour. "Before we go any further," he said, "I'd like to see your bank account." Zack took the cigarette out of his mouth, placed it carefully on the edge of the counter, and reached over to hit the dentist with his fist. His reach was short. The dentist walked quickly to the door with Zack's obscene epithets in his ears.

When Mark returned from lunch, Zack told him about the dentist's insult. "You donkey," Mark said. "You're offered a fine, educated woman and you look for insults. How many Greek women are there in America? You're lucky people will overlook your past! Or don't you have a dime in your pockets?"

"No one's going to insult me! I have my honor!"

"Eat your honor! We send you to shit, and you lose your ass."

It was the one and only time Mark tried to marry Zack off. The dentist stopped speaking to him and took his search for a marriage prospect beyond the county.

Of Mark's four daughters, Amelia, the next oldest, was intensely curious about Zack. She gazed with fascination at him and his friends dressed in suits from The Toggery, the creases in the pants pressed sharply, their hats looking newly bought. They had a joy, a carefree air about them as they stood smoking on the sidewalk, talking, laughing, diamonds glinting, so different from the hard-working, black-suited fathers like her own.

On their way to a movie serial one evening, Amelia and her sisters saw Zack talking to a grade-school teacher. He was smiling, showing the two rows of small, even teeth. No proper Greek-born man talked to women on the street. Amelia glared at him and would not speak to him for two months. She enjoyed, though, the nicknames he gave people. He called a Serbian who was regularly taken off to jail for assault "Jack Dempsey"; the fat, bald-headed school principal, "Hardy," after one member of the comedian duo Laurel and Hardy. Every Greek immigrant sitting in the coffeehouses had a special name. After school one day Amelia stopped in her father's store and heard Zack tell her father, "Horsethief came in to buy a gallon of olive oil." "Horsethief, hnn?" her father said. "What about you? 'The camel does not see its hump.' "

Zack used the Greek word for "horsethief," but the rest of the sentence was in English. The only time he spoke Greek was to damn someone with a proverb or christen someone with a nickname that referred back to bandits and heroes he remembered from his childhood. Amelia noticed that he never used English words mangled with Greekness: *carro* for *car*, *bootlekkers* for *bootleggers*, *tiketo* for *ticket*.

"Come here," Zack called to Amelia one day. She walked to the back of the store where he stood holding a mousetrap. A live mouse was caught in it. Its small black eyes were glinting beads, darting, frightened. Zack laughed, showing his small teeth, and tapped its head with a kitchen match.

Dazed, Amelia left the store.

The dentist married off his cousin to a man in Salt Lake City and Zack went to the hospital for a hernia operation. Except for the wartime flu, he had never been sick and never been in a hospital, but the nurses were friendly and solicitous. He closed his drowsy eyes, knowing he would be taken care of in the way of his mother and sisters.

Six weeks later he brought one of the nurses to Amelia's house in the middle of the morning. Amelia and her sisters jumped and clapped when Zack said they were on their way to Salt Lake City to marry. The woman was thin and flat-chested, her plucked eyebrows slanting downward in a pained expression, her straight legs hairy. She was wearing a black pin-striped suit. While Mark's wife was preparing the hospitality tray, the nurse talked about the suit in a voice so quiet, everyone sat still or a rustle would mask it. "I made it myself the last year I was in training. I didn't have a sewing machine, and I sewed it by hand." Her speckled hazel eyes lighted up. "By hand."

She asked to use the bathroom to wash her hands. While she was gone, the girls asked Zack if she were his nurse when he had his operation. Zack's peaked eyebrows went up, his eyes suddenly lively. "I didn't pay much attention to the nurses until this day the supervisor, she tells Florence she didn't do something she was supposed to, and

Florence said she did, and back and forth, back and forth, and"—
gleefully—"Florence, she threw a clock at her. She has guts."

When Florence returned and sat down carefully, the girls looked at
this quiet woman who had thrown a clock at a supervisor. Their
mother said nothing at all after Zack and Florence left for Salt Lake
City to be married in a Catholic priest's vestry. "He said he picked her
because she was a good woman," Amelia heard her father say to her
mother. "As if he would know what a good woman is."

On their return, they moved into a house near Amelia's. Only once
did Amelia stop there. It looked barren, although it had all the required
furniture: sofa, two armchairs, table, radio, buffet, stove, refrigerator,
and a movie-set bedroom—a dresser with two small, pink-shaded
lamps, the bed with a frilly pink lamp on the headboard and a long,
floppy-legged doll dressed in full pink satin skirt and lace pantaloons
on the bedspread. A record was spinning on the phonograph: "Just
Molly and me and baby makes three. We're happy in our blue heaven."
Florence sat in an armchair next to the portable phonograph, bony
hands clasped on her crossed knees, and stared. Her eyes were red. She
did not offer Amelia a cookie or a drink. Amelia was not surprised,
because, after all, Florence was an American.

On most afternoons Florence came to Amelia's house and spoke the
same words, "I tidied up the house and got cleaned up." Amelia and
her sisters dreaded seeing her. One day while her mother was getting
food ready for their Greek schoolteacher whose husband had just died,
Amelia looked out the kitchen window and saw Florence walking
across the lawn toward their house. Amelia's mother followed her
gaze. "*Ach, the varos,*" her mother whispered to herself—the burden.
Amelia was surprised that her mother, a grownup, also had such feelings about people.

Still, her mother always included Florence when she had guests. She
brought together widows, women who for some hidden reason had
never been asked to marry, the Greek schoolteacher with the rasping
voice and moles with stiff hairs growing out of them, and a recent arrival from Constantinople on whom the other guests fixed voracious
eyes—she wore bright lipstick, had cut her hair in a shingle bob, and
told slightly risque stories about Muslim holy men. Florence would sit
silently while the women spoke animatedly in Greek. Zack complained
to Amelia, who was then about ten years of age, "Florence, she feels
out of place. The women all talking Greek, and she don't know what

they're talking about." Amelia saw he had become different; although still dressed in well-pressed suits, that carefree, smiling air that had intrigued her was gone. Amelia told her mother it wasn't nice of the women to talk Greek all the time. She did not answer.

Sometimes, sitting on the porch with the sisters, Florence would become vivacious and laugh at everything while in the kitchen Amelia's mother made preserves and honey and nut pastries for guests. Her mother could even hurry out the backdoor on a special errand and be back before Florence got up to leave. When Amelia realized that her mother was not in the house and she would have to sit for a two- or three-hour visit with Florence, she thought, while Florence chirped on, what she would say to her mother when the house was quiet: "You think I don't know you go to women's houses, even that awful old woman Tikakis, to bring them things and do things for them and leave me here with Florence. I don't want to hear that people have to be helped. Just don't leave me with Florence again!" Amelia never said it. She knew her mother would lecture her on selfishness.

Florence laughed more when Amelia's mother was in the kitchen or elsewhere. She chuckled oddly at the names Zack gave people. "Zack calls him 'Mayor Fiorello LaGuardia'," she said of a short, big-stomached little man and slapped her thin thighs. "Zack don't care what he says," she said with that odd chuckle. Amelia wondered why Florence used the word *don't* for *doesn't*. In school they were drilled on proper grammar, and here was this woman who had gone beyond high school saying *don't* instead of *doesn't*. Amelia could not quite respect her because of it.

The girls asked Florence about her life and nursing school. Her father came from German people, her mother from Irish. They were Catholics and lived on a farm. Her mother had died while she was in nursing school in Denver, and "Mother Superior carried the telegram in her pocket for two days before she remembered to give it to me." Her father never talked. "When I came back and got work in the hospital, I had an appendicitis operation. He came to the hospital and sat next to my bed holding his hat between his knees and never said a thing. After about five minutes, he stood up and said, 'Well, I guess I better go back to the farm and water the horses.' "

One morning the girls' mother told them Florence had given birth to a baby girl. Amelia ran to the house. Zack was standing in the kitchen holding the dark pink, wrinkled little baby and smiling, just as he had while tapping the mouse with the match head.

Every day, his handsome face flushed, Zack had something to tell Amelia about the baby. He told her he bought special soaps at the drug store, castille that was better for a baby's skin and tar to make her hair shine. He learned to use a camera and took pictures of Teresa that Florence pasted in one album after another. Florence spent all her time keeping her house immaculate and taking care of Teresa. J.C. Penney clothes and shoes were good enough for her, but not for Teresa. She bought Teresa's clothes at the Golden Rule Store.

One night Amelia's mother awakened her and told her to go to Zack's house and sleep on the sofa. If the baby cried, she was to rock her. Florence was not there. When Amelia awoke, Zack was gone and Florence was in a bathrobe; the baby was still sleeping. Florence sat next to Amelia, all meekness gone from her face.

"See this bruise?" Florence pulled up her sleeve and pointed to a faintly blue mark. "*He* did that. I had to run out of the house, and I stayed all night by the railroad tracks. I found a cardboard box and curled up inside it trying to keep warm."

Amelia was appalled that Florence would show her the bruise, tell her this degrading thing—running away, crouching inside a cardboard box! "When we went to Salt Lake to be married, he signed a paper saying he'd let the children be raised Catholic and then he changed his mind when Teresa was born. I went to the priest and had her baptized secretly, and he found out and hit me. He's a sad-ist. I'm writing my brother to come and beat him up."

Her brother came, a big hulking man with whiskey on his breath. After talking with Zack, he shook his head and went back to the farm. Florence continued to visit and attend the luncheons Amelia's mother gave. From time to time Amelia's mother would explain in English what the women were saying. "I don't know why they can't speak English," Florence sniffed to Amelia, who was playing with Teresa as if she were a doll, "when I'm sitting right there." Amelia was annoyed with the women and their high-pitched talk. Such bad manners, even if they couldn't speak English very well, and some not at all. She despised, though, the hurt look on Florence's face. Why didn't she stay home when the women came to visit? Why didn't she invite American women to her house? And Zack still complaining angrily through his child's teeth, "The Greek women, they don't pay any attention to Florence. They talk Greek like she wasn't there. Last time, Mrs. Marangas, she said something that hurt Florence's feelings."

"He don't even pet a little before he gets on top of me," Florence said, self-pity sliding down her slanting eyebrows. Amelia hated her for saying such things.

During the Depression both families moved to Salt Lake City, where Amelia's father began opening grocery stores. He had been frugal, careful, all his years in America. Amelia, then in high school, was relieved that Zack's house was two blocks away, far enough that neither he nor Florence would know when they had not been invited to luncheons and dinners.

Florence became so preoccupied with Teresa that she would have had little time for luncheons. Teresa at four years of age began taking tap-dancing lessons. At the time, a child actress, Shirley Temple, was a movie idol. She had blonde, corkscrew-curled hair and dimples. She sang and tap danced. Teresa had one dimple and straight bangs, a Dutch Cut. Florence told Amelia and her sisters, "Mrs. Christensen said she thinks Teresa is cuter than Shirley Temple." She talked about Hollywood constantly. "And after Mrs. House saw Teresa tap dance, she said to me, 'If Teresa was in Hollywood she'd be just as big a star as Shirley Temple.' " Her eyes became slits and her mouth rigid. "If I could take her to Hollywood, but he . . ." and her voice trailed off and she sat musing darkly.

Florence came out of the darkness. "Men don't care. They only think of themselves." Suddenly she would turn solemn, her eyes sad, suffering under the pained eyebrows. "We didn't even know my mother was sick. My father came out of the bedroom and said to us children, "Your mother's dead." Amelia thought: hadn't she said she was in nurses' training in Denver when her mother died? And the mother superior kept the telegram in her pocket for two days before remembering to give it to her?

Soon Florence was taking Teresa to talent shows and to the Knighthood of Youth radio show. Teresa and Marilynn, a little girl her age, became friends, but when the director of the Knighthood show gave Marilynn a larger part in a program, Florence took Zack's gun to the woman's apartment and threatened to kill her.

"And Zack kicked Teresa yesterday."

"That's hard to believe, Florence," Amelia said. She was in college by then and had decided she would not listen passively to Florence.

"Yes, he did."

Amelia wondered whom she should believe. Not this crazy woman, and yet Zack had tapped the frightened little mouse on the head with a match. She asked Zack. He looked at her steadily, sighed deeply, and turned away.

When Teresa entered junior high school, she did not want to tap dance or go on radio programs any more. Florence murmured, eyes looking at the floor, "I'd like to have some fun too. I'd like to go to a show, but they never take me anywhere." She attended the trial of a man accused of raping and killing a girl. "I went," she said, avoiding Amelia's eyes, "from the medical standpoint."

After Amelia married and had her own house, Florence telephoned almost daily. At each ring of the telephone, Amelia stared at it, tried to will it not to bring Florence's voice. "He thinks more of the store than he does me. It's those girls in the delicatessen. That dark one. She's the one. I saw him. I walked in one day, and he had his hand on her arm. He said I was seeing things, but I saw him!"

"He thinks more of his friends than he does me. They come into town, and he takes them to Aleck's Cafe to eat. And you know what kind of friends he had! That one who talks fast, married to that woman who used to be a prostitute, and that other one who's got a social disease.

"And that schoolteacher, she taught third grade. I saw her outside Auerbach's two days ago, and she said she just stopped in to say hello to Zack. Why would she go say hello to Zack? She knows he's a married man. She said it to make me jealous. Right after we got married, we were sitting in the Palace Candy having a sundae, and she walked past us and she said hello to Zack but not to me. I saw the look she gave him!

"And ever since I had that hysterectomy, he don't think I'm a woman. He don't come near me.

"All he cares about are the fights. He never talks to me. He sits by the radio and listens to the fights and if I say anything he gets mad."

Store clerks shuffled their feet like guilty children when Zack's temper burst on them. "Whorelicker! Call yourself a vegetable man! Can't you smell something's rotten under there! You want this job or you want to stand on Second South with a tin cup?"

College boys Amelia knew from church who worked in her father's grocery stores after school laughingly told her anecdotes. "Boy, you sure have to watch your step around here. I went to the back room and drank a cup of coffee, and no sooner I got to the door when the cup whizzes straight at me. I barely ducked in time. I didn't rinse out the cup, and Zack's particular about things like that.''

Zack had ordered the employees to stay after hours to rearrange the gondola displays. He told them they would work until eleven and then quit. Under a big round clock high up on the back wall, they pushed and pulled, with Zack's glinting eyes on them. Suddenly Zack realized the clock had stopped and they had worked beyond eleven o'clock. No one had wanted to tell him. He went to the back of the store, returned with a step ladder, climbed it, axe in hand, and demolished the clock.

In 1941, when war was declared against Germany, Florence found work as a nurse in a pharmaceutical factory but stayed only two weeks. "Teresa cut her foot and I had to stay home and take care of her." She tried to find work again, but the location, the supervisor, something was always wrong. She was in a car accident, and Zack went into great detail in describing the oncoming car, the change in the semiphore light, all to show Florence was not at fault. Amelia looked at him with furrowed impatience, he who knew better than anyone how neurotic Florence was.

Teresa was now included in Florence's litany of reproaches. Teresa would not listen to her; she was in trouble in school, exposed as a member of a secret sorority. "She runs around with a fast crowd. She begs and begs to go places until it hurts me to hear her voice and I give in."

Brightly, "Do you have technicolor dreams? I do. Last week I dreamed the Virgin came to the foot of my bed. She was wearing a long blue dress with accordion pleats, and she said to me she said, 'Don't let them get you down.' "

She had gone to a dentist to have a tooth pulled and seen a pretty Greek woman there. "She's trying to take Zack away from me. She meets him secretly, I know. I told Dr. Kimball about him and how hateful Teresa is to me, and he says they are the ones who make me sick."

"Yes, Florence, you've told every doctor in town about how awful Zack and Teresa are. You've been saying it for years. Maybe you should stop."

"Well, the doctor told me to drink a glass of beer every night before I go to bed to settle my nerves."

"That's good."

"And Teresa goes with those rich people. And they bring her home late at night and she's in the car naked with them."

Suddenly the calls to Amelia stopped. The doctor had recommended a psychiatric hospital in California for Florence. Zack drove her there and had barely returned when she called him all through the day to come and get her. They had taken her clothing. She was naked all the time. Zack said, "I feel sorry for her" and brought her back.

Teresa did not finish at the university. She got a job at an exclusive dress shop and was soon a buyer. "It's only Mr. Berkoff's goodness," Teresa said, "that he lets me keep my job." Florence called him daily to rant that he was sexually abusing Teresa. Teresa moved into her own apartment. "She told Zack to call before he went down there." Florence said.

Teresa married in New York. "Teresa didn't want us there, because Zack wouldn't know how to act," Florence said.

Teresa got an unlisted number: "Mama calls and yells day and night," she told Amelia.

Teresa and her husband moved, and only Zack had her address and unlisted telephone number. His anger now was constant; he hissed invectives between the small, even teeth, tobacco-stained. Several times he stopped to sit on Amelia's patio and pet her daughter's golden retriever. He looked into the dog's eyes, amused at his panting and lolling tongue, smiling the same way he had smiled at the little trapped mouse. He began going to church. "The walls'll fall down for sure," Amelia's father said.

Amelia's husband decided to take Zack with him on a business trip to the Northwest. "It'll take him out of his misery," he said, "and besides he tells great stories."

They stopped for the night in Weiser, Idaho. Zack said he wanted to see if Fafoutis was still alive. Zack remembered the street and the exact location of Fafoutis's bar. He was amazed. "It used to be a bar, a dump. He's made it a high-class nightclub." Inside loggers, sheepmen, lumbermen, railroaders, businessmen, and women of all ages were eating, drinking, and dancing. Omaha stood at the cash register, still stately, now gray-haired, and looking like a respected grandmother. Fafoutis and Zack fell on each other laughing, hitting shoulders, exclaiming, "You bastard!" "You sonofabitch!" Fafoutis led the way to a corner table and said, his eyes tearful, "Karayoryis is in a Portland hospital. That syphilis got into his brain, all his joints. Go see him," but Zack said nothing then nor when they reached Portland.

A year later Zack had a prostate operation. It was cancerous, and he returned later for the removal of a growth in his chest. Florence had not driven for decades, and Amelia drove Zack to the hospital for chemotherapy. For days afterwards he retched, shivered, and could hardly get out of bed. "Let's not torture him," the doctor said.

Zack never spoke the word *cancer.* "Oh," he said once, "if only I had heart trouble, I'd be careful." Amelia brought their groceries and almost every day took Zack and Florence for a ride. Her jaw hurt from clenching her teeth at having Florence in the car seated next to her. Florence would not stay home, even though she sighed: "I'm exhausted. I'm just exhausted."

"Florence," Amelia said, "it isn't necessary for you to wash Zack's sheets and pajamas every day."

"It isn't only that. His friends come, and he expects me to wait on them."

"Why not serve a little Metaxa? No one expects you to serve coffee and cake."

Zack rasped, "That's what she gives them. Metaxa."

"It all adds up." Florence looked at Amelia with her thin lips pushed out. "It makes more work for me."

Twice they came upon a funeral procession, and on a later ride Amelia took an unfamiliar rural road and passed a graveyard. They were silent. Zack grew thinner. At the slightest bump in the road, Amelia saw that his face in the rearview mirror grimaced with pain. "Maybe we shouldn't go on any more rides, Zack."

"No. Pretty soon I won't be able to go out. I want to see everything I can."

"Besides," Florence said petulantly, "*I* want to get out. *I* don't like being cooped up all the time."

"When you complained," Zack coughed for several seconds, "I went to the hospital. Then you came and stayed all day and kept after me to come home. I told you I'd come home if you didn't make trouble for me. One day home and you started."

Amelia looked into the rearview mirror. Zack's face was gray, sagging, his eyes closed, his head leaning sideways. She thought: didn't he know that's how it would be?

"He don't pay any attention to me. I cut my finger yesterday, and he didn't even ask me how it was."

The skin on the back of Amelia's hands froze and a chill crept up her arms.

She arrived early one morning and found Florence giving Zack a morphine injection. "I'm giving Zack a little morphine to keep him quiet on the ride."

Amelia followed Florence into the sterile kitchen. "Florence, shouldn't you be giving the morphine only when the pain is really bad?"

"Well, if I don't, he won't want to go for a long ride. He'll want to come home after a little bit."

Amelia telephoned Teresa. "What can we do?"

"I don't know," she cried. "He says he can handle her."

One morning Zack was sitting on the sofa. His face was now skeletal, his eyes in black shadows, his shoulder bones showing through the wine-colored robe. His head was hanging to one side in infinite fatigue. Florence walked heavily into the room. Amelia stepped back. The hazel flicks in her eyes were sparkling insanely. Her jaw was strong, like a man's. "He don't let me get my sleep. I'm exhausted washing and cooking for him, and last night he came to my door and stood there waiting for me to give him his shot! I was so exhausted, and all he cared about was getting his shot! But the night before when I went into his bedroom and tried to get in bed with him, he told me to go away. Well, he just better start acting like a husband or I'll let his relatives take care of him!"

"Zack, did you get your shot this morning?"

"No, he didn't get his shot! I ran out! I'm going down to the drug store now! How can I give him a shot when I don't have any morphine in the house?" She left, slamming the door.

"Come on, Zack, you can't stay here. I'll take you to my house." Amelia gathered a few pajamas and the bottle of codeine tablets on the bedstand. They went down the steps, stopping after each one, his pale lips pulled back in horrible pain.

Amelia put him in her son's old room, gave him another codeine tablet, and called his doctor for a morphine prescription. She returned from the drugstore, boiled the hypodermic and needles, and gave him an injection.

He fell asleep. The telephone rang. It was Florence, screaming that

Amelia had stolen her husband. Later in the day Zack's attorney called: Florence had come to his office and wanted him to charge Amelia with kidnapping. He drawled laconically, "I got the picture and told her to go home and I'd get to the bottom of it."

Amelia telephoned Teresa several times until she answered. "I can't come. I'm not ready to face it. Oh, please don't make me."

"Your father's waiting for you. He can't go until you come. You get on the next plane."

"No. I can't."

Amelia called her many times in the next week while Zack dozed after the codeine and morphine. As the drugs began to take effect, he talked about his early years, chuckling about the Japanese he had cheated out of three thousand dollars by using a magnet under the carpet, spurting with anger at the dentist who asked to see his bank account before permitting Zack to marry his cousin. "I sent him to the devil, the sonofabitch!" Amelia often saw the plump, now silver-haired woman in church with her grandchildren. She wanted to be angry with Zack for cheating the Japanese, for his pique at the dentist that led to his marrying neurotic—no, psychotic—Florence. She gazed at him as he mumbled off and wished she cared more for him. It was this thing she got from her mother, the responsibility to help alleviate other people's miseries.

She put old *kleft* songs of Greek guerrillas fighting their Turkish masters on the record player. When she realized most of them had to do with death, she turned off the phonograph, but he asked for them. "I haven't heard Greek songs like this since I was a boy."

After a *mirologhi,* a lament for the dead, he said, "I'm afraid of the grave. I'm afraid of how cold it will be."

He asked for a rope, which he tied to the foot of the bed to pull himself up. He could not stand for long, and Amelia put a high stool in the shower stall for him to sit on. One morning after his shower, he shuffled into the kitchen, emaciated but smiling. "I don't have any pain. Maybe I'm licking it." His gray hair was wet and curly. He had given up wrapping a towel about his head to take out the curl. The brown stains on his fingers were fading.

Couldn't he die quickly? Amelia thought. He bit the inside of his cheek while he ate, a now frequent happening, and became very quiet. Within an hour, the pain became unbearable. After the shot had taken effect, he leaned back in the big chair by the record player. "If only someone would give me some pills so I can die," he said in Greek. It was strange to Amelia—Greek words coming from his mouth.

Each night she put a pitcher of ice water next to the codeine bottle, but he never took more than two tablets at a time. He was to call her when the pain began. He waited too long, and Amelia began setting the alarm for every three hours, then every two-and-a-half.

"When is she coming?" he asked after a horrendous night.

Amelia went into her bedroom and called Teresa. "Come now! Your father's waiting!"

"All right," she said quietly.

Amelia went into his room. "Teresa's coming."

He lifted his chest. "Now you can get me to a hospital."

Teresa came in a taxi directly from the airport. Amelia told her she had better stay with her because of her mother's behavior. "No, I can handle her."

Amelia shook her head at these delusions of Teresa and Zack. At two in the morning Teresa called from a neighbor's house. Florence had chased her from room to room with a butcher knife. When Amelia arrived at the neighbor's house, Teresa would not come home with her. She insisted Amelia go into her parents' house with her. Her heart fidgeting, Amelia entered at Teresa's side. Florence was docile. She said, "I took a glass of Ovaltine, and I feel better." She gave Amelia a friendly smile. "Yes, Teresa should come home to take care of her father. That's what I did. When my mother was dying, I left my nursing school and came home and took care of her."

He would go, the doctor said, any day. Florence disappeared. Teresa did not know where she was. Zack closed his eyes. Teresa talked in whispers without stop. "I used to tell her to visit her sisters in Colorado, and she and I went once, and they quarreled, and we came home. I told her to get friends, but she didn't know how to be friends. She said people talked about things she didn't know anything about and she felt inferior. And Daddy had no patience with her. When I was a little girl, he would shake his finger at her when he left for work and say, 'You touch her and I'll kill you.' How do you think that made me feel?"

Toward evening Florence came into the hospital room, smiling shyly. "I drove on the freeway, all the way to Ogden and back."

Teresa looked at her in awe and after a moment drew in a long breath. "That's good, Mama. You'll be more independent when Daddy's gone."

Teresa called. "They say he's going today." Amelia hurried to the nursing home. She, her mother, Florence, and Teresa sat about the bed. "He can have all the morphine he wants," Teresa said.

A breakfast tray was brought in. "I want to sit up and eat," Zack said, and Teresa and Amelia helped him up. Amelia wondered why a dying man cared about eating.

The young priest came. The women went out to the barren hall and returned after he left. Soon Amelia's father arrived. Zack motioned him to come closer to the bed. Zack opened his mouth, but words would not come out. Again his mouth opened. "I," he said and his Adam's apple in the withered neck moved up and down. Amelia followed her father into the hall. "He wanted to tell me something. Maybe that he used to steal from me. Every time he wanted a new suit or had too many doctor bills for Florence, the cash registers stopped working right."

Others came, Amelia's daughter and a brother-in-law. "Well, Zack, how are you?" her brother-in-law said.

Zack smiled. "I feel like getting dressed up and going dancing at the Coconut Grove."

Florence kept looking at the clock on the cabinet next to the bed. She said she was hungry and took out a paper sack and began eating. It was quiet in the room. Zack looked at the ceiling and out the window. The crunching of potato chips went on.

"What time is it?" Zack asked.

"Ten to three, Daddy."

He turned his head to face Amelia. "You know, more people die at four in the morning and four in the afternoon than any other time. That's what Florence says."

Teresa and Amelia looked at each other. Teresa faced the wall to cry. The clock ticked, ticked, Florence's eyes riveted on it.

"Amelia!" Zack shouted, his voice strong as it had once been, then in Greek, "Quick, the Our Father! Say it with me!"

Amelia clasped his hands and they raced through the Lord's Prayer in Greek. "Again! Again!" Twice more they hurried through it, Zack so rapidly Amelia could hardly catch her breath. Then with a bound he sat straight up, wild fear in his eyes, and throwing the bedcovers aside, jerked forward. He tried to get up, but Florence, Teresa, and Amelia held him down. He fought. "Let me up! Let me up!" For a few seconds he lay staring in horror. They let go. "Oh," he said and sat up clutching his chest. "Oh, how it hurts," and he closed his eyes, wincing. His eyes opened, startled. With a howl he lunged face downward to the foot of the bed. Great spurts of black-red blood shot from his mouth.

"Daddy!" Teresa screamed and fainted.

"Let's get her up," Florence said.

Amelia and Florence lifted Teresa onto a chair. Florence pushed Teresa's head between her knees. "Get a wet towel," she said. Amelia brought the towel, and Florence pulled Teresa up against the wall and wet her face.

Zack lay with his head sideways, his eyes half-closed, blood still flowing from his mouth and trickling from his nose. Teresa groaned, her head swaying. Amelia pulled the bedspread over Zack.

"I'm so ashamed of myself for fainting," Teresa said.

Florence pointed to the clock with a potato chip. "Look at the clock. It's ten after four. I told you."

For the funeral the church was filled with many friends from the mining towns and people who had suffered abuse while working for Zack. As the priest intoned final prayers over the open grave, Amelia thought of inviting the pallbearers to the traditional fish dinner, but looking at Florence, she was afraid to. She had baked a large salmon and arranged it with salads and vegetables on the dining room table in Zack's house. "Mama's afraid," Teresa said, "you won't have anything to do with her after I'm gone."

"We'll do what we can."

"She says she's going to start driving again and get a job." Teresa's eyes were bright.

"Teresa, your mother will never drive and never hold a job."

Several of Zack's old friends had come to the house uninvited, and as Florence sat there, eating hurriedly, Amelia saw the impatient thinning of her mouth: she wanted them to finish and leave. Amelia wondered at herself, angry that she had not invited his friends to the ritual dinner that completed the Orthodox funeral rites, angry that she had let Florence dictate the end of Zack.

After everyone had gone, Teresa showed Amelia a letter she had found in Zack's strongbox. He had written it to her on the night of her birth. The penmanship was beautiful. Amelia thought wonderingly: how had a ten-year-old boy with a few months' American schooling learned to write such fine, rounded letters? Amelia read the letter: "I am writing this letter to you, my little girl, on this, the best day of my life. You are in my heart. I will always do everything for you. I know you will grow up to be a fine, beautiful woman. . . ."

After Teresa returned to New York, Florence got a job in the Holy Cross Hospital, but she stayed only a few days. "Why, Florence?" Amelia asked. She looked down sadly. "I just can't seem to get along with people." The next day she demolished Zack's Buick backing out of the garage.

Amelia and her mother went to her house for an obligatory visit. They knocked on the back screened door. "Oh," Florence said looking at the stove clock, "it's eleven thirty-five. I was just going to make myself a sandwich. Well, come in for a few minutes."

In the allotted few minutes she told them she was putting her house up for sale and going to California where a niece lived. "I called her before Zack died, and she said I could stay with her until I got settled. I haven't seen her since she was two. She said she'd send Zack a get-well card and she did."

Florence stood up. "A letter came from Greece. I'll get it." She returned with the letter that had already been opened. Amelia and her mother read it. It was from a daughter of Zack's cousin Jim, one of the three with whom he had came to America and who had lost a leg in a mine accident. She wrote: It has been some time since you sent us any money. Couldn't you . . . ?

On their way home, Amelia's mother said in a hushed voice, "I never thought he ever sent any money back to his people. If I had known, I would have thought better of him."

Amelia thought of the dentist's cousin and then, angrily, that Florence was still alive while Zack was dead. She said nothing aloud; it was too tiring.

Two days later Florence called to say she had sold her house for twelve thousand dollars. "But Florence, your house is worth much more than that."

"I know, but that's all the money they had."

Amelia telephoned Zack's attorney. "I told her the same thing," he said, "but she's looney. Zack should have committed her a long time ago."

She wandered then from California to Denver, where she had gone through nurse's training, to New York, where Teresa lived, and back to Denver. Amelia never had a card or telephone call from her. One morning Teresa's husband called. Teresa was dead; an artery had burst in her brain. He brought Florence to New York for the funeral. "It's too bad Teresa died," she said as if speaking about an acquaintance.

A few years later, a woman Amelia had known in childhood was visiting from California and told her she had read in the newspapers that Florence had been beaten to death. With the twelve thousand dollars from the sale of her house, she had bought a fur coat and jewels. "This man thought she had a lot of money and he got friendly with her. Then this one day he asked her for money, and when she said she didn't have any left, he beat her up just awful. She only lived a few days, I'm not sure how many."

On days when Amelia takes flowers to her parents' graves, she looks down on Zack's marker and makes the sign of the cross. Under his name are the words: Beloved husband and father 1897–1961. For the first few years after he died, she would gaze at the words and think of him in his young years, a man who owned four brothels and knew nothing about women. She would remember him smiling showing his small even teeth while tapping the little mouse on the head. One day she realized it was not cruelty, but that the mouse was cute, like the little lambs trotting at the side of their mothers, like Teresa, small and pink after birth. She knew she really did not know him.

Father Gregory
and the Stranger

Father Gregory sat comfortably against a padded swivel chair and surveyed his desk with a pleased look. He did not like clutter, and on his desk were only four items: a black pen attached to a greenish onyx square, which the Philoptochos, the women's church organization, had presented him on his tenth anniversary as pastor of the community; an enlarged 1950s snapshot of his overweight father, mother in a long, sleeveless dress holding her folded arms high up under her breasts, his sister Penny in a circular, sequined felt skirt, himself in jeans, patched on one knee, and dirty Keds; another photograph of himself, a seminary graduate with jet black beard and full head of hair, standing with the archbishop; and a leather loose-leaf appointment book his mother had given him when he was sent to his first parish twenty years past.

The leather appointment book at his right had no appointments for the morning. He turned a few pages. All were blank for the following week, when he would be in New Orleans for the clergy-laity meeting. He had picked up his airplane tickets that morning and several times had taken them out of his suit breast pocket to make certain the date and time were correct. He lifted the telephone. "Fro, tell Father Jim to go ahead and put the announcement about the clergy-laity meeting in the bulletin." He returned the telephone to the cradle, feeling just a little guilty that he and his sister Penny had connived to have their mother visit her in Boston before she learned about the clergy-laity meeting. The airplane tickets from his sister had arrived the day before.

Father Gregory had taken his mother to the national meetings several times, and there was always the bother of having to have breakfast with her, introducing her to older priests' wives while he attended the meetings, and not having the freedom to talk later with his old friends from the seminary, just to sit around and have drinks, because he was always thinking of her, in the lobby, perhaps alone, or in her room taking a nap, or waiting for him to take her to dinner. And it was obvious to him his mother had no idea she was interfering with his freedom.

The telephone rang, and taking in a long breath, he picked it up. "Yes?"

"Father," his mother said in her didactic voice—she had called him "Father" from the day he was ordained to set an example for others, "Mrs. Kandylis called, and you must have been abrupt with her yesterday when she telephoned you. She's such a good-hearted woman, you should have listened to her . . ."

Such a good-hearted woman, Father Gregory repeated silently with a sniff. "Well, what was I supposed to do? Go to school and fight with her grandson's counselor? When these old women call you, don't jump to their defense all the time. You don't know the other side."

"Now, Father, from the time you were a little boy you had no patience. I think you ought to call her and be nice to her. You don't want to have trouble with her. She could make *trouble* for you."

Mrs. Kandylis addressed him like that also: Now, Father. "Yes," he said sarcastically, "that good-hearted woman could make trouble for me."

After a second or two of silence, while Father Gregory thought of his mother taken aback—after all she had done for him—she said, "Father," now in a more conciliatory tone, "no, I know she wouldn't. It's just, you know, she's an old woman. You don't want to alienate people."

"I'll talk to you when I get home. I have another call waiting for me." He repeated the word *alienate*. Probably heard it from that social worker at the retreat. He hung up and looked at the telephone. For five whole days he would be away from urgent and not so urgent telephone calls. He would be away from the string of visitors with their complaints. He would be away from retired men who "just dropped by to pass the time of day." As if he had all the time in the world to sit and hear their cryptic or open remarks about the cantor's singing or the assistant priest Father Jim's not arriving at the hospital fast enough. How that got to him: families knowing a parent had been dying for weeks calling up when the patient slipped into a coma.

And he would be away from his mother. Those telephone calls, wheedling Fro to put her through to him directly. Oh, what was the use? He should be more patient with her. Penny was the one who had been patient with all of them, their father, mother, and especially with him. He wondered if Penny were going through that change of life older men complained about to him. Her voice no longer had that cheerfulness when she spoke on the telephone. The last two times he had visited her on his way to a meeting were—he could not find the right word. His eager anticipation of being with her and her husband, now as portly as Penny and his long-dead father, had disappeared. Penny used to meet him with happy excitement and waited on him as she had done when they were growing up.

On the visit before last when he brought out his laundry, Penny had said, a little testily, as she emptied the pockets of his pants, "I see Mom is still emptying your pockets for you." On the last visit she had the coffee ready when he woke up, but she was somewhere else in the house. He had to pour it himself and eat an unheated sweet roll on a cold plate. Her husband had not even waited for him to get up and have breakfast with him. He had gone to work, which was, in a way, a relief to him. His brother-in-law had developed the unpleasant habit of telling stories about priests, bishops, and the archbishop. Father Gregory narrowed his eyes, thinking of his father, who'd had the same unpleasant habit. While he ate the tasteless roll, he heard Penny talking on the telephone about a woman's meeting and saying something about what men had done to women in this patriarchal Greek culture.

He had eaten the sweet roll absently. She had never rebelled when she and their mother waited on him, except to tease him, call him the Greek Prince, even when their father died and there was not enough money for both of them to continue college and she should have been the one to go. She had the straight A's. But she took it in her stride. Not now. It was all the fault of that woman and her book *American Aphrodite*. That Connie Someone who went around giving talks to get women to buy her book. If any woman in his parish tried to invite her to speak all that feminist nonsense, she'd just better talk to him first.

He looked ahead at the wall next to the closed door. He had mounted his treasure there, an old icon of the three Church Fathers, the two Gregories and Saint John Chrysostom. It was not a decoration, he told parishioners who asked about it; he always stood before it to make the sign of the cross when he entered and when he left his office. He sometimes prayed at the icon with grieving or distraught parishioners after they had unburdened themselves.

On the wall at the left of the door was a framed needlepoint Greek cross his mother had embroidered in a bronze color. Penny had designed it on graph paper and then transferred it to buckram. Where the arms of the cross bisected, she had drawn a circle of basil to represent Christ's head and his mother had carefully done it in petit point, a more delicate stitch, she had said.

Penny, named after their father's mother Penelope, whom they had seen only in a blurred photograph, was becoming remote to him as the years went by. She evidently had a large circle of friends, had always worked, and was not what he would call a regular churchgoer. If she lived closer, not two thousand miles away, they could have kept the old ties. She should at least be grateful that he had their mother living with him for twenty years.

There had been no question about it. His mother and everyone else assumed she would go with him from parish to parish and keep house for him. For twenty years he had returned home to a warm house with the good scent of cooked food, the table set, his clothes washed, ironed, drycleaned. Not like some of his seminary friends who lived alone. Penny didn't have to put up with their mother interfering with the grandchildren's upbringing, like that miserable Mrs. Kandylis did with her grandchildren. She didn't have to stand up to deliver sermons and hear their mother say afterwards, "You mumbled again. It was like you were bored to death."

He looked at the picture of himself with the archbishop. What hopes he had once had that he would someday be a bishop or—he blushed—the next archbishop! He had foregone marriage to make it possible. His closest friend in the seminary had recently been elevated, but Father Gregory knew it would never happen to him. He was too far away from New York; he was just another priest to the archbishop, not one of his inner circle. His face went hot as he thought of his mother telling him about the activities of bishops she read about in the *Greek Orthodox Observer*. As if he didn't read the *Observer*. She wouldn't even wait until he came home, but called him at the office. He had asked her not to, but he might as well have talked to the wall, as his father used to say when he hadn't done every little thing he had ordered immediately. He had an image of his mother with the open newspaper at the side of the telephone and circles around the bishops' names.

His mother. Now that she was older her cooking was losing its flavor. He had always looked forward to leaving his office, and especially after Sunday liturgies when his empty stomach yearned for food, to sit at the table and have her ladle out those Greek dishes which no other woman's could surpass, until recently. He often looked at the food lately and thought she must have forgotten an ingredient or two. Father Gregory was almost certain she was skimping on olive oil and butter. Also she had stopped making *dolmadhes* and *pastitsio*, those time-consuming dishes he had savored. At one time none of the Greek restaurants could match her, but lately he anticipated eating out.

A new restaurant had recently opened, and the cook was better than most. The owner, cook, and waiters treated him with deference, and he had to make it clear that he insisted on paying for his meals. That's what his life was like now—quietly enjoying the small pleasures. Like yesterday's sermon, which must have been a success: when he was passing out the *andithoro*, the consecrated bread, Soula Demas, the only woman in his congregation with a doctorate, smiled at him and said, "A good sermon, Father." His mother hadn't thought so; she complained the minute they walked to the car. "You talked way above their heads. Now, Father, you have to remember who you're talking to and come down to earth." He gave her an angry look, but knew he had been self-indulgent. While writing the sermon on early Greek mystics, he was thinking of impressing Soula Demas.

The small pleasures: a good dinner; a rewarding sermon; a nice visit with a parishioner who didn't want anything from him, but left him feeling better; and seeing his old classmates at the clergy-laity meetings, all satisfying pleasures. He thought of himself in a group of priests, their wallets open, showing him pictures of their children in caps and gowns. The pictures used to be of infants, then of children, and now young adults in caps and gowns. He lifted a palm as if rejecting a parishioner's complaint: no, he would not think about it. He had come to terms with life. People didn't always get what they wanted. What will be will be, as the song popular in the fifties said.

His good spirits returned. He was eager to visit with the priests he had known since his seminary days and those others whose paths and his had crossed. And to be away for five days! Yes, he was having a good day: the telephone had not rung, except for his mother's call, and he would be having lunch with Jim Kastoris, a good guy with an unlimited source of wonderful anecdotes about the immigrants who had come to America in the first decades of the century. A warm sense of well-being went through him.

The telephone rang. Annoyed, he lifted the receiver. "Yes, Fro."

"Someone to see you, Father."

"Tell him to come in," he said crisply and heavily set the telephone on its cradle. How many times, he thought as his lips thinned with exasperation, had he told Aphrodite to ask the person's name? What did the word *someone* tell him? It could be a woman, not a him.

The door opened, and a very tall man with light hair and amazingly innocent blue eyes came toward him, smiling. Father Gregory stood up and reached across the desk to shake his hand. He was thinking the man was a convert—he certainly did not look Greek—and gave him a firm handshake. "Sit down, please," he said.

"Paul Sarandos," the man said. He was between forty-five and fifty, about his own age, Father Gregory thought.

"I'm not familiar with your name."

"My parents are dead, and I've lived away for nearly twenty-eight years. I'm visiting here."

"Oh, I thought you weren't Greek at all."

"Oh, yes. My parents were both born right here, but their parents came from the same village in the Peloponnese."

Father Gregory nodded, no longer annoyed at having his quiet morning interrupted. He liked the man's face; it was interesting, even handsome, and the large blue eyes seemed familiar to him, although they certainly could not have been. He thought he might invite him to lunch at the new restaurant before he left for New Orleans.

"I used to sing in the choir," the stranger said and looked off with a faint smile on his full yet delicate lips. "I liked it all then."

"Is that right?" Father Gregory broke in. "You know when you walked in, I thought, 'Ah ha, a convert.' "

"Convert? That's a laugh. My mother was the Greekiest Greek mother alive. Talk about Jewish mothers!"

"I know what you mean," Father Gregory smiled sheepishly and added, "Paul."

"No, if I weren't Greek, I'd hardly be a convert. I'd probably be a Buddhist."

Father Gregory's smile slowly vanished. He looked into the wide-open blue eyes. "A Buddhist? Buddhism suits the mindset of the people of the East, but it's certainly not for people of the West."

"I wouldn't *actually* be a Buddhist. I used to do a lot of reading on religions. Years ago after I took a class in college on the religions of the world."

Father Gregory relaxed.

"Of course, Yoga is good," Paul continued. "It's been helpful to me. It's helped me relax when I've been confused and even thought of suicide."

Father Gregory leaned forward. "I hope you are over such thoughts."

"Yes, I've come to terms with myself."

Father Gregory frowned at the words *terms with myself*. "You could have achieved the same results with Christian prayers and contemplation. The early Christian mystics . . ."

The telephone rang. Father Gregory picked up the receiver. "Yes, Fro?"

"It's your mother, Father. I told her you had a visitor, but she insists it's important."

"All right. Yes, what is it?"

"Father, I forgot to tell you. No, I didn't forget to tell you, but I'm just making a stew, and I used up all the olive oil. You better stop and get a bottle before you come home or else we won't have any for the salad."

"Would that be a calamity?" Father Gregory said coldly.

"Now, Father, you'd be the first to complain if . . ."

"I'll take care of it." Father Gregory hung up, breathing rapidly. "These interruptions," he said shaking his head. He took a moment to recollect what they had been talking about. "Orthodoxy is the First Church," and after an almost imperceptible moment, he added again, "Paul."

"Well, I know, but what I'm here for is I want to know what my status in the church is because I'm gay."

A shot of fear ripped through Father Gregory's bowels, a fear that had once been familiar—a fear connected with wide, blue eyes. He forgot to breathe for a second. "What do you mean status?"

"I was reading in the *Greek American* that the church is anti-gay, which," Paul said seriously, his eyes still like a child's, "is pretty strange, seeing that so many of the clergy are gay."

Father Gregory's heart gave a nauseous twist. "How does anyone know that?"

"They know. Everybody knows," Paul said pleasantly.

"The church follows the Bible. Homosexuality is a sin, the Bible tells us."

"The Bible was written when no one knew what makes homosexuals. I didn't get up one morning and look in the mirror and say to myself, 'From today on, I'm going to be a homosexual.' "

"The church doesn't condemn homosexuals. It condemns the *act*. It expects *abstinence*."

"So heterosexuals can have the fulfillment of the sexual act, and we poor, stupid homosexuals have to deny ourselves the warmth of another human being?"

"The Bible and our tradition . . ."

"The Bible was written by men."

"But inspired by God."

"Then God should have done a better job. In the first place, why would He accept Abel's meat offering and reject Cain's vegetables?"

"Well, you have to look underneath the words to get to the real meaning."

"Are we supposed to be literary critics?"

"Oh, now, you're being"—Father Gregory was about to say silly, but he hesitated, and the stranger was talking again. Father Gregory's head was hot; he had a sensation that his brain was swelling and the stranger's words rushed at him and fleetingly vanished: *A just God! Abraham gets Hagar pregnant. Sends her and her son Ishmael to the desert. David sends Bathsheba's husband to get killed. Sack cloth and ashes. Okay, sons pay for his sins. Goofy Prophet Elisha, kids make fun of bald head, asks God to send bear to eat them.* He must get hold of himself, must listen to know how to answer. He must, must. He took a deep breath, looked at his cold palms, and rubbed one against the other.

The stranger Paul was going on as if they were having a congenial after-dinner conversation. "And in the New Testament Jesus lectures Martha because she complained that her sister Mary was sitting listening to Him while she was doing the cooking. Christ tells her what Mary's doing is more important. So what if Martha decided to sit and listen to Jesus? They'd end up starving."

This was going too far. Father Gregory stiffened, in control now, and lifted a restraining palm. He tried not to do this to parishioners because it reminded him of his father. But it was giving him time to think of a good answer. Then he remembered. "So much of the Bible is symbolism, you know." He looked down with a judicious purse of his lips and tapped his fingers on the edge of the desk.

"What's the symbolism in any of this?"

Father Gregory looked up and saw a calculating hardness in the stranger's eyes. Instantly it reverted to the kind innocence that seemed natural to the blue eyes. Confusion took away Father Gregory's ability to think.

"It seems to me the church takes what it wants and what it can't explain, it gives spurious answers. Take Revelation, for instance."

"Why?" Father Gregory's discomfort was beginning to turn into alarm.

"I've never heard Revelation referred to in the liturgy or sermons, and I asked one of my friends, a priest." (Father Gregory marvelled: this man had a friend who was a priest?) "Father Mathew told me it was because it was too extreme. It was the kind of thing fundamentalists latch on to. So it looks like the church can take what it wants and reject what it doesn't want. So why not reject all that homosexual proscription?"

"Then you don't believe in the Bible?"

"I believe the Bible is a literary history of the Hebrew people."

Literary History? Father Gregory wondered what in the world this meant. "Then I take it you're not a Christian?"

"Yes, I believe in Christ. I don't believe he was the son of God or in anything like the Virgin Birth. I believe he was the most nearly perfect man who ever lived."

Father Gregory lifted his shoulders, straightened his back, ready to rise, but he stayed in this position like a catatonic patient.

"I just don't approve of the church's views on abortion or on the ordination of women and certainly not their condemnation of homosexuals. It's all the work of men who lived and wrote in narrow, hermetically sealed sanctuaries."

Father Gregory reached out his palms and looked at them with surprise: they were trembling. Quickly he hid them under the desk and managed to say in a calm voice, "There's no question that abortion is murder. And as for the ordination of women, there were no women among the twelve apostles."

The stranger laughed mirthlessly, and a glint came into his eyes, but only for a moment. "I won't argue with you about abortion. Men again telling women what to do. And Christ had important women disciples, but, of course, they weren't apostles. How could women in those days travel around the country by themselves? They wouldn't last two minutes. That's the most evasive, specious explanation ever given for keeping women out of the priesthood."

Father Gregory fixed his stare on Paul, a triumphant stare. "How would you like to take communion from a woman?"

"Why not? Because they are biblically unclean? They cook our food, but their menstrual flow, their 'issue' makes them unclean?"

Father Gregory wanted the stranger out that minute. "Then I don't know what to say to you. You don't believe in the Bible or in the Orthodox tradition, so why do you care what the church thinks about your being gay?"

"Because we homosexuals have to let institutions know that we are here in numbers and that we count. That's why I want my baptismal record stricken out."

Father Gregory fell back, his mouth open. "That can never happen! Once a person is baptized, that's it! The oil of baptism penetrates indelibly into a baby's body, and nothing can remove it."

Paul smiled and looked far off. "Yes, I remember my grandmother, my *yiayia,* in her last years would get so angry at my grandfather, she'd say some kind of Greek expression about his tormenting her until he took the oil out of her. My mother had to explain it to me."

Then, a miracle happened: the telephone rang. "Yes, Fro."

"Father Jim called. He wants to see you before you go. He'll be down around eleven-thirty."

Father Gregory put down the receiver. "I'm sorry. I have an urgent call to go to the hospital. I'll look into your request, but I'm certain the baptismal records cannot be tampered with." He stood up, reached out, and shook Paul's hand lightly.

Paul jumped up. "I really didn't think it could be done, but I wanted you to know how I felt."

Father Gregory opened the right-hand drawer of his desk and took out a small folded cardboard icon of the Virgin and Child. He had a stack of them which he gave to visitors at the end of appointments. "Anyway, take this little icon and look at it from time to time."

"All right. Good luck to you, Father." Paul pulled his lips into a thin line, but his eyes were wide, no sign now of that hostility Father Gregory often saw in people seated across the desk from him.

At the door Paul turned, gave Father Gregory a long look, and closed the door behind him. Father Gregory sat down, quickly lifted up the telephone receiver, and whispered, "Fro, don't disturb me for any reason or for any person at all. For at least half an hour." He leaned back, slumped against the chair, and sat, stunned, looking at the hateful door, fury shaking inside him, then a yearning to be like the stranger—knowing, free. Then the shaking began again, then the yearning. Minutes passed and he was left numbed but still looking at the door the stranger had closed, shutting him in.

My Son,
the Monk

Chris Stavros sat in the shade of his brick toolshed, which was almost as big as the first house he had bought after his marriage over forty years ago. Slowly he turned his head to one side and looked at his tall, wide house in the same burnished brick as the toolshed. He thrust out his chin and gazed far ahead across a vista of lawn to a dark grove of trees.

He sat, knees drawn up, arms folded as he had in the 1920s behind the family washhouse made of old railroad ties. It had been his secret refuge, where the shouts and screams coming from the house were almost muted by the noise from the nearby railyards. His eyes on the house, painted blue, the color of the Greek flag, he would sit quietly, not to awaken his uncle or other boarder. They worked the graveyard shift in the railroad yards and slept on cots in the washhouse. He was not afraid of the boarder, but he was terrified of his Uncle Pericles, a bachelor who was always angry: he still had two more sisters in the village to dower before he could look after himself. He would pronounce the English words bitingly: *Look out for myself.*

He picked on Chris, especially, with insults and slaps. A twist of the ears, a back-of-the hand slap, another, and another, always three: "Donkey! In Greece children respect their uncles!" Uncle Pericles had been a privy hog too. He'd take the New York Greek newspaper that reached their western town with stale news and stay in there while Chris or his brother or sisters milled about the dirt yard waiting for him to come out. That old devil knew they were out there. He was a chicken shit, and he died just like he deserved, a bachelor in a cheap hotel.

Chris snorted: he had stood up to Uncle Pericles and married Katherine anyway, and then the bastard had to find someone else to pick on, and practically from the time Andy could walk, he chose him. He didn't dare do it in front of Katherine. Chris thought of the first picture Andy had sent from Mount Sinai. Wearing monk's habit and circular cap, he stood in front of a chapel. Close by, in the shade of a wall, a dog slept. By then Andy's hair reached half-way to his shoulders, but it was those dark, deep-set eyes looking straight at him that bothered Chris. He looked at them and then at the dog, back and forth, then returned the snapshot to Katherine. He had sense enough not to show it to anyone. Uncle Pericles, ailing though he was, would hear of it, smirk, and repeat one of those Greek proverbs that applied to every Pete, Gus, and Nick, but not to him, oh, no.

How that bastard Uncle Pericles had khee-khee'd outright when Andy left for Saint Catherine's monastery. Laughing so hard his face went red, he repeated all the dirty monk stories he'd heard in his village. They were worse than his priest stories. Sure, Catholics thought it was an honor for a son to become a monk; Greeks thought a person was some kind of a fool to shut himself up in a monastery, but that son-of-a-bitch uncle—Chris could still hear his cackling laugh.

That's what he thought of when he looked down on him in his coffin: his awful cackle. There he lay, his bald head and face skeletal, his thin veined hands folded piously over his caved-in stomach. On his narrow chest lay an icon of Christ rising into the sky, holding a staff of some kind in one hand, his long hair and white burial cloth floating backwards. Chris crossed himself, pretended to kiss the icon, and went back to the front pew where his family sat.

There he watched the few old-timers and people of his own generation file past the coffin, and he thought of the time his mother sent him to the Greek stores on Second South to find his godfather. She had cooked lamb with celery in a lemon-egg sauce, his favorite dish. First he looked into the grimy window of the Acropolis Coffeehouse, standing on his toes because the basil plants in rusty cans lining the sill were tall and bushy. Next he crossed the street to the Olympia, where men off shift were reading Greek newspapers and drinking Turkish coffee. Two of the men were yelling at each other, and Chris watched, hoping they would start fighting, which they did when one of them went over to the dingy wall and tore down a poster of the Greek king. The coffeehouse owner ran about, the dish towel around his skinny hips falling to the floor, and pulled the men apart. With his palms up, patting the air, he said something that quieted the men. Immediately he went to the counter and cranked the portable phonograph sitting on it. One of those old folk songs, tinny and muffled with scratches, floated out to the street. Chris was disappointed. He walked past the Athens Bakery. Still no godfather. He went on to the Byron Coffeehouse on the other side of a dark alley, the kind he and his friends liked to run through banging sticks against assorted trash cans and boxes of smelly refuse. Safely a block away, they'd burst into uncontrollable laughter.

Glancing down the alley the day he had gone looking for his godfather, he saw Uncle Pericles climbing the outside wooden stairs to a second-story landing. Chris and his friend Dominic had sneaked down the alley once and hidden behind some trash cans hoping to get a look at the painted women in the building. They wore Japanese kimonos and sometimes, Dominic said, came out to the landing to smoke cigarettes. Uncle Pericles was wearing his brown suit that smelled of sweat, and his big stomach looked like it made it hard for him to get up the stairs. He stopped at the landing and took a deep breath, then turned his head and looked down the alley. His black eyes paralyzed Chris for a moment, then sent him streaking off.

He was in bed when Uncle Pericles came home, and he listened, his body stiff, to the sounds of his mother reheating stew for him. "Where's that Chris?" Uncle Pericles said, chomping. "In bed," his mother answered. "Why? Did he do something?" "He was wandering in town." "Oh, that. I sent him to look for his godfather." Hatred for Uncle Pericles kept him awake a long time, and he hated his mother, too, for having to fawn over him and wash his shirts and underwear on a washboard. Other women in Greek Town had washing machines by then, but his mother still used the scrubbing board.

Uncle Pericles got him a week or so later. When American school let out, Dominic Pazelli and Mitch Tezak said they were going to Pioneer Park to look for money. People picnicked there, and sometimes money slipped out of men's pockets. Chris hid his Greek schoolbook and tablet under dirty newspapers blown against a wire fence and went with them. They had to pass the new Greek church being built diagonally across from the park, and who should be watching the brick go up but Uncle Pericles with two other men? "Be quiet," he said to Dominic and Mitch as they slinked past.

"Where you goin'?" Uncle Pericles shouted in English. "What you doin' with that wop and bohunk!" Chris stared at his uncle uncertainly and ran back for his book and tablet. Tears hurt his eyes: Uncle Pericles was supposed to be working the night shift. He could not keep his mind on the lesson, thinking about Uncle Pericles, and the teacher, the one people called "Assless," hit his knuckles sharply with a thick ruler.

Uncle Pericles was late at the coffeehouse that night, but he must have gone directly to the grocery store to tattle because when his father came home, he picked up a piece of kindling wood and gave Chris a good beating. Later in bed, feeling his skin warm and hurting wherever the wood had struck he thought of Uncle Pericles using those American words *wop* and *bohunk;* he did it especially to make Dominic and Mitch feel lousy.

Uncle Pericles gradually lost his hair, his teeth, and his big stomach, until finally he didn't look like the portly, short-legged ogre of the past. Barely had Andy left for the monastery when Uncle Pericles began to lose weight, almost overnight. Still, Chris couldn't feel one bit of sadness for him there in his coffin. He didn't feel anything except boredom on the slow ride to the graveyard, the return to the church hall for the funeral dinner prepared by the Philoptochos ladies, and the sad, expected smiles as people interrupted their eating to exchange the traditional words "Life to you."

"If there's a hell, you're in it, you goddamn sonofabitch," he thought. His chest lifted and fell, again and again. He remembered his blood pressure and his heart and tried to be calm.

Thank God, his father had died while Andy was only a priest, or else he would have joined in Uncle Pericles's khee-kheeing. His family had thought it was funny, oh, he knew they did, with their hypocritical long faces of sympathy, and the minute his back was turned, they were smirking. And why had it happened to him? To have a son who could have been anything he wanted, could have done anything he wanted, who grew up in a nice, big house, didn't have to work like he did, didn't have a terrible Uncle Pericles looking at him cross-eyed— why did he go become a monk?

Chris unzipped his khaki windbreaker a few inches, tugged and pulled at the neckline of his undershirt. Two sons, a granddaughter, and a grandson, that's what he had to show for almost seventy years on earth, and he didn't know why he was always worried about them. He looked ahead at the grove of trees left unmolested since pioneer days. In a hollow behind his house gardeners were working around the swimming pool and tennis court. Their voices came to him faintly. He knew he should go down there to supervise them. Since his Japanese gardener had died, he had found no one who kept the grounds a showplace.

He thought of the quarrel the night before. He should be nicer to Katherine. It must be hard on her too, one son a brainless yuppie and the other one locked up in a monastery. With quick resolution he stood up, brushed his rumpled khaki pants, pulled the waistband over his big stomach, and walked toward the back patio of the house.

The coolness of spring was in the air, and the scent of lilacs reminded him of the thick bushes blooming around the vegetable garden of his childhood. He had helped his mother irrigate the garden from the time he was five or six. He'd stop sometimes, lean on the hoe, and smell the sweet spring scent of lilacs. It hid the dry smells coming from the fenced-in chickens and penned rabbits.

Now he glimpsed the tiered slopes that encircled the pool and tennis court. Violets, early iris, buttercups, and icelandic poppies covered them in a wash of orange, yellow, pink, and violet colors. Beyond, among dense pines, a waterfall cascaded over red sandstone boulders. He thought of walking down to the gardeners, but he had to go into the house and say or do something to get things back to normal.

Katherine was in the kitchen standing at the restaurant-size stove.

Chris sat down at the table without speaking. Katherine usually spoke first after a quarrel. She had cut her gray hair shorter, and it made her look, well, like she didn't give a damn how she looked. She was wearing a dark blue skirt and a plaid cotton shirt, the same kind of clothes she had worn for years while her parents were in a nursing home. With her purse and sweater or coat near the back door, she had been ready at the ring of the telephone to hurry out. Her parents were dead now, but she still dressed that way.

He sat waiting for Katherine to bring him a cup of coffee. She poured herself a cup and went to the glassed-in alcove and looked out. Agitation churned in his stomach. It was a bad sign: even when they quarreled, she usually brought him his coffee. He wished she would say something, anything, but as long as she wouldn't, he went back to fuming over his family's laughing at Andy, a monk.

It had been miserable enough when he left to become a priest. He'd gone crying to his family when Andy announced six years ago that he was leaving teaching to go into the Greek Orthodox seminary. His family had pretended to commiserate with him. They told him Andy would come home after being under the thumb of those priests. Don't worry, they said, and looked at each other with sly looks. Then he knew. As soon as he left his mother's house where they had gathered, he knew they were making jokes about Andy. Even his mother, who looked proud at having a grandson who would become a priest, must have laughingly told them to stop. He knew because that's how his family was. They had got it from their father and Uncle Pericles, who would come home from work and entertain them at the kitchen table with gossip. Their father would change his voice and take all parts of dialogue. "Old man Sarangos," he'd say and assume a rumbling voice. "That assless Petropoulos," he'd chuckle and raise his voice prissily. His brother Pete had turned out just like them.

As the oldest son in the family, Pete had given Andy advice about the priesthood; he always gave puffed-up advice. That old-country, big-brother shit: "You won't make a good priest. You got to have an elephant's hide, and you haven't got it." In other words, Andy, you poor nephew, you're a sissy. Pete didn't care about Andy; he didn't care about anyone except his own children.

When Andy told them he had decided to become a monk, Chris, like a fool, had gone straight to his mother in the nursing home. Why had he gone? Hoping for sympathy? And she had railed at him, paralyzed, her white hair feathering about, blaming him and Katherine. "You should have put a stop to his foolishness! A priest yes, but a monk? They never wash! What good are they? Your woman let him do what he wanted, so 'now that you've danced, you pay the musician'!"

Chris set his elbows on the table, made fists of his hands, and clamped them on either side of his face. What possessed Andy to want to become a monk? A priest was bad enough. But a priest at least did some good, marrying people, baptizing babies, going to hospitals, and giving communion. Monks probably didn't do anything like that. What good were they? The whole thing made him feel like he'd lost his confidence. He hadn't had feelings like that for years. He had them often when he was just getting started in business—walking into a bank for a loan, trying to put on a business-like show to cover his uneasiness, all the time knowing the man across the desk thought he was superior to him, the son of a Greek immigrant with a Greek face and a Greek name to go with it.

Just two days ago he had come out of the doctor's office and seen his dentist in the hall. They talked for a few minutes about baseball, and he kept looking away from the pug-nosed face. He'd glance at him and then look away, just as he had with loan officers years ago. He felt meek, and he hated it.

Why had this happened to him? He'd worked hard from the time he was a child in Greek Town. He'd cleaned his father's little grocery store, which smelled of rotten vegetables and salty feta cheese. Yes, while Pete sat at the rolltop desk making a big thing of doing what little bookkeeping there was. Their father would leave for the coffeehouse next door the minute they came in from Greek school. And he, Chris, had been all alone one day when the Board of Health man walked in and told him to do something about those hanging slabs of salted cod. And how about those times his father sent him to deliver bootleg whiskey to the American doctors and lawyers up town? Making him feel like a criminal, and the way the pints were wrapped in Greek newspapers and tied with string, anyone could see right away they were whiskey bottles.

Why was he always the one? They always sent him for the midwife. His mother got out of control when one of the children was sick and hysterical if it was Pete. And so off Chris was sent to find the midwife to come and take away the evil eye or do one of her folk cures. Once when the midwife was delivering a baby in the mill town fifteen miles away, his mother in a frenzy chopped off a rooster's head and let the blood drip over Pete's head, with Pete yelling bloody murder. Well, it scared the hell out of him, and the next day his fever came down.

Ahh, he'd worked himself to the bones for the whole family, and which of them remembered how it was in the Depression? Certainly not his sisters, who could wheedle money out of their mother. Terrible, the way the economy was going now. The country could be in for another depression. You can't listen to the administration's lies. Just look at the homeless. Awful. Awful. There mustn't ever be another depression like the thirties. People would come into the grocery store for five cents worth of potatoes to feed a whole family. Five cents worth of potatoes. You could stay in the store all day Saturday and not once lift the lids on the barrels of Greek cheese and olives. The quarts and gallons of olive oil that came from Lekas and Drivas in New York got dusty on the shelves. His father was always moaning, "My miserable fate. My miserable fate. Why didn't I buy pints instead?" Reluctantly he sold the gallons of olive oil to Greek restaurants on credit that was once good. "They'll never pay you! They'll cheat you!" his mother screeched. "Catastrophe! Catastrophe!" She named former friends who she said used Wesson oil in the food they served on name days. They couldn't fool her, she said.

And how cold the store had been; they wore sweaters and jackets, and when his father was at the coffeehouse, Chris wore his cap with the ear flaps. His father didn't want people to think they couldn't afford coal. His godfather, that good old man who died too soon, told them to take the delivery truck down to the mines and bring back a load of coal. It was going for one-tenth the price in the coal yards in town, but if a person went down there himself and shoveled it into a truck, he could get it for just a little more than the cost of the gasoline. So they went, he and Pete; he was fourteen and Pete fifteen. They set off, Pete driving over those dusty untended roads with gouged-out holes left over from winters past, waiting for the WPA to fix them. Pete acted important as he drove through the outskirts, through farmland, and into pioneer towns that looked like they were dying.

The adobe and frame farmhouses thinned out. Chris looked far ahead to the horizon, but there was no sign of life. They drove mile after mile on a narrow road through sagebrushed land. The sagebrush was stunted and sparse under the pale gray sky. Not a single car came toward them. They were alone. His heart raced, his palms sweated, but he did not know why. He looked at Pete, and he might as well have been alone. It didn't help his fear. He felt cut off, abandoned, unimportant, a nobody. He prayed silently for the sagebrush to end, for some sign of life—a moving car, a sheep, a steer, but the empty, deserted land lay ahead, miles of it disappearing into the gray sky.

He had to stifle a gasp of relief when they came to a winding canyon road that kept getting narrower and higher as they drove. When the river and railroad tracks looked as if they were a mile below the road, Pete stopped the car, his face sweaty, and told Chris he was tired and he should drive. The road went higher and higher. At intervals trucks passed, all sizes, half-ton, two ton, and some cars with the backs cut out and made over into trucks, all hauling coal to the north. Chris had to hug the mountainside when the trucks passed, and once he had to drive the right wheels high up or a passing truck would have plunged into the canyon below. He held the wheel tightly to keep from trembling, and he went cold to the bones because he knew he would be the one to drive back through the canyon at night, keep the truck from falling into the canyon, and worst of all, cross the black, empty desert. He was limp by the time they returned home. His mother gave little claps of her hands and told Pete he had done a good job.

Under his eyebrows Chris looked at Katherine. She was still holding the coffee cup and standing at the alcove. He lifted his head to see for himself the pond he'd had cleaned and the surrounding ivy clipped of dead leaves. The ivy was climbing up the circle of tree trunks. He had better look into that; he had read somewhere that ivy can choke trees. He waited, hoping Katherine would say how nice the pond looked now. If she would only talk first, they could get it over with. She said nothing. He slurped his coffee. Still nothing. He rustled the newspapers and even removed some of the pages and dropped them on the floor. Nothing.

Finally she turned, and his heart thumped. She said in a hard, determined voice, "I don't want you to go. I want to go alone."

He pretended to be angry. "I said I'd go. Why do you think I got my passport for?"

"Because you were afraid," and her voice had that scoffing tone he hated more than anger, "someone would rob or kill me."

"It happens. You read about things like that all the time."

"We've gone all through that. Now I'm going, and you can stay home and tend to your wonderful business and gossip with your brother."

"Get off my back about my brother! And don't be sarcastic about my business! Where do you think you got the money to go to that god-forsaken Holy Land?"

"Oh, I paid for that trip. Oh, my God, how I paid for it."

"Tell me, just tell me how you paid for it. I'd like to know."

"I've only been telling you for forty-five years. No. I'm going alone. You'll only be miserable, and you'll make Andy miserable."

"Well, you're not going alone!"

"I've gone all over Europe alone! How come you're suddenly worried about my going to Mount Sinai?"

"I told you. I don't trust those Ayrabs."

"Oh, stop it!"

"No, I won't stop it! And besides we should give Andy a chance to settle down."

"Settle down! He's been there almost a year. Down deep you don't want to face him."

"Why shouldn't I want to face him? He's my own son."

"Yes, your own son. And you've always been ashamed of him."

"Just because I didn't want to walk down Main Street with him in that black dress and that black hat!"

"You know what I'm talking about! I'm talking about the years you ignored him. All the years you made so much over Tom, with Andy standing right there. Those times, like the day I brought home some religious books he ordered from Zion's Book Store and you made those ugly remarks about church books and threw a glass of water on the window. You didn't go so far as to throw the water on him. You threw it on the window. Oh, I could remind you of so many other scenes, but what's the use?"

He did not want to look at the despair on her face and picked up the pages of newspaper from the floor and put them back in place.

"Everything about him bothered you. You couldn't stand the way he held his books against his chest! You were so afraid he was a homosexual; you brought home awful jokes Pete told you at your so-called meetings! You thought more of your nephews than you did of him! You'd praise them to his face! You were plain mean!"

"I wasn't mean! He was born scared. You can't do much with a boy who was born scared."

"Andy-Pandy," "Scaredy-Andy," Tom and his cousins called him when they were little, playing outside. Chris was sitting on the patio one day watching a baseball game on the portable television set, and they were at the far end of the grass. The jeering grew louder, frantic; he could hardly hear the announcer. He looked up. Andy's head was bent. He was about five or six at the time. "Cut it out, you kids," he shouted and went back to watching the game, annoyed with Andy for not showing some fight. Where, he thought, had that memory come from—he hadn't thought of it until that moment.

"You could have helped him get over being scared—as you call it—but you never did a thing for him. You never even went to church once to see him when he was an altar boy."

"Oh, I did too. You're always exaggerating about him."

"You wouldn't give him a second look because he was different."

"Well, how the hell did you expect me to talk to him? What the hell could I have said to him? Those goddamn church books he used to read!"

When Andy was in high school, he had gone into his room. That room—it gave Chris the creeps. Books all over, neatly stacked on shelves with small icons in front of them, and a large icon of Christ on a small table by itself. A dried palm twisted into the form of a small cross leaned against the icon of Christ, and a dried, faded carnation from the Resurrection services stood in a whiskey glass next to it. In front of the icon was a glass of water and a small burning taper floating on a layer of olive oil. Andy was facing the door yet didn't see him. His eyes had that hazy look that had worried Katherine for years, but which Chris had never seen. With alarm tightening his heart, he walked quietly over to Andy and looked down at the open book on the desk. His eyes stared at words heightened with a yellow marker. He read: "If God is definable, he would then be circumscribable, something impossible in Christian theology. To attain union with God, the initiate must first pass through a divine darkness before reaching the luminous light which is God."

Perplexed at the words *definable* and *circumscribable*, he left the room walking carefully. "The luminous light which is God," he said to himself and shook his head.

"Yeah," he said now to Katherine, "he's different all right. He was always different."

Katherine put the cup and saucer on the table. Her arms dropped. "He was such a nice little boy," she said looking over his head. "A golden boy, his skin, his hair, golden." She was not talking to him; she was talking to herself, and Chris felt left out, as if he were not important enough to be included in her thoughts.

Andy in monk's robe and cap, and several Bedouin porters in striped caftans stood just beyond the airplane steps looking up at the open door. Katherine and Chris were the first tourists to come down the steps, each carrying an overnight bag for the two-day visit. Following them was a group of eager Greek-Americans led by a Chicago priest. As Katherine and Chris reached the tarmac, a lanky Bedouin took their bags, nodded to Andy, and hurried off. Andy smiled and put his arms around Katherine. "Hi, Mom," he said, standing in the shimmering heat. The hem of his black cassock was dusty with gray-brown desert earth. Andy held out his hand to Chris, who looked at it and then with a jolt shook it. He was still stunned at the great desert and jagged red-brown granite mountains and boulders he had seen from the sky. What was he doing here? he asked himself, and wiped the sweat off his face.

Katherine walked at Andy's side to the dusty van. Chris behind them riveted his eye on them, barely glancing at the few stone huts and Bedouin families outside their tents. He had never noticed before the gray in Andy's hair, now coiled in a knot at the base of his neck. His face was thinner, making his well-shaped nose more prominent. The skimpy beard could not hide his sunken cheeks. There was something different, though, in Andy's face, and he tried to think what it was.

The Chicago parishioners were interrupting the priest with questions in raised, demanding voices. "One at a time," he said, "one at a time," with the weariness of an exasperated guide who regretted undertaking his mission. Chris had made the mistake of being heartily friendly with the group in Jerusalem. It had helped take his mind off Andy and the monastery. One woman's parents had come from the same village as his mother and father. Impulsively he had invited the entire group to telephone him if they ever came through on their way to San Francisco or Los Angeles.

"Next year we're having our Arcadian lodge convention there," a new acquaintance crowed. Chris was sick of them.

Minutes later the van came to a stop in a cloud of dust. Other vans, campers, and four-wheel-drive vehicles were parked at the foot of the walled monastery. Tourists with cameras were taking pictures of it, the mountains, stone granaries, small retreat houses, and the desert. Several had mounted cameras on tripods. One of the tourists, his muscular, hairy legs straddling the rocky earth, was trying to photograph three black birds flying toward the airport.

Chris kept turning his head to look back at the inert, dead desert. It was endless, a wide expanse of rock and dirt, rippling sand, where nothing grew except on nearby boulders that sprouted bleached grasses. A Bedouin was cutting the grasses for fuel. Down below the mountain of boulders, the man's family sat under a tent, more a tarp suspended on four poles. In the far distance were more great barren mountains. Chris couldn't believe it, that Moses and his people had wandered there for forty years, but then Katherine said that in the Bible, God sent down quail and manna, like bread or something.

They continued over flagstones and up steps. Inside the monastery were the big church, smaller white chapels dedicated to the events of the Exodus—Chris had read in a brochure on the plane—and dark green cypress trees. Monks of all ages nodded greetings. A group of Bedouins was working with mortar to repair loosened blocks of granite. Tourists were chattering and exclaiming over the garden of cypresses, palm, and fruit trees, flowers, vegetable plants, and grape vines. A dog stalked a cat. Katherine was speaking, Andy pointing; Chris heard their voices, but he did not listen: he was overwhelmed by the great dead desert at their backs.

Andy led them to a room in the visitors' hostel, plain—a desk, a chair, two cots, an icon of Saint Catherine on one wall, and a dangling light globe. The walls were painted blue. "Greek blue," Chris said without mirth. The baggage was already on the floor. Chris looked at it, kept looking as if the bags would show some life. "I got to rest, Andy. Just let me rest for a while."

"Sure, Dad."

"I'll unpack later, Chris," Katherine said.

Yes, Chris thought, she doesn't want to waste one minute of this two-day visit. He knew he was being petulant. He took off his shoes and jacket and lay on the bed, but the barrenness of the room would not let him rest. He got up once and looked out the window and saw it, the great dead desert. Hurriedly he went back to the bed, which seemed harder the longer he lay on it. He closed his eyes in preparation for sleep, but immediately they opened. Turning on his side so that he could watch the door, he waited for Katherine to appear.

The room began to darken; he felt impelled to go to the window again. Darkness had seized the desert. Chris thought something unseen but terrible was ready to rise from it. He stepped back and saw a reflection in the glass pane, a bald man with a big stomach. With a spasm in his chest he thought he was looking at Uncle Pericles, but then, shocked, saw the reflection was himself. He glanced about the room, a booming in his ears. Back in bed nausea filled his insides: of all people, Uncle Pericles! To think he thought he was looking at Uncle Pericles! Mistaking himself for Uncle Pericles, that chicken shit! Minutes passed while the pounding in his chest and the nausea mingled and sharpened into a deep revulsion for himself. He didn't understand why. Slowly it subsided, leaving him weak; he thought every muscle in his body had gone flabby. He kept his eyes on the door, and then Katherine came in.

She washed her face and hands, put fresh makeup on while Chris wondered why she was so calm, as if this visit were an everyday occurrence, the two of them in a bare room with the great menacing desert beyond.

Now that Katherine was there, he closed his eyes for a few minutes' sleep. Almost immediately a monk walked outside the door hitting a wooden slab with a clacking sound, the call to dinner. Chris got up: even if he had the time, he knew he could not sleep anyway.

Andy came for them, and they followed him down to the long refectory. The pilgrim-tourists were talking in several languages; the American-born priest was telling his parishioners, mainly gray-haired women, that there was an old refectory dating back to the Crusades. Andy introduced them to another American, Father Nektarios, from a town near Pittsburgh. Father Nektarios was short, in his early forties, with a small dark face and coal-black beard. After an elderly monk gave the blessing, Father Nektarios jovially told them he had made a circuit of Orthodox churches in America giving a slide show on the monastery. He didn't look very ascetic to Chris, with his talk about the "States," laughing and chewing with gusto.

Chris looked at the Friday fare on his plate, chick-peas cooked with tomatoes and a large serving of chewy grains. The bread, though, was the kind his mother used to bake. When he was small, the women in Greek Town had outside earth ovens, the kind still seen on the Navajo reservation. They had lighted twigs inside it and placed a metal sheet against the opening. When the twigs burned to ash, they swept them out, eased round loaves from a paddle into the oven, and closed the door. He could smell the same scent of baking bread in the refectory, and he ate two thick slices of it.

Father Nektarios's cassock was stained with oil spots. No wonder, Chris thought, eating and talking at the same time, just like me, as Katherine would say. Andy was looking at his fellow monk tolerantly; he had hardly spoken during dinner. When the *sematron* sounded, a mallet hitting a paddle, summoning the faithful, Andy said he would be going to church. "I'll come too," Katherine said.

"Not me." Chris shook his head, then wondered if he would not be better off in church. "I've got to go back to rest," he added, but frowned, wondering if he could.

Katherine stood for a moment as if thinking, then said, "I'd better rest too, Andy."

"I'll show you the library tomorrow."

When Katherine turned out the light and the room was suddenly black, Chris longed to have her next to him rather than on the other cot that seemed farther away than it was. He knew she was too tired to talk and would be asleep in a few minutes. He thought of the blackness of the desert infringing on the walled monastery, of the great boulders, of the cold. He had to talk. "It's so bare. That desert. There's nothing there. It gives me the creeps."

"You've seen deserts all over the West."

"But nothing like this one. At least there you could see some sagebrush and in some places junipers, but here, there's nothing."

"Andy told me a Church father had said this desert made a person look inward and enrich his soul."

"It's terrible. It's so awful." Suddenly Chris broke into sobs, heavy, deep, his shoulders shaking. "Oh, God," he cried out breathlessly at intervals, but could not stop the sobbing. Katherine came to his cot, leaned over him, and put her arm under his shoulders. He turned to her and cried on, his head pressed hard against her. "It's all right," she kept saying until his body relaxed and he slumped on the pillow. She carefully removed her arm. "I'm cold," he said weakly. She found a blanket on the closet shelf and covered him, then went back to bed.

The frigid cold of the desert night came through the walls and window. "My feet are freezing," Chris said, his knees drawn up. Katherine rubbed them and wrapped them with a sweater. The cold deepened. She pushed the cots together, took the covers off her bed, and placed them on top of Chris's. She lay down, her body against his back. It was not enough. She got up, her breath making shivering sounds, and placed their coats on top the covers. Slowly Chris began to feel the warmth of their bodies and thought of their early years of such warmth, the touch of hands, the pat on cheeks that had gone without his knowing he had missed them. He slept.

The next morning Katherine asked, her voice lowered, as if she could be heard by strangers, "How do you feel now?"

Chris did not look at her, but the tone of her voice, which he had not heard for years, warmed him. He thought: in the end she's all I have. "I don't know what got into me last night. I should have brought some of those tranquilizers Doctor Lindquist gave me, you know, that time I was having all that trouble over that Murphy lawsuit."

"It's better this way."

"I don't know. It was the desert and Andy and—everything."

After breakfast Chris followed her and Andy over the rock-paved alleys, under arches. Andy pointed out symbols of the cross carved into the granite walls of chapels where Moses saw the burning bush, where he liberated Jethro's daughters from the shepherds at the well, where John of the Ladder wrote and studied. From a hermitage, Andy said, where Saint Catherine had been brought after her torture and death on the wheel, the monastery had grown over the centuries, third, fourth, fifth and on with small chapels, the old monastic cells replaced, a large bronze cross of the sixth century marking the passage of the Exodus. Chris listened to his voice, something in the tone of it, the weakness he had hated—gone.

Andy spoke, Katherine questioned him, and Chris wondered at her: didn't it concern her, that terrible desert, the isolated monastery set among boulders? Ashamed, he saw that she was stronger than he.

In the center of the compound was a mosque used by Bedouins during Ramadan and other services. Next to it was the three-aisled church.

They lighted candles and crossed themselves. Katherine placed an envelope with her offering before a large icon of Saint Catherine rising skyward. Through folding doors, carved with animal and flower motifs and the crests of Crusader knights above, they entered the nave. Centuries of precious gifts from far off dazzled them: exquisite gold and silver vigil lamps, a massive gold chandelier, gold icon screen made in Crete in the sixteenth century. On the wall above was a great mosaic of the Transfiguration, Christ standing in the divine Taborian light; there were icons many centuries old, faded, primitive ones, several of Saint Catherine, one of her holding her severed head in one hand, another with her left hand resting on the wheel of torture, and one of the saint, blonde, fifteenth-century Spanish, unearthly sweet. Chris looked at each icon intently. He had never given icons a thought: he had never been inside the suburban church Katherine attended. He had heard her on the telephone soon after the church had opened twenty years ago telling someone she liked the icons better than those in the old church. "They're more in the Byzantine tradition," she had said, whatever that was.

Katherine followed Andy from one great icon to the other. Chris lagged behind, then went to the stalls against a side wall, used by the old to support themselves on wooden armrests. He stood in one, put his arms on the rests, and closed his eyes. He awoke with a start and followed Katherine and Andy to the arcade galleries that housed the library and monks' quarters. The library gallery was crowded with icons of all sizes. The library itself was large and airy. Under glass were the ancient illuminated manuscripts embellished with colored motifs: Mohammed's document exhorting respect and honor for the monks of Sinai; a parchment manuscript, many inches thick, with Bible scenes; the original manuscript of Saint John Chrysostom's liturgy. Chris began to look at everything intently. Andy was saying that 3,200 manuscripts had been catalogued. Another 1,100 had been found later, and he was one of the monks at work cataloguing them. "That's where I work, inside there." He pointed to the locked gate and gazed at it.

They continued going from one illuminated manuscript under glass to the other. Chris lingered at a manuscript opened at a page of Saint Luke sitting in white robes on a bench, writing in a book with his sandaled feet resting on a raised block. Next to the saint stood a small desk; on it a sculpted gray fish held up an open book, and around it were the accoutrements of the scribe: curved knife, inkwell, and two speckled stones. A flush of heat brought sweat to Chris's face. Andy had had an identical icon in his room at home. Chris had gone into the room to tell him something one day, saw the icon on his desk, and said, "Why the hell don't you go out and get some fresh air? Sitting here with that icon staring you in the face." He had forgotten that incident until he saw the icon of Saint Luke.

Outside the library Katherine said she would like to walk about. Chris stopped at the chapel of the Burning Bush. "I'll wait for you here," he said.

"We'll walk up the path to Mount Moses," Andy said. "Not all the way. There are 3,700 steps to the top, but you'll be able to see the entire desert."

Chris shivered. Andy smiled at his mother as they walked on. His voice carried back to Chris. "We'll pass the charnel house. That's where hundreds of skulls and bones of the monks are stored." A light laugh. "I don't think Dad would appreciate *that*."

Chris bristled: who would, goddamn it? He watched them ascend the path to chapels and deserted hermit caves. Sitting on a ledge, somewhat shaded by a cypress, he gazed jealously at their freedom and closeness with each other. He felt abandoned. Slowly the heat took hold of him. He thought of the cool room in the hostel, but he remained on the low ledge, squinting at the monks, Bedouins, and noisy tourists who passed by. "Come with us," the Chicago priest beckoned. He was wearing jeans, sneakers, and a white T shirt. They don't pay them enough, Chris thought while waving the priest on; then, that was some way for a Greek priest to be dressed, like a teenager.

The heat became nearly unbearable, yet he would not return to the hostel. With great relief he saw Katherine and Andy approach. He stood up, feeling rescued and happy that Andy would leave him and Katherine to return alone to the cool room. Again his face flamed. Him, jealous of his own son! No, of course not! He looked at Andy intently and realized why he looked different. It was dignity. Andy had dignity now.

"You should have seen the caves the monks lived in, Chris, to be alone and think and pray."

Andy smiled ruefully. "I sometimes wish I could escape to them."

When it was time for vespers, Chris went with them. He was afraid of the bare, closed-in room when he was alone in it. In the incense-blue nave, he looked about with fresh eyes, listened to the chanting of the monks, and was mesmerized by the big brawny abbot in magnificent red brocade with embroidered bronze symbols and flowers made more than a century ago in Russia.

It was dark when they went back to their room. Chris had intended to take two dramamine tablets. He had heard someone say at his club that when he couldn't sleep, he took two dramamine. They were just as good for getting to sleep as they were for car sickness. He was concerned about getting the bed ready with covers and coats that he was in it with the light out before he realized he had not taken the dramamine. While trying to push himself to get up and take the pills so he would not be wide awake thinking of the dead black desert outside, he fell asleep.

The First Meeting
of the Group

Mary Soutas was a short woman of about five feet and had to have the car seat raised to its maximum height when she drove. Even so, she leaned forward and lifted her head to see the traffic ahead of her. She was in her early seventies but had little gray in her short hairstyle with long-out-of-style bangs that dated back to the fifties. There was a grim set to her round, finely wrinkled face as she drove toward the church. She had just had a telephone conversation with her daughter Diane that left her, as usual, feeling she was somehow passé, that she was out of step with the 1990s, that, in short, she didn't *understand*. Well, poor Gus was right when he kept telling her she was too much influenced by her: Diane's passing judgment on her clothes, on the books she read, on her friends, on her politics, on her ideas. She could hardly say what was on her mind around her. Like last week when she said to Diane that she didn't think homosexuals should be allowed to adopt children because they weren't good role models. That withering look and snappy, "Oh, you *would* think that."

Diane even found fault with the name of the Philoptochos which Mary had been president of for five terms, longer than anyone else, and which she secretly hoped she could go on for ten, a record. "Why do they spell it with a *ch*?" Diane had asked in that churlish tone of hers. "Why not just Philoptohos? People who don't know would pronounce it with a *ch* sound, like in chocolate."

For all she had done for Diane, helping her raise her children, staying at her house overnight when they had fevers and she was worn out—of course, she, her mother, was not worn out, oh no; she was made of iron, and what did it matter to Diane that she had to run to her own parents at all hours to make up for neglecting them? The few times Diane stopped in to see her grandparents, all she did was find fault. Like the time Mary's dentist had an emergency, or so he said, and she was two hours late getting to her parents' house. She had barely stepped through her front door when the telephone rang and Diane angrily said she had stopped in and *Papou* and *Yiayia* were so hungry they were trying to fry some lamb chops and made such a mess. So she, the princess, fried them, and—wouldn't you know?—left the kitchen for her to clean up when she finally got there. "Tell her to mind her own goddamn business," Gus said when she hung up.

Diane had just taken it for granted that Mary had no life of her own, that she wasn't doing anything, so she might just as well watch the children while she went to her club and met her husband for dinner and a movie. How many times she had changed her own plans, once a wedding she had really wanted to attend. "You do too much for Diane," Gus would tell her, but she kept on going until Diane's boys were teenagers and not only could stay alone, but very obviously didn't want her there. Not even a Mother's Day card from them.

Diane didn't think anything of her being the Philoptochos president for five years. She had never once come to the annual membership teas. Out of consideration for her mother, couldn't she pay dues and come once in a while? To show her mug, as the old immigrants used to say. How did it look to the women that her own daughter never came to the meetings? She had to put up with snide remarks from her cousin Effie: "Isn't the Philoptochos good enough for the little Greek princess?"

There were younger women Diane's age in Philoptochos, and some were not even married to Greeks. Yet they would come and take part in serving Thanksgiving dinners to the homeless and stand up all day at the festivals, the big fund-raiser of the year. "That kind of thing is just not for me," Diane said. "What do you do anyway, but slave for months baking for the festival? There's so much pain and misery in the world, and you women are concerned about whether you've made enough baklava and *kourambiedhes*." Mary showed her a list of the poor they had helped, and now under her presidency they were going beyond their own church community and contributing to the Red Cross and the United Way. "Let her alone," Gus said. "She just don't want to join."

She even confided in Gus, something she rarely did, that she wished Diane wouldn't come to the festivals at all. She'd come with her rich neighbors just to eat, an insult, which Effie made pointed remarks about. "You can at least help serve," Mary told Diane once, but she had shrugged her shoulders. This latest was too much. She had hoped she had finally shown Diane that the Philoptochos was a viable—the new, young priest used that word—organization. She had talked with Bessie Kasimakis, who had just retired from the county social service department about having the women get together to talk informally about their worries and problems. Well, it was Bessie, really, who had approached her with the idea. "We'll have to be careful how we handle it," Bessie said. "You know how our people are. They wouldn't admit they had problems, and never in a group. It's always someone else who has problems. We'll start out with general subjects. Whatever we do, we must not let them think these are therapy sessions. And we'll have to think of a good name for the meetings."

Mary was not sure women would come. "Even if just a few came, Mary, it would be a good start. I can tell you, we have dysfunctional Greek families, people with various addictions, women who are enablers, people with personality disorders. They cause so much pain in their relationships. And look at the Sunday School children. Some of them have emotional problems. They live under terrible emotional confusion."

Mary agreed, but hoped Bessie would not use words like *dysfunctional* and *enablers* the women would not understand. She knew what they meant; she had read an article in *Time* about it. The more she thought about it, the more excited she became. Now Diane couldn't say the Philoptochos wasn't aware of anything outside the kitchen and wasn't doing anything important. But when she told Diane about it, she got only a bored, "Oh, well that's nice. Maybe the men should go, too. You ought to take Dad." Diane could be so infuriating. That morning she had tried once more, called her, even went so low as to ask her to come as a favor to her. It would be a good start for women to see her there. Other young women would feel more like coming. "I haven't time, Mom. Besides I don't have any problems and I wouldn't share them there even if I had."

"Just come this once."

"No, I just can't," Diane whined, in the same way she had from childhood. Mary had always given in then, always looked at everything from Diane's point of view. "She gets away with murder," Gus often told her. Mary said, "Everyone has some concerns." She hoped Diane got what she was subtly saying: Diane's marriage wasn't that great. Diane cut her off shortly: "You're absolutely right." For some reason Mary felt a streak of pain in her chest. "Anyway, I've got an appointment."

Mary breathed in and out in shallow breaths. She hated this breathing. Whenever she had an argument with either Diane or Gus and even her mother when she was alive, it always ended with her breath coming fast, almost like panting.

Now she was driving through the old immigrant district. There stood the church, its old brick darkened by smoke from the railyards, but there with dignity, solidity. The sun shone on the bronze domes. Mary pulled back her shoulders. The church gave her reassurance when she was having problems, as when Gus was bullheaded, or when feuds developed in Philoptochos. Just to attend liturgies had helped her so much in her parents' long last years of illness. That was another thing: Diane only went to church during Holy Week, and not even all of Holy Week, usually just on Good Friday. Her boys would certainly not stay with the Church, and when Mary thought about how she used to take her grandchildren to Sunday School while their mother and father slept in—well! Gus had called her once, right in front of the grandsons, a horse's ass for doing it. That's what she got for marrying a man after a couple of dates when he was on his best behavior. So afraid she would be an old maid. "Who would you have found better?" her mother had said when she complained. "What's all this foolishness? And about something that isn't worth talking about." Then she had added one of those old village proverbs that could sting: "Manure on cabbages." Girls today were different.

Mary drove into the parking lot and was disappointed to see only a few cars there: the assistant priest's gray Honda; the secretary's Buick, which made Mary wonder each time she saw it how she could afford it; Bessie's Oldsmobile; her cousin Effie's black, shiny Lincoln Continental; and the Papastavros sisters' gray Ford. Then she became alarmed; she had always been the first one there. She could not understand why she was late. She hated Greek time. She always told her committee members to come a few minutes before meetings were to start: "Greek time was all right for our parents' generation, but we were born in America." Something was wrong with her thinking! Oh, she mustn't end up acting like her mother.

She hurried into the side door of the recreation hall. The women were seated in a circle around a coffee table in front of the stage. Even in her confusion she thought there should be something they could do to make the hall more inviting, less like an institution. "Mary!" Bessie called, round face smiling, looking much younger than her sixty-five years, but, of course, she did not have a husband, and her one child lived in the East.

The Papastavros sisters nodded to her politely but briefly. They were leaning toward Mary's cousin Effie, who was pursing her thin, garishly lipsticked mouth and raising eyebrows that over the years had become black drawn-on pencil lines. Just like Effie, Mary thought, not to have the courtesy to stop talking long enough to greet her.

"Mary," Bessie said brightly, "did you forget we were going to have coffee before the meeting, not afterwards?" Then Mary remembered Bessie had offered to bring a breakfast cake, low-fat, low-calorie, and they would brew a pot of decaffeinated coffee. It was Diane making her forget, with her awful way of twisting her insides.

"I had three telephone calls just as I was going out of the door," Mary said, looking away from Bessie. She disliked telling white lies next door to the church. "I had to answer. You never know. It might be someone who was in real trouble."

Bessie brought her a cup of coffee and a slice of cake on an oblong plate. The Philoptochos had bought the set the year of Mary's first presidency; it did away with the need of having two plates. Every time Mary used the plates she remembered that Effie, the rich widow, had balked at spending the money for them. Effie never thought twice about spending money on herself, though. She always had money when they were little; even later, in the Depression, she always got what she wanted. Mary never got the butterfly skirt that was popular, but Effie was the first to have one. Effie's mother had spoiled her rotten. Mary was moist under the arms. She was certain that her face was moist also. She should have checked her makeup before leaving the car. Effie was talking about a church board member who had been seen in several places with his blonde secretary.

"Of course, if you told Dena her husband was playing around," Effie pulled her mouth down, "she wouldn't believe it anyway. You know," and she mimicked a little girl's voice, "Tommy is so worn out when he comes home. Tommy says. Tommy went. Tommy did. Hah!"

The Papastavros sisters looked miserable. They were trying to be more Christian-like now that they were very old. Mary ate the cake, tasty, a little brown sugar and chopped nuts on top. Eating something sweet always made her feel better. Her mother got that way, too, as she aged. She stopped chewing for a moment; her mother was not much older than Mary when she died. She glanced at the other women; she knew she looked pretty old. Effie was still so conscious of her face-lift that she was preening, lifting her head up to show her new, tight chin. "You look fifteen years younger, Effie," Koula Papastavros said. "I wish I hadn't stopped dyeing my hair. When I look at you, I feel so old."

Effie smiled insincerely. Mary hated that condescending false smile. Effie had used it on everyone, including Mary's mother, to get her way, to worm herself into people's good graces. Both mothers, Mary's and Effie's, always made her give in to Effie. If Effie wanted her doll, Mary's mother made her give it up. "Let her play with it. She's little." And there was only three months' difference between them.

Mary chewed and looked at Effie, now talking about a Philoptochos member who was having chemotherapy. Effie was the only one of their generation who hadn't married a Greek. Even though her mother raised a big commotion at first, Effie not only married Howard, but in the Greek church. Over the years the family sang his praises and, except for Effie's mother, condemned her for being selfish and mean to him. Effie got a new Lincoln Continental every few years.

Mary sipped the decaffeinated coffee and glanced at the door, expecting other Philoptochos members to walk in, but no one did. If it were a fashion show, they'd be there, all of them, dressed up, hair and nails done. Still, she hoped that suddenly she would glance up and a group of the younger women would enter.

Koula Papastavros was telling one of her never-ending stories. She talked slowly, looking about, her face wrinkling up with smiles. She had a call from Tina Pappas. "And Tina said she had just come back from a baptism in Las Vegas, and the priest said"—twinkling eyes and a moment's interruption while she gave the women a chance to anticipate the humorous anecdote—"this was last October—now that was seven months ago!" Koula barely raised her voice to emphasize the incongruity of her story. "Seven months ago the priest was in Greece, and he met this woman, and she gave him this package to take to us, her cousins!" Koula shook her head slightly, savoring the memory. "The priest said, 'I told her. They live a thousand miles away, but those Greeks in their little tiny country just don't understand distances.' They asked him then to *mail* the package. So the poor priest, whether he wanted to or not, had to take the package with him. And he never got around to mailing it. So when he was introduced to Dena and found out she knew us, he gave her the package. Then she had it for *another* three months because we were gone for a few days, then she went to see her son in Seattle, and we *just* got it yesterday."

"And what was in it?" Effie demanded.

"Oh, it was very nice," Philanthi said, even more slowly than her sister. "There was a large package of bay leaves, nice big ones. If you bought them here they could cost as much as a hundred dollars, and a large plastic bag of *oreganon*, and another of chamomile." Smiling and leaning her head to one side, she gave a little sigh. "We have no idea what to do with the chamomile. I know mothers used to make tea for babies' upset stomachs." She smiled at every woman in turn.

"You forgot the cherry preserves," Koula said in soft reprimand. "The *vysino*. Oh, dear. It leaked all over."

"But thank goodness, the packages were plastic, and we just wiped them off with a wet cloth."

"Then we ate the *vysino*." Koula gave a high tinkling laugh at their ingenuity.

Mary felt sorry for the Papastavros sisters, although it gave her a sad satisfaction that at least they were older than she; Philanthi, the older, was nearly eighty. The sisters had never married, and until they were sixty had still expected to. She remembered a day decades past when their girls' club met at the Papastavros house and the sisters opened their cedar chests to show their dowry linens. Philanthi had stroked a sheet embroidered in white with cutwork flowers. "Yes, I know, cutwork takes a lot of work by the time you do the solid stitch and then cut out the inside, but there's nothing like it."

Koula had laughed. "I haven't the patience. I just crochet around the edges," and she held up a sheet with a wide band of crochet. "I've got matching pillowcases," she said and spread them out. Their old widowed father had sat in the kitchen reading a Greek-language newspaper.

The sisters had waited on their father hand and foot. "Yes, he's strict," Philanthi had said, "but it's because he cares about us so much." It wasn't until the Depression became so bad that he allowed them to take secretarial jobs in the welfare office. They had shrunk with the years and now sat like two emaciated birds, their hair thin and white, looking more and more like each other. They never missed anything: the Senior Citizens' luncheons prepared by the Philoptochos; the Daughters of Penelope activities; the Cultural Association meetings; all the church festivities for Christmas, Easter, the March Twenty-fifth anniversary of the Greek revolt against the Turks, the Dormition of the Virgin in August, Sunday liturgies, and feast days for their dead parents' and other relatives' patron saints. "We go to everything while we can," Philanthi had said and smiled deprecatingly. "Who knows next year this time where we'll be?" And that's why they were here, Mary knew. It was a diversion, a place to go to get out of the condominium while they could.

"I don't know where the others are," Mary said. "If it were some kind of entertainment, they'd all be here."

Philanthi smiled and leaned her head to one side. This was a habit from the time she was a girl. Mary and Effie had made fun of her then; they had been inseparable as girls. "It's because they have families, Mary. They have so many things to do. I'm sure they would be here if they could."

Mary gave her a small smile and thought: almost eighty years old and still following her mother's admonition not to say a bad word about anyone. Mary's mother used to lecture her about it. They were never to gossip, never to pass on what they'd heard, never to criticize, because the day would come when families would be looking for brides for their sons and girls with loose mouths would be passed over. Poor Philanthi and Koula, the little old birds with the thinning hair, always did the right thing, never criticized, never gossiped, and never

married. Mary finished the cake and placed it on the coffee table, and
Bessie quickly poured more coffee into her cup. "Well, Mary," she
said, "no use waiting. Should we begin? Do you want to say something first?"

"No, no, it's your program, Bessie. Go ahead." Mary liked Bessie's
tact. She had seen her on television with a group of social workers discussing the Supreme Court decision to withhold federal funds from
clinics that counseled patients on abortion. Mary agreed with Bessie:
women should have the right to choose, although she would never had
resorted to it. She hoped Father Michael hadn't seen the program or
heard about it because then he would have made trouble about Bessie
leading the group.

"I'm sorry," Bessie said, raising her voice, to get the women's attention. Effie said something to the Papastavros sisters, and they did
not know whom to look at first, Effie or Bessie. A frantic look was on
their faces. Mary stared at Effie to show her displeasure: Effie always,
always had to be the center of attention. "Ladies, I'm sorry that more
women didn't come," Bessie continued, "but let's not be discouraged.
It will build up. One of my friends in Denver said they started with a
small group, and now they have a good-sized attendance every month.
Father Michael had an errand, and he'll come by when he's finished."

"So what are we going to do exactly?" Effie said, with that bellig-
erent little tightening of her thin mouth Mary knew so well. She had
told Diane, "While she was getting that second face-lift, why didn't
she have her lips done? Like actresses have something injected into
their lips to make them look bigger?" "She's a kook," Diane had said,
"a real ass. All that makeup and dyed hair." Mary was pleased that
she and Diane had agreed on something, even though she didn't like to
hear her say words like *ass*. At least she didn't say the *f* word and the *s*
word. Mary stared. How did she know what Diane did behind her
back? And some of her stories didn't add up. She lifted her hand and
gave it a shake: she mustn't get into thinking like that.

"I can't believe Greeks will sit around and talk about their personal
problems," Effie said and folded her arms across her white wool suit,
an Ann Klein, according to Diane.

"Oh, no," Bessie said quickly. "We're not going to talk about personal problems. We're going to talk about issues in general."

"We hear all that on television."

Mary could see Effie was on her high horse, Gus's words, but she
would just ignore her, pretend she wasn't there.

"That's not exactly what we'll be doing," Bessie said. "We'll be talking about women and their relationships with their families."

Mary nodded: she approved of Bessie. She had such a pleasant face, and no one would know how hard she had worked to go through the university and then the two extra years to get her master's. No one would have expected her to get that educated, considering the kind of family she came from, the father a cook, the mother a little bustling woman who had taken in boarders when her children were little. Mary didn't like this thought: she and Effie had scorned Bessie in those years for wanting to get an advanced degree when her father was only a cook. Mary lifted her head high to give herself dignity: well, she, at least, had outgrown such stupid ideas. Not Effie, of course: if a woman didn't have a big house, a Cadillac or a Lincoln, and eight-hundred-dollar dresses, she was a nobody.

"We're going to talk about general subjects," Bessie was saying, smiling at each woman in turn. "We could look at our lives. For example, how has television affected us? Or we could begin by talking about priorities. We can't do everything. We can't run ourselves ragged taking care of our old parents, husbands, getting involved in our children's problems, our grandchildren's. We can't rush around from one meeting to another. We can make a list and place the most important things at the top, then go down the list and cross out the nonessentials."

The women looked at her. Only Bessie now had an old parent to worry about, her aged mother in a nursing home. Only Mary had a husband. Effie's had died, the Papastavros sisters had never married, and Bessie had divorced her husband twenty years previously. As for children and grandchildren, Bessie had a son and two grandchildren all living away; Effie had one child, a son who had never married and was rumored to be gay. Mary's children lived in the city, Diane and her two children, her son Mark and his three. And as for running around from one meeting to another, she knew without a second's thought that Effie and the Papastavros sisters were there because it was something to do. She wasn't sure now about this group idea of Bessie's. She had a feeling it might not go well.

Bessie began again. "Another subject we could look at is guilt. Why at our age are we still carrying guilt around with us? Are we going to go to our graves feeling guilty about our choices and unresolved issues?" Bessie laughed lightly. "You can't believe how much guilt I carried with me like a suitcase until I went into social work. From the time I was little, if I didn't use the polite address to Mrs. Manopoulos or

Mrs. Hadjiyorgos when I held out the tray to them—oh, my God, the guilt! A few slaps in the face along with it," she nodded knowingly. "All through school, American school, Greek school, if I said or did something I thought afterwards I shouldn't have, oh, dear God! I was a walking mass of guilt."

The women looked at her with deep interest. "Another subject is the church. We can talk about our feelings toward the church. About women's place in it. You know there are women who think we should have women priests."

"Oh, no!" the Papastavros sisters said in unison, shaking their heads slowly from side to side, also in unison.

"God!" Effie gave a short, derisive laugh. "What nuts! Wanting to be priests."

"Well," Bessie went on, "but to get on to something more immediate. For example, how do you feel about the archbishop choosing the national president of Philoptochos? Do you think women should vote on it?"

The Papastavros sisters moved their thin bones on the chair seats. Effie leaned forward. "You mean the archbishop chooses who he wants? What's all this about the Philoptochos having national conventions if the archbishop chooses who he wants as president?"

Bessie's eyes glinted with excitement. "Yes, that's right!"

"But, Effie," Philanthi Papastavros said in a small voice, her head shaking slightly from palsy, "we don't know all the women around the country, and the archbishop knows who's capable." Her sister nodded, two little birds with denuded heads moving back and forth.

"Oh, don't give me that! It's the same old crap! Women don't know anything. Men do. That's how we were raised. We'd have to listen to those puffed-up peasants who made a little money in America with their damn speeches about the Greek language and customs, and we were always put down. The boys got to do anything they wanted, but we had to be nice and demure." Effie mimicked the last words, pursing her little mouth primly. "I had to press my brothers' pants and shine their shoes before they went out on dates."

Mary couldn't believe Effie had said that. She had done no such thing. Her mother had done it. And it was she, Mary, who had to press her brothers' pants and shine their shoes.

Bessie leaned forward, a kindly look on her face. "It sounds like your carrying a lot of anger, Effie."

"Don't try to analyze me! I don't need a therapist."

Mary tried to look serene, understanding. "We have to remember," she said, "that our parents were just carrying on the traditions of the old country. They were just doing what they thought was right."

"Well, they were in America, damn it! I never got to do anything I wanted to. All the time I was in junior high and in high school," Effie breathed in so deeply that the muscles of her neck became two thin ropes on either side of a bony windpipe, "all the girls were having fun, but *I* had to go to Greek school, *I* couldn't date; *I* had to bring the tray with baklava and coffee to all those visitors. Years and years of holding out the tray to those goddamn women giving me the once over to see if I was good enough for their shitty sons!"

The Papastavros sisters gasped.

"You weren't the only one, Effie," Mary said keeping her voice even. "We all had the same kind of upbringing. We didn't like to be left out, but we survived. It wasn't so bad. And there were compensations." She was thinking of Effie, first with the latest fads, a piano she didn't look at after a few lessons, and getting out of Greek school with all kinds of lies and excuses.

"It wasn't so bad, huh? You just took it and never made a peep! I remember you. You were such a goody-goody."

"Now let's . . ." Bessie began, but Mary raised her voice, then brought it back down and said with a strained smile, "Effie, what are you making such a fuss about? You did what you wanted. You married an American. So how can you sit there and complain?"

"Yes, I married an American. They weren't going to stop me one more time!"

Mary clutched her hands together, but still smiled while something made its way from her stomach to her throat. "You had a good husband. He let you have your way about everything. He left you plenty of money. He . . ."

"That doesn't make up for those awful years in high school! All the girls were having dates. Going to the senior hop. I wanted to go to the senior hop so bad and be like all the other girls!"

Mary took a deep breath. "Well, for heaven's sake, that was fifty some years ago! What in the world's the matter with you?"

Bessie reached out her hands, saying something, her face agonized.

"You didn't care that we couldn't date! You just put your nose in books! If you had stood up with me, we might have got somewhere!"

"How could we have got somewhere? You're talking silly!"

"Silly, am I? You were like a little lamb! They took you to that Ahepa convention to find you a husband, and you got Gus! Well, I wouldn't let them do that to me!"

Bessie took two steps forward and said, "Girls!"

"Now listern here, Effie, you married a wonderful man! You ought to be grateful."

"Well, I'm not grateful! That doesn't make up for not going to the senior hop!"

Mary slapped the coffee table. "Did anyone ever ask you for a date to the senior hop? No one ever did! You were fat and had b.o. So don't come around fifty-five years later blaming everyone because you didn't get to go to the senior hop!"

Effie stood up, eyes sparking, and stamped out of the room on her specially ordered high-heeled Italian shoes. Mary sank on the chair. The Papastavros sisters looked at each other miserably.

Bessie's mouth sagged, and she looked her age, old. "Don't feel bad, Mary. It was a good start. Effie will feel a load lifted off her. She'll be back."

"No, she won't be back, and I don't think we should have anymore of these meetings."

Quickly, before Father Michael arrived, the women placed the dishes and saucers on a tray. Philanthi rinsed them, and Koula arranged them in the dishwasher. Bessie wiped the coffee table with a paper napkin and sighed deeply. Mary wondered what people would say when they heard about the meeting. She thought of the strain at family dinners when Effie wouldn't speak to her, and she had to think hard on how she could tell Diane about the meeting without making it sound so awful.

The Great Day

It was soon after the Second World War, a Thursday in the Busy Bee Cafe. Dean ate there every Thursday because Fat Bill, the owner, cooked a Greek dish. The Busy Bee had never been painted since Fat Bill bought it in 1920; springs pushed against the leather booths and made sitting uncomfortable, and Fat Bill with the big face and hairless head was a sour man. His food, though, was good enough that Dean overlooked these drawbacks.

On this certain Thursday Fat Bill came out of the kitchen wearing a soiled white apron that came to his ankles, with a young man behind him. "Deno," he said gruffly in Greek, "meet my nephew, Thrasim-voulos. Just come over from our country."

Dean shook hands with the short-legged, wide-shouldered young man and told him to sit down and talk to him. Thrasimvoulos, who was about nineteen, looked at him, eyes eager with gratitude, a smile, tentative and innocent, and at that moment Dean set out to help him. "First thing," he told him after learning he had come from the same Peloponnesian village as his mother, "is to cut your name. You can't go around with a name like Thrasimvoulos." Dean thought, remembered the old Tracy Collins Bank, and said, "Tracy. That's a good name," and he wrote it down on his card.

From then on Dean ate at the Busy Bee two or three times a week, often with old friends he had known from Greek school days. He found out where night school classes for immigrants were held and took Tracy to register. When he bought his son David a new car—yes, he knew he spoiled him—he gave Tracy the old one. "God will remember you," his mother said, "for your kindness. People should make life easier for those who need help." He couldn't remember his mother being especially charitable, but he liked himself for giving Tracy the car.

Dean's wife Georgia said, "All right, now you've given him the car. Don't get too involved. Remember the time you paid Ted Kapsis's tuition his last year in law school and then never heard from him again."

Dean waved his hand in front of his face. "This is different. I know what I'm doing."

"In the courtroom, yes; outside you jump without looking."

"I like Tracy. He's like me, a go-getter." Georgia sighed audibly.

Tracy wanted to remodel and clean up the cafe, but Fat Bill told him to mind his own business. If it was good enough for him, it should be good enough for the nephew he brought over and who found the table already set. Tracy was secretly looking for other work when Fat Bill had a stroke and died.

Dean helped Tracy get a loan and found subcontractors to remodel the cafe. Dean suggested a new name, The Great Burger. It became a popular gathering place for university students and for young Greek immigrants. Dean felt comfortable there, especially after defending a hard case in court. It didn't matter if his suit was rumpled and his shirt damp from perspiration. He could eat without having one eye out for a judge or an attorney from one of the big firms stopping at his table with a greeting. He didn't have to worry about his manners at the Great Burger, and the immigrants were more interesting than the Americans with important family names who ate at the Grill.

The immigrants had come to America around the same time as Tracy had, most of them, like him, with a year or two more than a grade-school education. There was something about them, their haircuts, something Dean couldn't put his finger on, that immediately told people they were immigrants. He remembered how he was taunted when a boy. "Foreigner! Foreigner!" boys shouted at him during recess at school.

The immigrants were always glad to see Dean at The Great Burger and asked for advice. He was gratified to give it. He made telephone calls for them, sent them to employers with his card, remembering how he had spread manure over the university grounds in return for his tuition. "You're a generous man," the immigrants said. "Other Greeks born here don't look at us twice."

Their Greek talk carried to Dean's booth while he looked about to see if there was something that he should bring to Tracy's attention. He and his friends were amused by the frenzy the immigrants would get into over some supposed insult. Often it had to do with American-born priests who expected them to pay dues, which they hadn't done in Greece. The government paid priests back there. Dean smiled; when he was little his father and his friends banged fists on the oilcloth-covered table and shouted that they would go that minute and "demand to know the reason why." He never remembered their going anywhere; they remained seated in the kitchen drinking wine.

The young immigrants talked about women, where to find them, spoke dirty, and made Dean, although not his grinning friends, uncomfortable. He had to remind himself that he and his friends had been no different when they were that age. One of the immigrants was big-toothed, fat-lipped Ernie Peperonis, his thick hair swept back with hair oil. He had a better education than the other immigrants and at every opportunity reminded them of it by telling anecdotes about what had happened to him in high school and in the two years beyond. He liked sex, he said. "I gave it to her front and back," he snickered about the wife of an automobile dealer.

Dean motioned Tracy from the cash register. "What do you think of that, Tracy? I don't know if it's true or not, but what do you think of a man who yells something like that for everyone in the place to hear?"

"Don't pay no attention to him. You know Ernie."

"No, I don't know Ernie. I think he's a horse's ass."

A few days later Dean almost forgot what he had heard: Ernie Peperonis could be entertaining. Dean saw him and the other immigrants congregated at church functions, weddings, and baptisms, always in tight groups. Even there they complained and criticized. Ernie Peperonis strayed away from them, went about the crowded, noisy gatherings, clapped well-to-do American-born men on the back, laughingly carried gossip to them, imitated the talk of the current priests, and told jokes. Dean heard Ernie in The Great Burger jingling the coins in his pocket and sneering at those same men, "They have money in their pockets and don't look at us." Dean didn't think Ernie included him.

Ernie was especially attentive to an elderly bachelor who had come to the country in the first decade of the 1900s. At church and lodge buffets, he brought him drinks, wouldn't let him stand in line, and served him heaping plates of food. Soon Ernie Peperonis was the owner of an insurance agency that everyone knew the elderly Greek had made possible. Dean helped him out by buying insurance for one of his investments, a building in the industrial park. "I wish you hadn't," Georgia said. "You shouldn't trust him. You know how two-faced he is."

Ernie never acknowledged the old man's help and stopped jingling the coins in his pocket. He prospered so well that he seldom came to The Great Burger. He ate in an uptown restaurant frequented by the wealthy American-born and two immigrants who had gone to the university; one had become an attorney, the other a CPA. The attorney had never talked to Dean about his cases. He didn't have to; many immigrants who came after the Second World War retained him. He didn't have to struggle for clients as Dean had in the Depression years, when he would have starved if it hadn't been for old-country Greeks and Serbs.

One night Dean's building burned down, but he was never able to collect the insurance. The policy was defective, and Dean was humiliated that he, an attorney, had not read the policy carefully. He had skimmed through it while Ernie watched, and to show he trusted him, he signed it. He grabbed Ernie by the lapels and called him a bastard, a liar, a cheat, but there was nothing he could do about it. Gossip came back to him that Ernie Peperonis was telling people that Dean had cheated him, had tried to dirty his name.

"Me," he said, stabbing his index finger against Tracy's chest, "me! He cheats *me* and goes around town telling everyone he meets that I cheated *him!* Trying to save his ass!"

Ernie's lies came back to Dean and Georgia at intervals. Dean would rage, then forget about them until he heard another report. He avoided the restaurants where he might see Ernie Peperonis. He was free of him at The Great Burger.

Tracy sat with Dean during lulls and one day introduced him to a small, dark girl who spoke very little English. "We're engaged," Tracy said. "We're gonna get married." Dean's first thought was that their children would be short. He remembered his father lifting his wine glass at his and Georgia's engagement dinner and saying, "Let's drink to their children. Not be short like Georgia and not have Deno's mug." Dean was six-foot-two and Georgia about five-foot-four. He wished his father could see how successful he had become.

Dean thought he saw an expectant look in Tracy's excited eyes. He told Georgia about it. "I think he wants me to offer to be his best man." It troubled him. "I think I'm too old for that, and I'll be in the thick of his friends all the time. You know how those clannish imports are. Every time there's a wedding and baptism, they'll think they have to invite us." Georgia suggested he tell Tracy the truth, part of the truth, tell him that it was better to have someone his own age as his best man, someone who wouldn't be too old to be godfather of the first child, according to custom. "By the time the child is grown up, you'll be an old man," Georgia said.

Tracy said he was disappointed. About Tracy's wedding Dean remembered one sharp detail. Tracy, his best man, and the ushers were short men. The American-born priest was slightly taller than they and had increased his height with two-inch heels. "Did you notice the priest's shoes?" Dean asked Georgia afterwards. Georgia said, "It doesn't occur to Tracy and his friends that they should be taller, but the poor priest has those American ideas about being tall and masculine." Dean thought it was interesting. If he had been short as a young man, besides being the son of an immigrant, it would have been the last straw.

Dean saw Tracy's children, a boy and two girls, in the cafe from time to time. He saw them growing tall as they went through grade school and junior high. "America makes kids taller," Tracy said. Dean seldom saw them during high school. "Too much homework, too much activities," Tracy said. Dean didn't see them at all while they were in college, but duty-bound, he asked Tracy about them.

One early morning he was awakened by the telephone. Georgia answered in the kitchen, and Dean heard her blunted exclamations, then her running footsteps—she, at least, had not gained weight with the passing years. Her eyes were flecked with excitement, and he felt a pang over how she had once been. "Pick up the receiver," she said. "Becky has something to tell you."

"What's up, Doll?"

"*Papou!* I got engaged last night! I'm going to get married!"

"What? What the hell's going on? Who's the guy?"

"The guy," Becky said slowly, with controlled mirth in her voice, "is Mike, Tracy's son."

"Tracy's son Mike?"

Dean was stunned. It had never occurred to him that his granddaughter Becky, fourth generation in America, would give the son of immigrants a second look. No one had said anything to him. He thought: yes, Tracy had been smiling secretively. Tracy knew they were dating, and that was the reason for those smiles. Georgia said she hadn't known either. He had a suspicion that Becky and her mother had kept it a secret because they were afraid he would spoil it. "Don't be paranoid," Georgia said. He picked up the receiver and telephoned Becky. "Why didn't you tell me? Did you think I'd spoil it? Didn't you think I'd be happy about it?"

"I wanted to surprise you, *Papou.*"

"I guess your dad and, of course, your mother are glad."

"Of course. They like Mike a lot."

Dean sat up in bed, shaking his head. "I used to make fun of my mother always talking about fate. *Tihi, tihi,* she used to say until it came out of my nose. Now with Becky marrying Tracy's boy, I'm beginning to think there's something to fate after all."

"Oh, fate," Georgia said and raised her eyebrows.

"But just a minute, Georgia. You remember when Tracy got engaged, remember I told you I had a feeling he was hoping I'd ask to be his best man? Like the old-timers from Greece?"

"Yes," Georgia said looking at the door.

Dean knew she wanted to rush into the kitchen to telephone her daughters and sisters with the news, but he persisted. "Now, look, if I had been Tracy's best man, then I would have been Mike's godfather and then our little Becky and Mike couldn't get married because they'd be considered related."

Georgia lifted her gray head and pursed her lips as she did when thinking out an answer. Instead, she laughed. "Remember when Nola and Bill Maheras married? They didn't have children, and the mothers said it was because of that taboo about having the same godfather."

"Ah, that was more than fifty years ago. If you ask me, nobody told the priest Nola and Bill had the same godfather."

Georgia folded her arms. "Well, if you want to think it's fate, then go ahead. Anyway, I don't think American-born priests would pay any attention to that old Greek custom."

"You always throw cold water on everything I tell you. I say it's fate I wasn't Tracy's best man."

"I don't care. Fate or not, they'll have a wonderful marriage." Her face turned sad. "Anyway, I hope so."

Pacified, Dean dressed and drove to the cafe to talk about it with Tracy. It was the middle of the morning, and a frothy joy rose in his chest. It was wonderful! Becky and Tracy's son Mike! The last of the grandchildren marrying and for once marrying a Greek, and there wouldn't be that tug-of-war over which church the children should be brought up in. He'd had a hard time with Becky's father, his son David, but he had to admit David had finally settled down and become a good father to his three children. "All's well that ends well," Jeanie, David's wife, had said when he started paying attention to his business. As if she hadn't been all for partying as much as David. Oh, but it was great having a really close family, not like some people he knew. And his wonderful granddaughter Becky who always hugged him and sat next to him at the family gatherings!

Dean drove over the speed limit, looking guiltily in the rearview mirror: he was afraid of traffic police. He drove into the parking lot and with a start pressed hard on the brake. Sitting at a table against the plate glass window was a group of Tracy's friends. They were looking at Ernie Peperonis, who was evidently telling them an anecdote, something funny. The others laughed, flinging out their hands. That import, that banana, that d.p., Dean whispered furiously, put the car in reverse, and drove to his office. He was too distracted to look at the papers on his desk and called Georgia. "So who's down at Tracy's holding court but that sonofabitch Ernie Peperonis. Sitting in a booth telling stories to a bunch of imports. Laughing like he was their best friend."

"Oh, no."

"The dirty bastard! Sitting there, laughing it up!"

"Deno, don't let him ruin things again. We've got the wedding to think about. That's the most important thing on our minds."

"It just sticks in my craw what he did to me. Cheated me, then went around telling people I cheated him. Blackened my name and he's still doing it."

"People know him. They know what an egotistical, jealous person he is. They know he's got an ugly mouth."

"Yeah, but he's so cunning, the way he tears people down in that laughing way as if he's not doing it maliciously, he's just telling facts."

"Try not to think about it. It happened a long time ago."

"I'll never forget it as long as I live! That phony, slimy Greek. Been in this country all these years. Still talks with that stupid accent and goes around putting on airs like he's so goddamn educated!"

"Deno, you're getting into a condition again. Stop thinking about him. He's not worth it."

Dean hung up but kept his eye on the wall clock and at 11:15, before the lunchtime crowd filled The Great Burger, got into his car and drove to Tracy's cafe. Ernie Peperonis's Mercedes was not in the parking lot. Dean jumped out and hurried into the restaurant. Except for three men sitting in a booth, it was empty. He was about to walk into the kitchen when Tracy sprang through the doors, still youngish looking, only a little gray at his temples. "Deno! Come on. Sit down. I'll bring coffee."

Dean sat in the booth by the plate glass window. He knew Ernie Peperonis would not come in if he saw him. Tracy brought the coffee and sat opposite him. "So we're gonna be related after all?" Tracy smiled that same open smile he had on the day Dean first saw him. Dean noticed that his teeth had yellowed.

"We're happy about it, Georgia and I; we're happy. How come you didn't tell me the kids were seeing each other?"

Tracy put out his palms, pulled the corners of his mouth down, and lifted his shoulders. "I didn't know, either. I guess the kids, they thought better not say nothing so the families wouldn't get involved."

"That was smart of them." Dean wanted to get to Ernie Peperonis, but he thought it would be unseemly to bring him up too quickly. "You know, Tracy, who would have thought that first day Fat Bill introduced us our kids would get married someday?"

Tracy shook his head slowly in unbelief. "It's fate. It's *tihi*."

Dean blurted, "I was here earlier, but I saw that shit Ernie Peperonis through the window, so I didn't come in."

Tracy leaned his head to one side and lifted his shoulders—he had brought all those Greek expressions with him. "Well, what can I do, Deno? I can't tell him to leave. You know, I'm running a business."

"Yeah. The bastard. I hear the recession has cut down his insurance business. So he's going around to every Greek restaurant and business in town, slapping people on the back. People he thought he was too good for."

Tracy lifted his palms to signify: yes, but what can be done?

"Started going to church every Sunday, Georgia tells me."

"That's what I heard, too."

"What gets me is he's so goddamn jealous if someone does better than him, he makes up lies, twists things, and then those same stupid people he throws mud at end up talking to him again."

"Yeah, he's got a bad mouth all right. Now for the wedding, Deno, I know you're paying for everything. Becky, she said that, but I want to cook the food."

"No! The hotel's going to do it all. This is my party. I want to control everything."

"Ah, come on, Deno. For old time's sake. You helped me so much to get started."

"No, it's my party." People were beginning to come in. Dean stood up. "Your customers are coming. We'll be talking."

"Okay, but . . ." Tracy turned to Greek, "my woman, she insists she'll make all the pastries. She already called Georgia."

Dean left, thinking and trying to sort out why he hadn't handled himself very well. For one thing, he shouldn't have brought up Ernie Peperonis's name so quickly, and he didn't know what Georgia would say when he told her about it.

Between that meeting and the wedding, Dean saw Ernie Peperonis's Mercedes parked in front of Tracy's restaurant several times. He drove on, hating the red car.

The house was in upheaval: telephone calls, comings and goings, cars driving up and down the driveway. Dean had never been involved with past weddings of children and grandchildren. For one reason, he had not yet retired, but mainly it was women's work. In the fifty years he and Georgia had been married, he brought home the money and she took complete charge of the house, the children, the family feasts. With this wedding, he left his television sports programs to sit at the dining room table among books, catalogs, and brochures. He was especially interested in the guest list. Becky's mother Jeanie brought the list and said, "Add any names you want," as if she were paying for the wedding instead of him.

"Don't make any of your snappy remarks," Georgia warned him as the plans were being discussed. "We want this wedding to be extra-special."

"What do you think I am? I want it to be special, too. It's our last hurrah. We'll bring them all together. Our friends, the relatives, whether we like them or not, and what's left of the old-timers. Like saying goodbye. Who knows where we'll be next year."

For a brief moment they were silent, but there were too many details to think about, to decide, to make telephone calls over. Dean asked about flowers, even looked at swatches of fabric for the bridesmaids' dresses, and discussed the dinner menu for over eight hundred guests. His dress suit from past weddings was tight under the arms and around the waist, and rather than have it altered, he bought a new one. It still seemed strange to him who his granddaughter would be marrying.

A week before the wedding Georgia gathered her daughters, sisters, and friends and, working four full days, made a thousand stuffed grape leaves, another thousand feta cheese pastry triangles, and great bowls of *taramosalata,* orange caviar dip. Every morning Georgia cooked a pot of lentils or bean soup for the lunch respite of excited talk and much laughter. Dean ate with them the first day, but felt strange seated in the kitchen, the only man with nine women. His father, uncles, and brother never had anything to do with food or kitchens. "Is that all you've got, lentils?"

"Yes, that's all we've got. We're too busy to cook banquets. Why don't you just go down to Tracy's?"

The next day there wasn't a coke in the house. "Deno," Georgia said, "I wish you'd go get us some Cokes."

He was about to be annoyed, but then he thought: What the hell? She'll throw it up to me someday that I didn't do a thing for the wedding. "Okay, anything else?"

"What I'd really like you to do is cut about nine hundred grape leaves, nice ones for the appetizer dishes."

"There aren't nine hundred leaves on the vines."

"Get the rest from Tracy's garden. He's got plenty. But don't bother the women. They're making the pastries."

Dean left, feeling like an errand boy, but thinking of Becky, he felt young, buoyed.

At the wedding every detail followed the exhaustive plans. Enormous bouquets of white gladioli banked the icon screen and in half circles formed a bower for the wedding party. Becky in voluminous white satin embroidered with seed pearls, the lace train flowing over the elevated platform and down the red carpeting, smiled, her smooth cheeks a radiant pink. When the white flowered wedding crowns attached by wide ribbons were placed on their heads, Mike gazed at her lovingly. The young priest chanted low, a hint of melody in his voice when it soared. Dean and Georgia's great granddaughters, frilled and beribboned, and their great grandson, the ringbearer, behaved as they had been drilled. The choir Becky had belonged to sang the responses softly. To Dean the bridesmaids and ushers gave off an aura of unsullied youth; they looked fresh, strangers to drugs and free sex. He knew that's what he wanted to believe.

As Dean and Georgia followed the bridesmaids and ushers down the aisle, women who looked as if they had just left their hairdressers smiled at them happily. Men nodded to them; one old-timer winked. The wedding had been perfect.

As soon as they reached the door of the church, Dean and Georgia hurried down the steps and to their car. Dean had parked it at the corner curb to prevent their being delayed by well-wishers. He carefully settled his big body behind the wheel, not wanting to wrinkle his suit, turned on the ignition and drove unnecessarily fast through the streets to the hotel. "You're driving too fast," Georgia said placidly, preoccupied with the vision of their granddaughter facing the icon screen.

"I just want to be sure those cases of Metaxa got there."

"Of course they got there." Georgia wondered why she felt sad.

"Just seeing her up there was worth all the money we dished out." Dean said and clicked his tongue.

"If only we could be sure they'll always be happy."

"It seems like only yesterday when I first saw Tracy. I don't know where the years've gone. His son a college graduate and married to our Becky." Dean shook his head. "Time sure does fly." He lurched the car down the ramp into the underground parking, turned off the ignition, and bounded out of the car.

"Remember your blood pressure," Georgia said as she removed the car keys and locked the door. Dean ran up the escalator and was already at the top when Georgia stepped on it. Inside the ballroom Dean hurried to one end and talked with three bartenders behind a long white-silk-covered table with a large bouquet of white flowers on either end. He turned abruptly, circled the flower-decorated tables, and walked hurriedly toward the other end of the ballroom, where six musicians were taking out their instruments and setting up sheet music on stands. The musicians were sons and grandsons of his friends. Dean threw out his hands while talking as if he were angry with them, which he was not. Georgia shook her head: it was his way when he became excited, but the guests wouldn't know that.

The tables fanned out from the elevated bridal table and filled the ballroom. In the center on a round table, the many-tiered wedding cake rose like a fairyland castle. Georgia walked from table to table, looked at the centerpieces of white roses and greenery, and checked each dinner plate for the traditional white almonds tied in white net with white ribbon. Next to each table was a stand holding a small silver tub with two bottles of champagne in ice. She glanced at the bridal table. Festoons of green garlands and stephanotis were swathed across the fall of white satin. White orchids rose in the center and continued to the ends of the table. Georgia thought: was it ostentatious? Was it too much? She had been critical of others. She gave her gray head a shake. Dean had said it was their last hurrah.

Georgia gave special attention to the tables directly in front of the bridal table: one reserved for her two daughters, their husbands, and their married children; next to it a table for her three sisters and their husbands, the two flower girls and the ring bearer; and adjoining it, a table for Dean's older brother, a widower, his two sisters with their husbands, and the oldest of their children. Georgia suddenly saw her mistake. She should have put her relatives on one side of her daughters' table and Dean's relatives on the other side. The two families' mutual pretense of good feelings at family gatherings was a mask for the snide remarks that would come later. She could not believe she had forgotten such an important detail.

Satellite tables for grandchildren proliferated beyond the main tables. Farther back were additional satellites for cousins, godparents of children, the elderly distant relatives Georgia and Dean called aunts and uncles. The rest were reserved for friends and business acquaintances. Georgia gave a long, sweeping gaze around the ballroom. She wanted to give Dean's sisters no cause to criticize with their usual, "It was nice, but . . ." They never dared say the damning words to their brother.

The guests had begun to gather in the foyer, and some were slowly coming into the ballroom, looking about. Several heavily madeup women in bright silks or sequined dresses with string upon string of gold chains over their chests tipped chairs against the tables for late arrivals. Georgia did not know why this displeased her. It wasn't quite elegant. Three old women in black, the last of her mother's friends, were entering the ballroom shepherded by an obese younger woman. She was the daughter of one of the women, Mrs. Papayiannis, and had never married. Her dark face, devoid of cosmetics, was shiny with perspiration, and her fat was no longer girdled. Georgia hurried through the buzzing crowd, greeted the women, and led them to a table against mirrored walls. "You'll be out of the way of the traffic going to the bar," she said, "and, Diamond, I think the food will be all right for them."

"I told you not to worry, Georgia. They just won't eat dessert." Diamond laughed. "I'll end up eating it. That's why I look like I do."

Georgia gave each of the old women a kiss on her withered cheek: Mrs. Karafoundis who got up in church fifty or more years ago and clawed the mouth of a girl, not even one of her own, until a wad of chewing gum fell out; Mrs. Halamis, the smallest of the women, plump at one time, pretty, educated by immigrant standards, now a stringy diabetic; and Mrs. Papayiannis, the flat-faced, dark woman Mrs. Halamis had once dismissed with an impatient flap of her hands as being an illiterate villager. A sadness came into Georgia's eyes: the old women had come together in their old age because they were the last of their generation.

"Georgia," Mrs. Halamis whispered in Greek, and Georgia leaned forward to hear her, "you are so good to remember us old women and invite us. We hardly ever go out now."

"It seems I'm always taking you out," Diamond said huffily in the same village dialect as her mother, Mrs. Papayiannis. "I'm forever taking you to doctors and hospitals."

"True, true, Diamond. What would we do without you?"

As if caught in a lie about her saintly concern, Diamond reached over and patted Mrs. Halamis's hand. "Auntie,"—she called all elderly women "auntie"—"just enjoy the day. I don't get the chance, either, to get invited to big doings like this."

"I wish your mother were with us right here at the table," Mrs. Halamis said mournfully.

"Yes," Diamond said quickly, "but we're not going to think of those who've gone."

"I'll be back," Georgia said, and Diamond rolled her eyes.

Georgia walked back to the foyer. Most of the guests had seated themselves at tables, and those of her generation called out the old Greek exhortation, "*Na sus zisoun!*"—May they live! Those of their children's generation shouted above the din, "Beautiful wedding, Georgia!" "Becky looked just stunning." Their grandchildren's generation waved to acknowledge her. Probably, she thought, they didn't know exactly who she was. One of Dean's childhood friends cupped his hands about his mouth and said loudly, "Georgia, I guess ol' Deno'll shell out twenty grand for this shindig." He laughed, and his wife playfully shoved him.

Georgia smiled wryly. The din grew and almost overcame the orchestra's melody. Three groups had formed in front of the bar. In one, two young university professors were talking with a structural engineer and three attorneys, grandsons of the aging, overweight men in the adjoining group. In that group were Dean's friends from childhood; he had gone to Greek school with them, kept up with them, stopping to see them in their restaurants and businesses. They were husbands of the women decorated with gold. The husbands were dressed up in dark suits, except for one of them in a sea-green suede suit. Georgia stopped. Immigrants who had come after the Second World War made up the third group, and in the cluster around Tracy was Ernie Peperonis. Her breath left her. She looked quickly about the banquet hall for Dean, then back at Ernie Peperonis. How did he get here? Who invited him? A clammy moisture rose from her neck to her scalp. Again she looked about for Dean: she must tell him before he saw Ernie and caused a scene.

There he was, escorting the priest and his wife to the bridal table. Georgia's head shook as if she had palsy: What to do? What to do? Becky and Mike entered the ballroom. The musicians stopped the music they were playing and began a lively rendering of the Lohengrin march. Guests rose, clapped, and shouted as Becky and Mike made their way to the bridal table. Becky's parents followed, and Mike's small mother, dressed in blue satin with several strands of pearls and a gold and emerald necklace swaying across her ample chest, marched officiously toward Tracy and pulled at him. Waitresses and waiters were filling the champagne glasses.

Georgia hurried to the bridal table. Becky was leaning over Dean's shoulder. "Oh, *Papou*, I'll never forget this day as long as I live. Thank you, thank you so much." She kissed Dean on his thinning hair, and Mike solicitously helped arrange the clouds of white satin about the chair and then sat at her left.

Georgia and Becky's mother had set the place cards with Becky and Mike in the center, the best man at Mike's left, then Tracy and his wife, the bridesmaids, and the ushers. On Becky's right were the priest and his wife, her father and mother, Dean and Georgia, the matron of honor, and the maid of honor. Dean was standing up to see that everyone was properly seated. Tracy looked up at him and gave him a thumbs up. Dean nodded, his face flushed with happiness.

Georgia pulled Dean by the sleeve. He looked at her, annoyed. "Sit down," she said and, frowning, he sat. "What's the matter?"

"Now control yourself. Don't get excited."

"What! What's wrong?"

"Pretend everything's all right. Don't look to the right. Ernie's here."

Dean's face grayed; his chin jutted, rock-like. "Where? Where?"

"He's way over at the table next to the orchestra. Don't look."

"The sonofabitch, the sonofabitch. How did he get in here?" He turned, leaned forward, and looked at Tracy. Tracy was laughingly saying something to the priest. Dean looked ahead.

David was standing up, hitting a glass with a knife until the buzzing in the ballroom lessened. He was almost fifty; baldness was creeping toward the middle of his head, and although his face showed deep creases about the mouth, his body was still like a young man's. Georgia's heart shivered: Dean was looking at their son, perplexed, as if he were a stranger. Georgia leaned toward Dean. "We've got to pretend everything's all right. You can take care of it later." She sat back, her shoulders sagging, aching, feeling a miserable anger at Tracy.

David raised his champagne glass. "You're not going to be bored with speeches," he said. "Let's give a toast to the bride and groom and remain standing for Father to give the blessing."

A commotion of chairs pushed back, hundreds of people coming to their feet, and David said, "May Becky and Mike have a long and happy life and everything else we heard Father say in church." *Didst bless Isaac and Rebecca . . . thy wife shall be a fruitful vine, thy children like a newly planted orchard round about thy table . . .*

The priest asked the usual supplication of God for his blessing on the wedding feast, as Christ had at Cana. A unison of hands made the sign of the cross. The guests noisily seated themselves, and the orchestra began playing old Broadway favorites. "Wave to the kids," Georgia said, and Dean looked down at the tables where their great granddaughters in flower-girl finery were sitting, wearing little crowns, their empty ribboned flower baskets on the table. They were waving frantically. Their ring-bearer great-grandson in white dress suit, was yawning, slumped in his chair. Dean waved.

Dean's brother was shouting at him, hands cupped about his wrinkled mouth, but Dean lifted a hand and gave his head a shake. His sisters were whispering to each other. One of them had recently had a facelift, especially, she had said, for the wedding. "Don't tell Dean, Georgia, I can't wait to see his face," she had laughed.

Georgia's sisters were looking at her, nodding and smiling. Tomorrow morning they would come to her house. They would sit in the kitchen, drink coffee, eat pastries, and talk about the wedding: little details that one or the other might have missed, conversations overheard, comments made. It had been a ritual established by their mother after a name-day party, a wedding, or a baptismal dinner. Those mornings of tranquil recapitulation had been almost better than the actual events. The work, the anxiety were over; they were at ease. Taking little sips, tasting the pastry, their mother had been satisfied that they had behaved, as she had said so often, *san anthropoi*—like human beings. Georgia's hand went up to her throat. Mama, Mama, she said silently.

Slowly Georgia turned to the matron and maid of honor and told them how beautiful they looked. They thanked her politely, then faced each other and talked with intense animation. Dean and David's wife Jeanie sat next to each other and had nothing to say. They had known each other a quarter of a century, had feuded when she first married into the family, then had become accustomed to each other, making small talk unnecessary. The dinner proceeded, and dully Georgia looked at the plate of appetizers set before her. It was as she had wanted: a stuffed grape leaf with a wedge of lemon, a small feta cheese pastry triangle, and on a shiny flat grape leaf, a piped rosette of creamy orange caviar. She stared at it. She did not want to eat it. A woman—an American, of course—squealed, "Ooh, look at this Italian food!" Crab cocktail followed, then green salad with artichoke hearts, prime rib, rice, asparagus, tropical fruits, everything that Dean had chosen.

Georgia listened to Dean's heavy breathing. Her own breathing became hurried: he was afraid of dying, and what if it happened there at the table. She leaned as close to him as the chair allowed. She wanted to say something to him, but could not think of anything. She thought her brain had hardened and could no longer think. Dean's face looked like gray granite. "Pretend you're eating," she said, and he lifted his fork several times.

Georgia automatically surveyed the tables, beckoned to waiters to take more rolls, more champagne to the tables. She saw the happiness of their guests, the talking, the laughing across the tables, the lifting of champagne glasses to each other. At one table was a family of brothers whose father had been killed in a mine explosion when they were children. At the adjoining table was a group of elderly single women, friends of Georgia's. They had been bitter that they had never been asked to marry: "No, we weren't good enough for the Greek boys. They had to marry American floozies." They were happy, too, dressed in their best, their hair salon-dyed and set.

Near the door to be close to the restrooms, the remnants of the early immigrants sat, two with wives, the others either bachelors or widowers. One of the widowers had eloped with an American woman during the Ku Klux Klan attacks of 1924 and had returned to find a cross burning outside his restaurant. Another shrunken man had been a gambler and a procurer, the equally shrunken woman at his side, an American woman he had married to protect him from the Mann Act, but decades passed and they had become like any married couple. Hardly anyone remembered their story.

The old people ate on doggedly, bent over their plates. All through the ballroom were men and women in their late sixties and seventies. Georgia had belonged to a girls' lodge with some of them, their tunics edged with the Greek key design; Dean had belonged to the Sons of Pericles lodge band with many of the men. Georgia felt nothing now as she gazed at them. Glancing at Dean from time to time, she saw that he did not look at them at all. A loud merriment came from the tables where Tracy's friends sat.

Plates were removed. Tall glasses of fresh strawberry parfait and squares of white cake with silver almonds in the center were served. Coffee came next, and the waitresses went about the tables with large silver trays of Greek pastries. Georgia watched. Mike's mother had insisted that she would take care of the pastries. Dean had told the headwaiter that he, David, and Tracy would take the trays of Metaxa to each table. Now he waved him forward and told him to have the waiters serve the liqueur.

David was carrying on a light conversation with the priest, and Georgia felt relieved of the obligation to make pleasant talk with him and his young, round wife. Then Becky and Mike were standing at the wedding cake table. Together they inserted a long silver knife into the fairyland cake. When he heard the prolonged clapping, Dean asked Georgia if they had cut the cake.

"Yes, they did. Just now." Georgia frowned and looked at Dean carefully.

"You see how these imports stick together," Dean said, as if suddenly aware, his chin jutting forward. "All I did to help Tracy goes out the window. Those bananas are more important to him than I am. The hypocrite!"

"Shh, shh, don't ruin it for Becky."

"It's ruined for me. I'd like to kill that bastard Tracy. I thought he was different, but he's a goddamn shit. That damn smile of his, just a coverup for the snake he is."

"Shh. Think of the consequences. Think how it will be for Becky and Mike."

"I'll think of myself for a change."

"People are looking. Don't do anything you'll regret. Don't, please don't. I'll hold it against you the rest of your life if you do."

"Okay. Okay."

Georgia leaned back, worn out, lips tightened at having to be on her guard, of having to remind Dean of propriety, of warning him against losing his temper. She took a deep breath and felt her cheeks droop.

With a peal of the clarinet the orchestra began playing Greek music. From all over the ballroom teenage children and young men and women swarmed to the dance floor. The great-granddaughters and great-grandson chased each other around the table. Becky led the first round, her train wrapped several times around her right arm. Mike took her left hand, and the ushers and bridesmaids completed the circle until suddenly the flower girls and ring bearer ran to join the dance. Georgia shook her head slowly and wondered, as if detached from the room, the wedding, what it all meant, if the Greekness meant anything to them, and how long they would keep it up after she and Dean and all the other grandparents were dead. Clapping errupted and from the immigrants' area whistles and shouts of *"Hronia pola!"*—Long life. Becky's parents excused themselves, "Father, we have to visit with the guests." "Of course," the priest said.

"We have to be going in a little while anyway," his wife said. "We have a new sitter, and you know how it is."

Georgia nudged Dean. "Move over. Let's talk to Father and *presvytera.*"

"You both look tired," the priest's wife said. "I'm sure you've had lots of parties, and the work you must have done to have such a wonderful reception!"

"You won't know how much," Georgia said, "until you marry off children and grandchildren. And you've got a long way to go." She put a smile on her face. Below, rushing past, Tracy and his wife waved to Dean and Georgia, "Come on. It's our turn to dance!"

Georgia smiled at Tracy's wife. "Our feet hurt."

"Ah, it's for good luck," Tracy said and hurried to the dance floor.

"Some old idea about good luck they brought from the old country," Georgia said.

The priest's wife pursed small pink lips. "You should hear some of those old-country things people tell Father."

The priest gave his wife a sharp look under thick eyebrows. "Some of the old-timers, you know," he said.

They were the only ones sitting at the bridal table after the priest and his wife left. Georgia said, "We should go around the tables too. And whatever you do, hold your temper. We can't spoil it now."

Georgia led the way, half-turned to be certain Dean was close behind. Some tables were completely empty, the guests had either gone closer to the orchestra to dance or clap and sing along. Others were visiting at other tables, and there was a steady number of guests going to and coming from the restrooms. "That champagne makes you have to go," a woman in her seventies, who had always been sedate, laughed coyly.

The old-timers had gone. Diamond was herding her black-dressed charges out of the ballroom. "We've got to go, Georgia. Mrs. Halamis fell asleep twice, and the noise is getting to my mother. You know she has this tinnitus in her ears I've told you about. Not that it hasn't been wonderful! Everything has been just perfect. I'll call you after a few days. Give you a chance to rest first."

"Diamond," Mrs. Karafoundis said, "when are we going to eat?"

"You just ate, Auntie," Diamond said grimly.

"I wish your mother had been here," Mrs. Halamis mourned, and with Diamond taking charge, slowly the little group made its way through the crowd.

"Glad you could come, Tom," Dean said, shaking hands with a son of the miner who had been killed in the explosion.

"Deno, you sure did it. This wedding will go down in history."

Dean lifted his hands in imitation of old-country Greeks and spoke one of their proverbs, " 'We ate the donkey. Are we going to leave the tail?' " Everyone at Tom's table laughed. Dean did not.

From one table to another, guests made the obligatory remarks, and Georgia and Dean answered with their obligatory remarks. "Oh, Georgia," one of the sequined women, her face painted like a doll's, sighed, "Becky's gown is just fabulous!"

"It didn't have to be that fabulous," Georgia said and was shocked at herself.

Now the bride and groom were also stopping at the tables and greeting guests. "I went to Greek school with your grandfather," a bald rugged man said to Becky. "As soon as we got out of American school, we used to sneak a cigarette before we went to Greek school, and boy, did we get it from the Greek school teacher! He had this ruler, you know, with a metal . . ."

Someone slapped Dean on the back. He turned and looked down on Tracy. "Deno!" Tracy's face glowed, red and shiny; the lines radiating from the corners of his eyes crinkled from his wide smiling. "Deno, the greatest day of my life!"

The muscles of Dean's jaws moved. Georgia clutched his elbow. In a low, frigid voice, Dean said, "Who invited that shit Ernie Peperonis?"

Georgia tugged at Dean's sleeve. "Well, what could I do, Deno? He kept asking about the wedding. Everyone was coming, and he's been wanting to make up with you. My boy getting married. You know, it's hard to be put in that position."

Dean's voice was suddenly loud. "And I had to pay to have that sonofabitch eat at *my* table?" Georgia tugged again, pulled. Dean jerked away from her. There was a sudden quiet around him. "You left me looking up the monkey's ass, Thrasimvoulos!" Becky's horrified eyes were on him. Georgia took a deep breath of something like dust— no, ashes. She gazed at Dean with profound pity and thought of the two of them standing alone on a great, barren plain.

A Note about the Author

Helen Papanikolas is a Fellow of the Utah Historical Society. She has been writing on ethnic and labor history for several decades. She is currently adding to her short stories on Greek ethnic life in the United States.